ANGEL
UP MY
SLEEVE

Ezra Scott

FONTANEL BOOKS

PUBLISHED BY FONTANEL BOOKS

For information, address: Fontanel Books,
P.O. Box 29234, Santa Fe, NM 87592
Online at www.fontanelbooks.com

Publisher's Cataloging-in-Publication Data
Scott, Ezra.
Angel up my sleeve / Ezra Scott.—1st ed.
p. cm.
ISBN 0-9709048-7-8
1. Angels—Fiction. 2. Mysticism—Fiction.
3. Cabala—Fiction. 4. Symbolism—Fiction.
I. Title.
PS3569.C5955A64   2001
813'.6   QBI01-700465
Library of Congress Control Number: 2001092635

Printed on acid-free paper

Design consultants: Zi Pinsley, Marcie Pottern
Cover design by Casey King
Digital imaging by Michael McGuire
Cover illustration © 2001 by Casey King. All rights reserved.

Printed in the United States of America

10 09 08 07 06 05 04 03 02 01   10 9 8 7 6 5 4 3 2 1

For the Choirmaster
and for
HH & GMG

Chapter One

A Strange Meeting

Though Dana had lost count of the days, a month had passed since she'd been locked in the closet and curiously freed. The moon had been full then. She'd seen its light trickling under the closet door where her brother had left her, forgotten and alone.

Somehow she'd slipped free, but just how Dana still couldn't tell. She'd felt darkness tightening around her, airless and hot. Fear had shrieked in her ears, even as her own shouts went unheard. Then came the glow of moonlight, a sliver beneath the door . . . and in the next moment she was free, standing in her room. How? she'd thought, and pondered it for days, always with a shudder. How?! For the closet had remained locked. In the end, Dana gave up trying to reason it through. A trick of her brother's, better put out of mind.

Now the moon was full again. Dana had seen its light the night before and again upon awakening, hanging as a pearl in a clear sky. It lured her gaze as she arose, light-headed and suddenly nauseous. Turning from her window, she dashed for the bathroom, afraid she'd bring up yesterday's dinner, but it was too far down.

Dana stayed home and that sick feeling spread from her stomach to her head, leaping past her chest and throat. Her mother said it was a fever running up the thermometer, so she cooled her down with wet cloths while a tilt-a-whirl spun in Dana's head. "Hold the bed still," Dana moaned, but her mother's hands were busy dipping and wringing and placing cold cloths. Dana held on and rode that bed until the mattress and fever settled down.

"You'll be okay alone, while I run out for a chicken, will you, Dana?"

"Okay, chicken," said Dana. But she didn't hear her mother leave. All she heard was "marble."

"Marble?"

"Marvel—not marble, marvel. Like, marvelous!"

And there he was, sitting on Dana's knees where her bed covers made a mountain. Down he slid to her lap. He clambered up and slid down again, this time tumbling to her chin. Then he tipped his red jelly-cap and smiled.

Dana smiled too and said, "You're a dream—a dizzy fever dream."

"A dizzy dream, eh? So you say! Can a dream tap-dance on your nose?" And he did it, springing from Dana's chin to her nose, leaping from nostril to nostril.

"S-so . . ." Dana's eyes crossed. "So, anything can happen in a fever dream."

"I'm not a dream," he said simply, kicked his heels together and bowed. He was no bigger than Dana's hand, with a tiny green face, like a bud before it becomes a leaf.

"I know then, you're an elf, or a dwarf, or something like that," Dana guessed.

"Something like that, piffle!" The tiny man's arms flung out wide balancing a wobbly pirouette on one heel. He danced, hair flying about like fall leaves in the sun, flashing gold and red and brown. His tiny eyes shone like mustard seeds, black as rich earth, peering out from a very far place.

He danced his way up Dana's cheek till they were eyeball to tiny eyeball, and Dana thought she saw forests reflected there, and shining pools, deep and green. Then down he slid to the tip of her nose stirring a wind and a whiff of old pine trees, rotting apples, and ancient leafy must. Dana sniffed and sneezed the smells out with a blast sending her visitor end over end to her lap. There he landed on his feet with a flourish, slapped his legs, hitched up his pants, and bowed twice. "No need to be snooty, fair beauty, my queen."

Dana opened her mouth to speak, but stopped—catching her breath.

"There see? You know it's true," he said.

Dana's lips came together slowly and spoke unsurely, "Wh-what's true?"

"That you're my queen and oh so marvelous our meeting!" Again he danced, this time singing:

> *Oh, by joy and wonder,*
> *by marvel do I fawn,*
> *to greet my queen,*
> *in timeless reign,*
> *hither to forewarn.*
>
> *By birth to birth,*
> *through age on age,*
> *slipping down the years,*
> *Arise again,*
> *my boundless queen,*
> *gathering our tears.*

Dana blinked, and blinked again, rubbed her eyes and swallowed. Still he was there, now doing a clog dance under his red jelly-cap. "It must be up to a hundred and three!" Dana shrieked. She grabbed the thermometer and shoved it into her mouth.

"Much, much, much older than that!" The tiny man danced and spun, coattails flying.

"Odeh deh wha—" Dana began . . . pulled the thermometer from her mouth and repeated, "Older than what?" as he raced up her chest. "I'm talking about my fever!" she said and put the thermometer back into her mouth, folding her arms tightly.

"I'm talking about your age," he said and leaped to the thermometer, walking along its scale. "As for your temperature . . ." He looked between his green leather boots. "Normal!"

"Nohmeh!" Dana yanked out the thermometer. Normal it was, as the tiny green man lurched and fell, but held on by his hands.

"No fever, see?" he said, dangling at the tip.

"Yes," she said, "I mean, no! It must be broken." She shook

the thermometer furiously. The tiny man dropped to the bed and sprang to the window sill. "Then what did you mean about my age and calling me your queen?" Dana demanded.

But now he was quiet, peering outside. He seemed smaller and a paler green, almost gray, faded. When he looked back at her, Dana saw tears like dewdrops quivering in his tiny eyes. A sadness gripped her then, and a loss, deeper than any she'd ever known. Dana felt it in her chest, a dull thudding ache—grief. The tiny man was grieving with a sadness so thick it choked Dana's air. Dana grieved too, dismayed at how quickly it came upon her. And as she looked outside her window, she saw the daytime sky turning oddly to night.

Dana followed the tiny man's gaze skyward to where a shadow covered and seemed to melt one edge of the sun. She could look but a moment before the shrinking sun's glare made her squint and turn away. Yet the tiny man held his dark stare.

"An eclipse of the sun," Dana assured him. "Better not look into it," she warned, "or you'll go blind."

"Too late for that." His gaze remained fixed, steadfast as ancient stars.

Dana peered into those mustard seed eyes, past their black glaze and through watery pools, feeling she was peeking down two tiny wells. Down she looked deep to the bottoms, to where two lights were shining. One, the sun. The other, the moon. Her glimpse was fleeting. For no sooner had her eyes reached bottom, than they suddenly reeled back and up through the wells, the sun and moon disappearing down below. And again she was looking at the shiny surface of the tiny man's mustard seed eyes. She looked away and then toward the window, squinting to see the eclipse out of the corner of her eye. "It'll pass, you'll see," she said. But she was feeling uneasy.

The tiny man shook his head sadly. "No, not this time." Then woefully, "I'm afraid it's too late!"

Shadow continued spreading like a dark ocean across the sun. Gradually, the sun was draped in a black, cold coat of night. Dana shivered. "An eclipse," she said again, "it'll pass." But her voice rang hollow, sounding far away and uncertain.

As they watched, the ball of the sun, once bright as fire, now wore a dark mask. Only a ring of light shone at its rim and soon this too faded to black.

"Gone!" cried the little green man. "And it's only the beginning!"

"But look!" Dana called hopefully. Out of the darkness where the sun had been, the moon appeared, full and aglow. White light beamed off Dana's face and lit her room.

The little man held his unblinking stare. "So you don't yet know, my queen? Then it can't be stopped!"

As they gazed up at the moon, it began to shrink—not in its regular fashion, but all at once. From its edges, the moon withered to a small and smaller disk. It dwindled in silence to the size of a pinprick. And the light on Dana's face dwindled with it.

"Oh, I can't bear it," grieved the tiny man, slouching in a heap on Dana's window sill.

Then as Dana looked on at the tiniest of moons, there occurred a blast. Before her eyes, the pinprick of a moon exploded into white light.

With the peal of a thousand thunders, the moon burst into shreds. Sparks of light flew out, darting and falling, careening and disappearing into the night sky like countless shooting stars. And the moon, like the sun, was no more.

The little man looked up slowly, reluctantly. "Then it's done. Over and done. I didn't find you in time."

Dana stared, breathless and lost. "This must be a dream. Yes, a fever dream, a nightmare!" She crawled under the covers, shaking in her nightgown. Hunched down and curled with chattering teeth, Dana kept her eyes shut tight. Nothing stirred outside her covers. Inside all was hushed in black. The awful silence was heavy and leaden, pressing, crushing its stillness. "He must go away," she told herself, and pleaded, "Dana, oh Dana, wake up!"

A sound, slight and slender, tripped about her bed covers. It rose and fell, muffled like boot steps in the snow. Though afraid and trembling, Dana parted a corner of cover. Her eyes opened warily, first one, then the other. Each was like a small moon, eyelids parting, lifting cloud and shadow. Half-open half-moon eyes fluttered fear and peeked out.

There on the sill he shuffled, the little green man taking three steps forward, three steps back, solemnly, with care. Tiny eyes and coat buttons glowed gold in Dana's night light. Now she heard his singing, silky and soft as mayfly wings:

> *Muck and muddle,*
> *moon in trouble,*
> *sun on the run,*
> *gone a-blow!*
> *With a hoof and heel,*
> *woof and reel,*
> *whither to gather,*
> *hither to claim her,*
> *whether she knows me or no,*
> *I'm Ibbur*
> *and ready to go!*

> *Ibbur, I am*
> *sprung of Dana,*
> *Dana, your splendor,*
> *bestow!*
> *I come as your guard,*
> *your shadow,*
> *your bard,*
> *dream or an elf?*
> *You know it yourself,*
> *but memory's*
> *slow to re-grow,*
> *I'm Ibbur*
> *and ready to go!*

Dana looked on and listened. Her breath came in spasms: quick, short bites of air. She was frightened and confused, but charmed by his song, enchanted with his dance. Her eyes were full moons as he continued with deliberate step forward, a gentle bow of his head, and measured step back. He paused, then tilted his head to one side and the other, as if listening for a sound. And his gaze was fixed on the moonless night. . . .

> *By scattered and splattered*
> *moon glow,*
> *a puff on the wind,*
> *as I go,*
> *Willing and wild,*
> *ancient and child,*
> *a speck of a friend*
> *unseen,*
> *A spark to the heart*
> *of my queen!*
>
> *Soul in the dark,*
> *guide at the start,*
> *I was*
> *and I am*
> *and I know,*
> *I'm Ibbur*
> *and ready to go!*

To herself, Dana mouthed, "Ibbur," trying out the name. Again, in hushed tones, "Ibbur." Strange, but somehow familiar. The name felt sweet on her tongue, like a crumb of chocolate lost between her teeth and later freed.

The song faded to a murmur—a ripple of leaves skimming across a distant, hidden lake. Dana strained to hear. Yet her own heart beat too loudly in her ears. She waited. The rustling voice floated and drifted away till it was gone. With that, he turned to face her.

"Come, we'll be going now, my queen."

"Going? But where?" Dana jerked her head to stir her senses.

"To the worlds before this one. Surely you've just seen for yourself. Moon and sun gone! And not a moment to lose before this world too is consumed and scattered like the ones before it!"

"But you said it's done, over and done!" Dana sat upright in her bed. "Anyway, I—I don't believe you're here!" She closed her eyes and held them shut, counting to herself, her face tight with concentration.

"Yes, it's done and too late to stop it," replied the little man. "But hopefully, with your help, it's not too late to repair the damage—not too late to restore worlds!"

Dana continued counting, plugging her ears with her fingers. "I don't hear you, or see you, you're gone!" Moments passed, then . . . "There!" she said, and opened her eyes.

"Come my queen, get dressed!" He'd leapt back to her bed and was pulling down the covers. Dana moaned. But with her moan came a flutter, a sweeping of wings at her window. On the ledge there alighted a raven, unlike any other. For this one was giant-sized and silver-white as the moon. It paced restlessly, preening, its breath forming clouds on the window-pane. Dana gaped, and spellbound, unknowingly dressed—jeans, flannel shirt, and sneakers.

The little green man, Ibbur, held out his hand and she took it. His touch was soft and warm as moss bathed in sunlight; cozy and intimate around her finger, as a hand of her own.

"Ibbur," she said. "But my mother, she'll wonder—"

"She'll not have time. We'll be gone but an instant. Please hurry!"

Together they raised the window sash. Up stepped Dana, dark wind whistling at her feet. And he, springing like a grasshopper, jumped up the sleeve of her shirt.

White wings prodded and caressed them to a broad silver back. Dana straddled the restless bird, sinking deep into feathery saddle. Her head grew light, weightless, then too her shoulders and arms, on down to her feet.

Having squirmed up her sleeve and under her collar, Ibbur trod Dana's shoulder anxiously. His tiny voice called, "Here's off!" and the bird, though eager, did not stir from the ledge. "Why then, dear queen, you've forgotten this too? So much of what you know—lost?"

A giddiness shook Dana then. Nervous laughter pressed behind her lips. While in her head, behind her brow, birds rose and flew and swooped in flocks. Then she knew, or thought she knew, a trace of memory long forgotten. Like sparks into

flame it swelled in her mind and burst from her lips with words
. . . "Here's after!"

"Well then!" piped Ibbur. "I'm off!"

To which Dana replied, "I'm after!"

As if by command, the great raven stirred, its eyes glowing
like stars in a head of white light. Wind began to swirl and the
raven lifted. Together they rose—the three of them—on raven's
wing into moonless night.

Chapter Two

To the Mountain of Wind

Past boundless skies the raven rose on a slanted path, great wings pounding the night, scattering gloom. Dana shivered fear and excitement, her fingers deep in feathery down. Black sky swept by at dizzying speed. Stars whirled in clouds like tornadoes of light bending and breaking into dazzling color.

Abruptly, the mighty bird turned and shot upward. Dana felt herself slip. She screamed into space and grasped the raven's neck, clutching tightly around its throat. The raven slowed and struggled.

"You're choking his breath!" came the tiny voice at her ear. "Grip with your knees at his sides, hands at his scruff." Dana dared not move, afraid she'd fall from the feathery back. "Remember, remember! How does a queen fly? Think!" cried Ibbur. "How we fly, how we've flown!"

The raven's head cocked back, eyes ablaze searching Dana. They pierced and saw through her, down the ages, past yesterdays lost. Sharp eyes gripped her and held her like talons. They drilled into memory, chilling her bones, awakening her mind.

"Cling with your heart," a voice seemed to say. And though frightened, Dana began to relax and ease her hold round the raven's neck. She grasped the bird's scruff and gripped with her knees. Now she could feel the raven's heart beating beneath her, in time with her own. The raven streaked with new vigor, like an arrow, headlong and straight up.

Wind whistled melodies in Dana's ears. She heard tones rising and falling, trilling as from a pipe or flute, leaping one to the next. There were ten tones in all. Each somehow seemed to be a song in itself, vaguely familiar to Dana, as lullabies sung at her crib side. Gentle breezes flitted about her head, rocking the mighty raven's back like a cradle, lulling Dana with drowsy pleasure.

She was on the edge of sleep and dream, when the breezes picked up. The ten lullabies began to twist in her ears. The sweet lilting tones became a garbled babble. A confusion of sound. Dana brought her hands to her ears to muffle the noise, and again began slipping from the raven's back.

"Queen Dana, hold fast!" called Ibbur. "Or all is lost before you've begun!"

Dana's hands shot back to the raven's scruff. The great bird, which had faltered, again flew upward, but not as swiftly as before. For now winds blew down from above and from all sides, crashing like waves. Storm winds buffeted the trio, whipping around in darkening tornadoes. Dana screamed. Her voice twisted off as fast as it left her mouth, sucked away in the swirl.

Ibbur crawled under Dana's collar and clung there. Winds seemed to seek him out. Like fingers they dug down grasping at his tiny form. They tore him from hiding and would have whisked him away had he not grabbed hold of Dana's flying hair.

Twisted in wind-pleated strands behind Dana's neck, Ibbur blew to and fro. "He'll not—" Ibbur's voice swung by Dana's ear . . . "let you go—" Dana heard on the next pass . . . "dear queen!"

"Who?!" cried Dana. The question ripped from her mouth.

"He's unleashed—" came Ibbur's voice again . . . "his hordes—" swinging past . . . "his demons!"

Dark whirling clouds parted as if slashed from within by a knife. From this gash poured blotted forms and bestial shadows. Like darts they flew on wings of black fire, charred lightning flashing from sockets in their heads. Dana's own eyes saw and reflected glazed terror. She screamed wildly and fell limply against the raven's neck. The great bird staggered in flight.

Throaty cheers welled about Dana. Dark squadrons charged. "Demons, holy shades, consume her!" screeched one at their lead. "She folds without resistance! Heartless queen! She's a coward, as our master foretold."

On storm winds they rode with flaring wings, shrieking curses. "Foul queen!" Their lightning struck fire, igniting clouds to spew steam. Nearing Dana, they let fly fiery brands. Dana raised her head once, glimpsed sight of the deadly shower, and fell back in a faint.

"Queen Dana, awaken!" called Ibbur at her ear. "What has become of you? Queen Dana never shrank from evil. How far have you fallen?" But Dana lolled uselessly, burning spears whipping past her head. "Precious queen!" Ibbur cried, tugging at her hair.

Dana half-heard Ibbur's voice, muted as the call of a thrush in a faraway thicket. It sounded in her ear, insistent, "Queen Dana, remember yourself!"

Dana moaned and slowly came to, peeked out warily with one eye, then buried her face. "Go away!" she shrieked, muffled in down. "Please go away, please . . . !" She continued prayerfully mumbling, "Please, please, please . . ." over and again into the raven's neck. Finally she ended, "There!" and lifted her head, expecting all had vanished. Bent shadows and fiery points filled her vision. "No!" she screamed and gripped the raven's scruff, calling in desperation, "Here's off! Off! Off!!"

Ibbur replied jubilantly, "Then after! Here's after!!"

The raven revived with new force. With words of power girding its flight, it soared upward.

The demons gave chase. Blazing wings whipped the air into flaming swirls. "She flees like a slave," mocked the one at their lead, "and as a slave she'll succumb to her master."

Dana flew through clouds of black fire. She cringed, holding fast to the raven, certain she'd burn. And though she felt the dark heat, somehow she didn't burn. This must be a dream then, she thought to herself.

In the fire appeared colors shining like shards of glass. Dana eyed them in wonder, now certain she was dreaming, for it seemed each color sounded with song—ten in all, as the melodies she'd heard before. More remarkable still, it seemed to Dana that she didn't so much hear the sounds, as see them. And likewise or reverse-wise, she didn't so much see the colors, as hear them. Her mouth gaped. A dream like no other, she was sure.

Her reverie was broken by a clamor coming from behind. In a buzzing dark swarm, demon rode upon demon flinging lightning shafts and curses. In unison they laughed with the sound of oceans dashing against cliffs. Dana cried out, but kept her hold. Demons advanced, riders spurring their mounts with jabs of lightning. "By fury and shade, overtake her!" called the leader. And the smallest demons, the swiftest and meanest, poked their mounts deepest, charging recklessly for Dana.

The raven was outpaced. Demons dove upon Dana screeching like bats, prodding her with fire-tipped bolts. "Cursed queen, back to dust!" they taunted, spitting sparks at her face.

Their leader flew at Dana's side. "Faithless queen, our master is heartbroken by your sudden departure." Then he laughed, molten fire drooling from his mouth like saliva. Dana could taste terror in her own mouth. At the same time, her eyes were drawn to the hollow sockets of his head, where black fire burned.

From behind folds of Dana's hair, Ibbur spoke. "He speaks deceit, dear queen. And drips lust for your death."

"Who is he—any of you?" Dana screamed.

"The tiny fool lies, little girl," spat the demon. "He hides like a coward and leads you astray!"

Dana shut her eyes tightly. "Oh, please—wake up!" She kept her eyes closed, hands firm on the raven. "Now . . . !!" Her scream faded to a whimper. Dana hunched forward, clinging to the raven's back, weeping despair.

"Queen Dana, take heart. You've more power than you know!"

Through her sobs and fear, Dana heard Ibbur like a thought or memory long buried, now stirring. Behind eyes shut and wet with tears, she saw or imagined a spray of light. What is it? she thought and surprisingly answered herself. . . . The well of my tears! And to her fascination, hope began to fill her.

"Awake, little girl, you're dreaming!" rasped the demon.

"No, Queen Dana. You're remembering!"

"She's losing and lost!"

Dana was sobbing, the lighted spray gone from behind her eyes. In its place appeared a veil of black, falling like endless night.

"Now you see and you'll see, humble queen," mocked the demon and lifted a flaming bolt high above his head, its tip pointed at Dana. "By our master's decree, in tears you'll die!"

"By her tears she'll live!" shouted Ibbur.

Dana felt the raven lurch. All at once, the great bird was well ahead of the demons. Its wings churned the air into thrusting winds. Opening her eyes, Dana saw a glow spreading over the tips of the raven's feathers. As a corona encircles the moon, the bird became sheathed in a ring of light. One ring spawned another, becoming two, then three, ring breaking from ring until there were ten. Again Dana heard or thought she heard ten tones, each a melody in itself, each sounding from another ring of light. And her tears gave way to amazement, to wonder.

"The gates of worlds are never closed to tears," Ibbur spoke into Dana's ear. "The weeping of our queen pierces all barriers . . ."

In a flurry of wind, Ibbur's voice trailed off. The raven had entered a hollow of stars, a cave-like channel in space. Through this hollow, Dana flew at furious speed leaving the demons and their curses far behind.

"It's a narrow way now, my queen," called Ibbur, shinnying down Dana's hair to her shirt pocket. "We'll squeeze through the Pillar of Stars. It's the only way there."

"But where?" asked Dana.

"The world above the one behind. A world you once knew." Ibbur pointed up through the hollow of stars. "There! To that windswept world—brew of a billion breaths. There to find your place. To begin to learn and fashion the tools you'll need. There!" A tiny green finger pointed . . . "To the Mountain of Wind!"

Up the Pillar of Stars, Dana whisked through a tunnel of wind. On and on, rising on winged muscle. Stars whizzed past her eyes in a spiraling, spinning blur. Dana shuddered and shouldered the rush. And the pounding wings stirred the swirling glitter into whirlwinds of jewels and starbright confetti.

Through it all pointed Ibbur—tiny green finger, a beacon in a sea of wind. Dana called to him, "Ibbur!" but the wind took his name, twisting it into crazy echoes . . . Ibbi-ubi-ru! Dana was amazed. Again she called, "Ibbur!!" And back it came, different . . . Uri-bub-burri!! . . . twisting on and on up the Pillar of Stars.

Dana buried her face in the raven's neck. She felt as if she were riding a moonbeam or a streak of sunlight, or the wind itself, not a bird.

All at once, the rushing wind stopped. The raven slowed, banked, and descended. There was ground below, reaching up . . . closer . . . as the raven circled down and alighted, like a feather floating to rest.

Dana found herself on a cliff ledge, climbing through feathery down to the ground. Ibbur coaxed her climb. "Very well, handhold, grip, easy, don't slip, please my queen, careful, don't crush the pocket!"

When she had dismounted, Ibbur sprang from Dana's shirt, somersaulting to stony ground. High cliff walls towered above and plunged beneath them. It was neither day nor night, but a dusky, eerie dimness.

There was a great flapping of wings, and the raven was gone, rocketing from the cliff. Dana watched, dizzy and breathless, as the giant bird flew off, shrinking to a vanishing point. She closed her eyes. "When I wake up, this will all be gone. What a fever can do!"

Chapter Three

ANAVAK'S TALE

When Dana opened her eyes, she saw that Ibbur had stepped to the mouth of a cave. He was hopping on one leg, then the other, calling into the black:

> *Hickory stick, baggedy sack,*
> *by Pillar of Stars,*
> *bringing her back!*
> *From Mountain of Dust*
> *to Mountain of Wind,*
> *Fountain of Light,*
> *no middle, no end!*
>
> *Source of my drink,*
> *boss of my right,*
> *queen of my left,*
> *sheen of my night,*
> *wink of my day,*
> *shine of my sight—*

"Ibbur, enough! Many thanks, thank you," came a voice from the cave. It crackled and crinkled like dried-up leaves. "I knew you were here," the voice came closer, "yesterday!"

A pair of eyes gleamed through the dark like moons of green jade.

Out of the black she stepped, stooped over a stick. First came her hand—Dana saw only one—withered skin shrunken over bone. It shone in the dark like a night light, lit from within. But where the other hand should have been, a sleeve of satin draped a bony stump. Dana shrank back. Next to emerge was her nose, green tip first. Then yellow-nailed toes leading dirt-crusted feet. Cheekbones next before her shriveled face.

So she appeared, bent under robes, tattered black satin worn green. She was four feet tall, hunched at her shoulders with neck and head jutting straight out before her. A wild mat of hair tumbled over her chest. Like her robes, her hair had gone green, not gray, with age.

As she hobbled out, Dana saw gusts at her feet sweeping stones and twigs from her path. The old woman's voice cackled, "Ah, darling, dear queen, you've come home. Good, good!" Her arms reached out for Dana. "And very oh very many thanks to Ibbur." Her eyes flitted his way. "On him you may always depend!"

Ibbur bowed deeply, so low that his cap slipped off. He hurriedly returned it to his head, green ears flushing purple. The old woman neared. Dana stepped back from the knobby old hand.

"Ah, ahh now, there sweet, dear sweet Dana. You fear tired old Anavak? How strange! Strange I say," and she chuckled, discarding her walking stick. Ibbur tittered too. "But then . . . ah!" The old woman lowered her hand and stood before Dana. "But you've forgotten, of course! So? Then soon you'll re-member. And I'll teach you. As you once taught me . . . when you were old and I was young!"

Again she laughed. And for an instant Dana saw the old woman change: the crusty feet and wrinkled face turned beautifully white and smooth. There stood a young woman in pink velvet robes draping two fine, delicate hands. Dana blinked. . . . She was gone. The old woman returned. She looked into Dana's eyes, searching, holding her stare. Old lips smiled. "A fleeting glimpse then? So you remember old Anavak after all? How lovely I was! Was I not?"

"Well, I—" began Dana, "yes . . . I mean, well, I guess yes. Yes you were, I think, but I'm not sure. Such crazy things! I thought it's a dream. Now I don't know. I wish I were home in bed!"

"Sick in bed? Come now, come now. No need for that! Aren't you feeling well? Better than before?"

Dana thought. Her stomach and head felt fine. But before she could answer—

"Good, good then!" The old woman reached out her hand, kindly, with care. Dana took hold and felt safe. And together with Ibbur they entered the cave.

The old woman, Anavak, fed bundles of twigs to a fire. Flames leapt, glowing orange in Dana's face. Smoke curled up and out an opening high in the cave ceiling. Ibbur reached for a plume of smoke rising from the fire. His tiny hand held it like a string. Dana gasped. "But your hand should pass through it!"

Ibbur nodded and grinned, holding firmly to the smoke. He gave it a tug and up he went as if holding the tail of a kite.

"You're a ghost!" cried Dana.

Ibbur rose with the smoke to the ceiling. As he went he sucked in puffs and blew them out through his mouth in different shapes. First came simple smoke rings, then spirals and tiny tornadoes. From off his lips streamed birds, horses and elephants, flying, galloping, trumpeting through the smoke hole. Tigers of smoke jumped through rings and floated away.

"He's a show-off, but down deep he's an angel, all good," said Anavak.

"An angel?"

While above them both, snug in an armchair of smoke, Ibbur sat singing:

> *Come whiff it,*
> *come waft it,*
> *come air,*
> *Come Ibbur aloft in a chair,*
> *A ghost for a guest,*
> *an elf you had guessed,*
> *now nix it, I dangle,*
> *a pix for an angel,*
> *a pinket, a pigsy, a pisk,*
> *a spook or a sprite*
> *or betwixt?*

"An angel—no more, no less," said Anavak and with a wave of her hand she stirred the rising smoke. Ibbur tumbled down to her palm. "Beguiling, ah, but he'll guide you, Queen Dana. He's noble and he knows his business." With a finger she stroked Ibbur's head. "Don't you dear Ibbur, my dear?" as she set him down in Dana's lap. Ibbur crinkled his nose and purred. "Ah, now then," said Anavak, "a tale—"

"But please, if you will," Dana broke in, "I mean, I hardly know, though I'm trying. . . . First Ibbur and the eclipse, and he called me his queen, and it seemed that I knew—then sounds and colors—and demons! And now you! And what about the moon? It shrank and exploded. I saw it!"

"You are so very excited and why not? Such upset for a queen!" From a kettle near the fire, Anavak poured tea for Dana and gave her a biscuit from a bundled scarf. "Now drink and nibble. Rest . . . ahh, rest." Anavak soothed her. "I'll tell what you need to know. It's what you already know. Remember?" And Anavak began her tale. . . .

"Before and before and before," told Anavak, "there stood a great Mountain of Light. Such a place, ah! You can't even imagine, not now. But once you were there, you'll see. The Mountain of Light stood like an island in the Sea of Light which spread without end in every direction. There every tree, every stone, every bird and walking animal was spun of light, just as here all things are twisted of wind.

"Atop that Mountain stood Light Castle. It shone as a crown of pure gold, each of its towers a point in the crown, and each one brighter than the next. Dazzling! Yes? Ah! But there was greater dazzle still. For high in the brightest tower of Light Castle, one thing shone still brighter—the Princess of Light! She came from before all the befores, from a place that is no place. Not fire. Not water. Not air. Not earth. No place. Neither solid, nor liquid, nor gas. Nothing to speak of. Nothing to see. Nothing to hear. Nothing to touch. No beginning. No end—"

"You mean—but excuse me," Dana cut in, "if you don't mind, you mean the princess came from outer space? On a spaceship or a rocket powered by light? Maybe—" Dana stopped short. Ibbur had burst out laughing. He rolled on the cave floor kicking up dusty winds, shaking under his jelly-cap. Green tears flowed down his twitching face as he tried to stop and catch his breath.

Dana blushed, offended and annoyed. She poked a finger at Ibbur. "So what! What place is no place, before and before? Space! Rockets fly there! Don't you know about them? And solar energy? You, you! You who could be the Man in the Moon!"

"There, ahh, there now," cooed Anavak. "Ibbur means no ill." Her eyes fixed on the squirming little man, "Ibbur?" as he quieted down. "We are lucky, dear Ibbur. Our queen is bright for she thinks! Don't mock her. Need I warn you? She'll put it together. She knows more than you or I both!"

Anavak turned to Dana. "Spaceships? How could you think otherwise? Before all befores, I say. Before rockets, my queen. Before planets and stars. Before space. No place. No thing. Hard to imagine. Harder even to imagine than a world of light. But don't let it bother you. Ah! More tea?" Anavak poured another cup of tea for Dana and handed her the bundle of biscuits. "There, my queen. It doesn't have to make sense, not yet. The princess, the king's daughter, came from no place to the Mountain of Light. There she took charge of all light!"

"All right then," said Dana, "but how? How did she take charge?"

"Ah! The princess, with one arm outstretched, held the moon and sun in their place." Anavak stretched out her arm . . . "Like so!" and a whirling image of light took shape at her fingertips. Two balls of light spun, one within another, like mingling clouds. Dana watched, then saw them fade as smoke melts into air. "For the Princess of Light it was just so simple," said Anavak. "From the brightest tower of Light Castle, she kept watch on the moon and sun. Ah, but such a moon and sun, different by worlds from the ones that came after. For that moon and sun were the first— and one! One shone within the other and the other within one. They flowed together like one sea. They pulled like one ox. They breathed with one breath. They flew—two wings as one!

"Ah! It was a world of pure light. Almost. Within all that light—where everything was light from the smallest ant to the largest whale!—there was but one dark spot. One spot without light. And that spot had a name—"

"Var!" cried Ibbur.

"Indeed! Contained in all that light, all that good, there was one evil spot, Var! May his name be stricken!" Anavak jabbed a log into the fire. Flames leaped and licked at her hand, but she brushed them away like flies.

"Var poked his ugly head through the Mountain of Light and swallowed a single spark. There in its place remained no light, no! But a spot empty of light."

While Anavak told her tale, Ibbur stepped around the fire of sticks, stalking, lurking in pantomime. His eyes grew fierce, his lips curled, snarling, baring his teeth. He thrust a hand into the fire to snatch a fistful of flame. Flame jumped in his hand, while Ibbur, miming Var, gathered it to his lips and swallowed it down. An empty hole gaped in Anavak's fire where that spot of flame had been.

"Now," said Anavak, "one spot empty of light in an endless sea of light, might not be so bad. No thing is perfect, after all. Ah! No place is perfect, only! But Var didn't stop there. He swallowed more! Spark after spark and still more."

Ibbur mimed each of Var's swallows. His tiny darting fist poked hole after hole, taking handful by handful of flame. Soon the leaping fire of sticks appeared as a blazing Swiss cheese, dripping with melting holes.

"Bit by bit, spark by spark, Var devoured the Mountain of Light. Swallow by hungry swallow. Until he reached the sun itself. With jaws expanding as the fangs of a snake, Var clamped and crushed and crunched the sun! Then he turned to the moon, so many times smaller than the sun, its mate. With the sun in Var's dark belly, the moon was left completely alone. Unguarded by the sun's mighty fire. So Var, with cruel smirk and spiked teeth began nibbling the moon, that first of all moons. Nibbling because he was full, yet greedy for dessert. He ate in from the edges, slowly, savoring the moon as if it were a scrumptious cookie. Then with one last bite—too big for his slobbering jaws!—Var crushed the last spark of moon, the very heart of light itself. It exploded and shattered! Sparks scattered and fell. Var flew as a whirlwind gobbling each falling spark—"

"But what about—sorry," Dana put in, "but what about the Princess of Light? She was in charge of the moon and sun! Couldn't she stop him?"

"Sadly, she couldn't. She was then too young. She didn't yet know how." Anavak looked intently at Dana. "But she is now much older and wiser. Ah! She knows so much more." Then Anavak added, thoughtfully, "But does she know enough? Will she know what to do when the time comes?"

"She must!" cried Ibbur.

"Yes, she must," agreed Anavak, "and she will!"

Dana had more questions, but she kept them to herself. For now a creeping feeling churned in her stomach. Her head began to pound. The dizziness she'd felt at home returned. Dana longed for her mother and thought, by now she's back with that chicken.

"Never mind the chicken," said Anavak, holding a cup of tea to Dana's lips. "Drink, drink, my sweet," in soothing tones. "This will calm your royal fears." And it did. Anavak continued. . . .

"The princess dashed about frantically, desperate to gather any sparks she could. She'd save a few, but then Var would rip them from her hands and greedily swallow them down. Var strained after every spark of that first moon, till at the lowest depths of shadow, he found the very last spark. For a moment it clung between his lips, for his mouth was too full to close over it. So stuffed with light was he! But he gulped to make room and in it slid, though only for a moment. That last spark proved too much for Var. Light welled in his stomach and in his gullet and mouth. Sickened, Var lay down, and retching, he puked it all up.

"Sun and moonlight burst from his lips tearing a hole through the lowest shadows of the Mountain of Light! Light streamed down to a world below. And Var followed, lusting after the light he'd stolen and lost."

Anavak gazed into the fire. Flames danced in her eyes.

"Was it—Var—who sent his demons—after me?" asked Dana, words sticking in her throat.

"Yes, my queen, but also no."

"But—" Anavak held up her hand. . . . "So confusing," finished Dana.

"Confusing, so? Of course! So listen, then remember." And Anavak resumed her tale. . . .

"On shafts of light, Var entered a second world—the Mountain of Water, below the Mountain of Light. There all was water, rushing rivers, rippling streams, lapping lakes, churning oceans of life."

The old woman waved and fluttered her hand and for a moment Dana saw tiny streams of water pouring from her fingertips, before they vanished.

"A world of water flowed through all things. All animals, stones, and trees were alive and formed of water as above they'd been formed of light. Hard to imagine?" asked Anavak. "Perhaps harder to imagine than the Mountain of Light. Ahh! . . .

"There in the Mountain of Water, the light of the first moon and sun entered a new watery world. Each now shone with its own light, in watery form. Understand, my queen?"

Dana wasn't sure whether she did understand. She tried to imagine a world in which all things were made of water. She pictured fields of flowers flowing like streams, trees like standing waterfalls, clouds spun of whirlpools. She saw a horse running, its body all of water, cantering with muscles and limbs all flowing like a river. Then too, she saw the sun shining in sea waves and the face of the moon rippling on the surface of a lake. Yes, she could imagine a world of water. In silence, she nodded, meeting Anavak's eyes.

"Good, good, my queen." Anavak went on. . . .

"The Mountain of Water rose on waves at the center of the Sea of Water which spread without end in every direction. There the Princess of Light again took charge. Now she was called the Princess of Water as she floated high in the highest tower of Water Castle. With arms outstretched she held the second moon and sun in place as she had the first. But this moon and sun were separate! Each was only half as bright as it had been before. One dripped the waters of day and the other the waters of night. They bobbed and sailed across watery skies, guided by the princess. While deep at the bottom of the Mountain of Water, a shadow lurked in a murky pool—"

"Zar!" cried Ibbur.

"Zar, indeed!" Anavak spat into the fire and watched her spittle sizzle and hiss on an ember. "In the Mountain of Water, Var became Zar. Half evil. Half evil as Var, but two times worse!"

"But—I don't get it," Dana broke in. "How could Zar be just half evil but two times worse than Var?"

"Ah, my queen," said Anavak and without another word, she began to smile. As Dana looked on, half of Anavak's face smiled sweetly, while the other half twisted into an angry snarl. "What do you think?" Anavak asked.

"Think—?" Dana's voice was dry with fright. "Why—why it's impossible to know whether you'll offer me tea or tear me apart!"

"Exactly!" Anavak spoke from her two-sided mouth. "You don't know what you're looking at. You don't know whom you're facing! You don't know if I'm your friend or your foe. If I'm good or if I'm bad. That's why I say Zar is two times worse than Var, who is all evil. Var's evil is totally crushing, but it doesn't have the trickery of the evil that followed in Zar. So beware, Queen Dana, of Zar! For Zar distorts evil and good. Which is which, my queen? With Zar you can't tell. He'd gladly invite you to dinner for a chance to serve your head on a platter!"

Dana stared wide-eyed at Anavak, slowly nodding her head, half-afraid it would roll from her shoulders if she shook it too much.

"Now," said Anavak, her face relaxing, "Zar groped the bottom of the Mountain of Water, turning stone after watery stone, for he knew what he was after. He poked and prodded with scaly claws, scratching, lifting. He sniffed with flaring nostrils. Soon he found it. Ah! The holding stone! He lifted that stone and giggled like a baby unstopping a bathtub. And all the world began to drain through. Then Zar—half-evil but two times worse!—set his mouth open twice wide at the bubbling hole. And as the living waters rushed down, Zar slurped and drank them in.

"While atop Water Castle, the princess felt ripples of disaster below. Yet she couldn't leave her position. For weren't her outstretched arms needed to steer the moon and sun through the skies?"

"Yes, of course!" Dana blurted before she could think. "That's how it was!" Her certainty surprised even herself. Yet she felt so oddly sure.

"Of course!" agreed Anavak. "As you remember, Queen Dana. Zar gurgled through ever-widening jaws, drinking on and on. Soon the tugging flow spun at the feet of the princess. She strained to swim free, but down she was pulled, and the sun and moon with her. When the princess reached Zar's lips, he stretched his jaws twice wide again, swallowing her down with the moon and sun behind her.

"Then Zar, full of water and twice full with himself, could not resist the urge to grin a twice-wicked grin. But as his teeth parted ever so slightly, a droplet escaped his lips. Others followed, droplet by trickle by spill, till a torrent burst Zar's jaws ripping through the hole at the bottom of the Mountain of Water!

"Water washed down to the next world. In that rush went the princess with the sun and moon at her heels. And as they drained away, Zar followed, lusting after the sparks of water he'd stolen and lost."

Anavak warmed her gnarled hand and stumpy wrist above the flame of her wood fire. When she drew them back, once again Dana saw tiny streams flowing from Anavak's fingertips. But this time, the streams dissolved into mists, and then tiny tornadoes, before vanishing.

"Zar entered a third world—the Mountain of Wind, below the Mountain of Water, below the Mountain of Light. In the Mountain of Wind," told Anavak, "all things were formed of wind as above they'd been formed of water and above again they'd been formed of light—"

"Yes!" cried Dana. "I was carried, it seemed, by wind. By that raven flying like wind!" She caught her breath and looked around, puzzled. "But this cave is stone, not wind . . . and this fire, it's fire—and you—"

Anavak smiled a green toothy grin. "A cave is a cave and appears as a cave whether formed by sparks of light, water, or wind. Here all that entered became wind, my queen. Energy, as you say. Moving, forming, changing. Taking shape from one world to the next. A single spark shines as a spark for its essence is the same, whether its nature is light or wind. You see and shall see. . . . Now hear and remember. . . .

"The Princess of Light, then Water, was now the Princess of Wind. She flew high in the windiest tower of Wind Castle atop the Mountain of Wind. Here the princess held the third moon and sun in place as she had the second and first. And the third moon and sun now shone as wind. Understand? You must! The sun blew the winds of daylight and the moon breathed the winds of night. But the evil one—"

"Tar!" cried Ibbur.

"Yes, Tar! After Var, who was all evil. After Zar, who was half evil, but two times worse. In the Mountain of Wind entered Tar, who is four times worse! Half evil and half evil again. A checkerboard of evil and twisted good is Tar. A patchwork of faces is Tar!" Anavak pointed a crooked finger at Dana. "Don't fall for his treacherous tricks, my queen!"

She fanned the fire with her robes. Embers glowed brighter and flames reached higher. "In the Mountain of Wind," spoke Anavak, "Tar hid himself in folds of wind and emptied his lungs of air. Then with cruel breath—four times deep and long!—he sucked in. All things of wind whished down—whirling leaves, blowing beasts, all breezes, all of windy kind. All down his throat in a vacuum! Tar snuffed down castle and princess, and the moon and sun too, like air sucked from balloons. Then he clamped shut his lips and, this time, did not dare smile. The Mountain of Wind blew inside him, trapped.

"But wind, dear Dana, is a ticklish thing. It pressed Tar's cheeks and needled his mouth. It pestered and teased his lips until Tar could not help himself. A snicker passed his lips, then a chuckle. And with it, a puff, then a gust and a gale! Cyclones tore from his mouth to the next world below. In that storm flew the princess along with her sun and moon.

"Again Tar followed, lusting for the wind he'd stolen and lost." Anavak sighed, poured herself some tea and inhaled its steamy fragrance. Ibbur sprawled face-down on the ground weeping bitterly to himself. Dana too felt tears. They welled in her eyes.

Now Anavak asked, "And what came next?"

Dana tried to speak. Words caught on her tongue. "N-next? I—what next?" Dana strained to know or remember and almost did, but the thought got away. She shook her head.

"Ah! Hard to hold on to? Don't mind. It'll come. Very well then," and Anavak returned to her tale. . . .

"On twisting winds, Tar entered a fourth world—the Mountain of Dust, below the Mountain of Wind, below the Mountain of Water, below the Mountain of Light.

"In the Mountain of Dust, all things were formed of dust as above they'd been formed of wind, and above that, water, and above that, light. Ah! My queen! But the Mountain of Dust— you know all about that. Why that's where Ibbur found you!" Anavak bent over Ibbur, smiling, stroking his back. "Searching all those years. Dear Ibbur, we thank you!"

The old woman turned to Dana. "In the Mountain of Dust— sweet queen, you must know!—all things were formed of dust. The fourth moon and sun, dust too. Fireballs of dust in a sky of dust. As before, the Princess of Dust held the fourth moon and sun in place. Dusty life stirred at her fingertips—"

"At my fingertips—how?" Dana asked. "When Ibbur found me, I was in my room—not some castle of dust!"

"Certainly, my queen. For in the Mountain of Dust, so far from no place, it is easy even for a queen to forget. Our princess held her position until her purpose was slowly lost in the swirl of dusty forgetting. And gradually she settled—as dust will."

Dana shifted her gaze from Anavak to Ibbur and finally to the fire, silently trying to comprehend, to see.

"In the Mountain of Dust," continued Anavak, "Var, twice worse Zar, four times worse Tar, was divided into evil again. His shape and name now ever changing. Vart! Zart! Zvart! Zat! Vat! Rat! And worse! Parts of each and every evil. Twisting evil as good and good as evil. All shapes and sizes, and cruel combinations. The many faces of good and bad. The masks of evil too, and masks of good hiding evil! More than those that came before. He's the one who crunched and shattered that fourth dusty moon and sun. As you saw from your bedroom window. He's the one who sent his demons to stop you!"

Fear had come to settle in Dana. She didn't know what to make of Anavak's tale, or of anything she'd seen and heard or remembered since Ibbur first danced across her bed covers. Now her stomach felt uneasy and she wondered, would this dream never end? And if it wasn't a dream—panic fluttered in Dana's belly—how would she ever get home?

Chapter Four

A Farewell

Anavak grew silent. With eyes closed, she drew a deep breath and began blowing a soft, steady stream of air into her fire's dying embers. The coals reddened, glowing hot. Dana thought she heard a faint whistling in the glow, and the coals seemed to jump, then burst into flame. She felt the heat of the fire on her face.

"All is not lost—if you'll help, dear queen," said Anavak, opening her eyes.

"But how? How can I?" Dana tried to stand up, but her legs wobbled beneath her and she had to sit back down. She looked fearfully at Anavak. "And the world I left behind, where Ibbur found me—" Dana hesitated, her lips trembling, gone almost numb. "Is it still there? My room, my house, my family, my friends? What's left behind?" Dana pleaded. Cold sweat dripped down her forehead, stinging her eyes.

Anavak blew lightly across Dana's brow and face, drying her sweat and tears. "As I say, all is not lost, my queen. That's why you're here." Anavak's eyes widened. "What's left behind? Why something was left in each of the worlds. More than shadow, more than emptiness, more than a vacuum! Each of the worlds—down all the ages!—has been waiting. When all seemed lost and done, we knew our princess would return, grown into a queen. You, Queen Dana." Anavak smoothed the hair from Dana's forehead. "It's how we knew it would be. Whether you remember or not."

Ibbur stood up and bowed, tiny eyes on Dana. "Will you do what you must?" he asked.

"But what? What must I do?" Dana hung her head and began to weep.

"There, ahh, there," said Anavak, patiently, lovingly, "there, my queen, ahh . . . as you feel," until Dana stopped crying.

"What was left behind in each of the worlds," explained Anavak, "were the very seeds of that world, fallen sparks of each moon—enough to sustain each world in ruin! In the Mountain of Light there remained three sparks of light." Anavak's eyes grew brighter, reflecting the lighted coals. "In the Mountain of Water, three sparks of water remained. In the Mountain of Wind, three sparks remained formed of wind. And in the Mountain of Dust, only one, one dusty spark of the fourth and last moon remained. These are the seeds you must find. Without them we'll perish!"

Dana stared long and wearily into the fire. She fixed her mind on memory and tried to see for herself. Could it all be true? How strange. And if it weren't true? Then where was she, and why and how?

Memories passed through her: games, school, holidays, people and places she knew. Could they all be gone as Anavak told? Dana wondered again if she'd ever get home. And how would she get there? She'd given up closing her eyes, wishing it all away. That simply didn't work. Whatever they were—Ibbur and Anavak—it seemed they were on her side after all. Questions and thoughts filled her head. Anavak's story came back in small pictures behind her eyes: light and water and wind. Dana held out her hand and, instantly, there at her fingertips, was a tiny glowing moon!

"Bit by bit, it will all come back to you, fair queen. If only you'll begin. If you'll set out to gather what's left—"

"Then I will!" cried Dana, surprised at herself, for her voice spoke in her head, not from her lips.

Ibbur sprang to the moon at Dana's fingers, spun and skipped on its surface. It faded beneath his dancing feet and he dropped to her hand.

"You will indeed!" cried Anavak. "It was always to be so, was it not?"

"But how—"

"I'll set you on your way. And not alone. Not without some assistance. Ibbur will go with you, dear Ibbur of many talents! He's more than he seems. The most gifted of angels, from high places and low!"

Ibbur bounded from Dana's hand and perched on her shoulder.

"You'll make your way from the Mountain of Wind, through the Mountain of Water, to the Mountain of Light. In each of the worlds you'll seek out and gather the three remaining sparks. Nine sparks! Nine seeds to restore the worlds, my queen!"

"And then?"

"That's enough for a start. Get through and you'll know what's next. For in the Mountain of Light lies hidden the Spring of Beginning. Reach it and grasp what to do. More I can't say or don't know. But you'll find out. You must!"

"But the last world, the Mountain of Dust. I'll go there too, won't I? The last spark, the one of dust is there. And my home!"

"And the worst of evils too! So build your strength as you go. Each spark you find will empower you. But I must warn you! Evil shadows stand in your way. Var and Zar and Tar! He and his shades remain guarding each spark. Cruel and hidden in the worlds he destroyed!

"Remember what I say. Each spark will help you forward. For each holds a charm—magic you may use. Nine charms and then one more. But I've said too much. It's for you to find out, as only you may."

With these words of counsel and warning, Anavak became silent again and closed her eyes, breathing deeply, slowly.

Now from a corner of the cave there emerged what to Dana seemed to be four flying scarves. One was red. Another, yellow. A third was blue and the fourth, green. They flew about, circling the old woman's head. Dana saw how the scarves seemed to melt into air and out again, like colored smoke, but without the smoke. Not like scarves at all, but something else. . . . "Tiny winds!" Dana gasped amazed. Four tiny winds, each shimmering a different color.

Anavak's eyelids fluttered open. Her eyes fastened on Dana,

staring through her. Dana dared not speak, but quietly returned Anavak's gaze, eye fastening on eye. It was Dana who blinked first.

"Ah!" cackled Anavak. "There was a time when you held my stare as if forever and it was I who'd blink first. No matter, not yet. But when the time comes and you must hold a stare, don't falter! Or you'll lose everything!" Anavak waved her arms. The four winds drifted over to Dana and began slowly circling her head. Anavak smiled. "My winds, my pets. They adore me— and now you! They'll go with you, dear queen, to the boundary of the Mountain of Wind. By then—hopefully!—you'll have gained the three sparks of wind. Three charms to empower you further."

Dana tried to fix her mind on what Anavak said. So important to remember, she kept thinking, but how will I ever do it? Rescue sparks of lost worlds. Impossible! Yet here I am getting ready. Somehow—I don't know how!—but somehow I am who they say.

Dana spoke aloud, "You call me your queen, and I think, well, what else could any of this be? Because little by little, there are things I remember. But I just don't know, and if I refuse to believe you, how will I ever get home?"

Anavak extended her arms. Her old skin now shone brighter, lit from deep within. And once again, but only for a moment, Anavak's withered skin turned smooth and beautiful. "I blush with youth to be near you, my queen," said Anavak shyly, shuffling Dana to the mouth of her cave. Ibbur watched from Dana's shoulder as the four winds swirled before them, sweeping their path.

They emerged from the cave to the cliff ledge. There the four winds wove themselves into an airy blanket sweeping under Dana. Dana stood aloft four colors of wind, shifting her feet for balance.

"Grip with your toes!" called Anavak.

"How—?" asked Dana trying, and finally finding her footing. She looked into Anavak's eyes. "Will I see you again?"

"Perhaps, my queen."

"And my mother—my home?"

"If you succeed," said Anavak. "First gain the sparks—your charms, our hopes!"

"But where—where do I start?"

Anavak pointed a crooked finger. "The very longest of journeys, my queen, begins beneath your feet!"

With those words, the winds churned and lifted as a cloud. Before Dana could say good-bye, Anavak was far below, green-black robes whipping in wind, waving farewell.

Chapter Five

BEHIND THE MOUNTAIN OF WIND

Dana sped off through pale sky aboard the blanket of winds, a shimmering glow of color pulsing beneath her feet. She kept her balance, awkwardly at first, and then with greater control, gripping with her toes through her sneakers. Wind whipped her hair, pressed against her face, flew down her throat and out again with a whistling sound. From Dana's shoulder, came a small voice—Ibbur singing to the whistling tune:

> *On wind,*
> *ti fi dum, ti day,*
> *On colors of four*
> *we're away!*
> *By windy mouth music,*
> *how easy she croons it,*
> *Queen Dana,*
> *ti fi dum, ti day!*
>
> *Ti fi dum,*
> *ti fi dum, ti doe,*
> *by Mountain of Wind*
> *we do blow,*
> *To gather each spark,*
> *three hidden by dark,*
> *ti fi dum,*
> *to find them,*
> *we go! . . .*

Ibbur sang through the wind, holding fast to Dana's hair. The whistling continued until Dana's mouth tired. She closed her lips and the whistling stopped. But when she opened her mouth to speak, the wind again blew a throaty whistle. It was "Ibbur . . ." and all melody after that, until Dana cupped her mouth to block the wind. With her head to one side, she spoke through cupped hands to Ibbur.

"Ibbur, please, do you know where these winds are taking us?"

Ibbur smiled, green teeth beaming. But he only shrugged.

Dana tried again. "Then where do we find the first spark of wind?"

Ibbur scratched his head through his jelly-cap, then answered, "We'll find it in the dark, where it is!"

"Oh? And where's that?"

Ibbur scratched and thought again. His forehead wrinkled with worry. "I'm afraid, my queen, we'll find it where Var four times worse has hidden it!"

"Var four times worse? That's Tar!" Now Dana was worried too. For what did she know about facing such a thing as Tar? Anavak had warned that the sparks she sought in the Mountain of Wind were guarded by Tar. It wasn't likely he'd surrender them willingly. Tingling fear crept up Dana's back. She wondered if she'd left her courage, and strange but powerful memories, far behind with Anavak. She closed her eyes, shivering, feeling very small, smaller even than Ibbur.

"Ibbur, I'm afraid—!" Before the words had passed Dana's lips, there appeared in the distance, a dark cloud. Or so it seemed. The blanket of winds sped closer. Dana fretfully opened her eyes in time to see the cloud looming larger. . . .

Closer, and Dana saw that the cloud wasn't a cloud at all, but a shadow. Closer still, and she could see behind the shadow—a gaping hole. Dana's memory reeled back. She saw things Anavak had never mentioned. Parts of the story left out. Memories too fleeting and fast to hold on to . . . lost quickly in rushing air.

They neared and the shadow widened. Ibbur ducked under Dana's collar and slipped down her sleeve. Dana wished she too had a sleeve to crawl into. Just as she wished, the blanket of winds wound around her. And wrapped in four colors, Dana soared through the shadowy hole in the windy sky.

Once through the hole, shadow was all there was. Dana sped through the dark, twisting and turning around curves. But for her blanket of winds, nothing stirred. All was silence about her. She could see nothing.

How long Dana rushed through shadow, she couldn't tell. Moment upon moment, hour upon hour, day upon day upon year?

The rushing stopped all at once. With it went the shadowy dark. Dana came to rest, but where?

The four colored winds unwound and floated to Dana's feet as ribbons unwrapping a gift. Dana stood in a forest thick with trees. Odd to behold. For the air all around was checkered. Things appeared as if seen through sunglasses with lenses divided into black and white squares.

Ibbur's head peeked above Dana's shirt collar. "I don't like it," he said.

"Do you know this place?"

"No. Never. Checkerboards! Impossible to see! I don't like it!"

"Well," said Dana, "neither do I. And listen . . . there isn't a sound. Not a bird. No wind in the trees. Where are we?"

"Where we were headed, my queen. Tar's shadow world behind the Mountain of Wind."

Dana worried to herself, what now? As if in response, the four colored winds entwined again to lift her. They bore her away with Ibbur, on checkered air, to a valley cut by a stream. They followed the stream, slipping slowly through reeds along the bank. Bit by bit, Dana's eyes adjusted. The checks seemed to fade from the air. Drop by drop the stream appeared normal.

"That's better," said Dana. "The checkerboard is gone!"

"Tar's tricks, my queen. Don't be fooled! The air is still as it was—a patchwork of Tar's evil! But Tar makes you see differently, as through his eyes. Don't let him! In Tar's world, good and evil blend. Good veils evil. Evil veils good. Who can tell them apart?"

"Can you?" asked Dana.

"I know where I am, my queen, that's enough. Slowly you'll

learn—and before it's too late!—to lift veil behind veil behind veil . . . and see clearly."

The blanket of winds wove breezily through stands of cattails. They soon came upon a patch of wild flowers. Here the winds halted and hovered.

"Moonflowers," said Ibbur.

"Yes, I know," said Dana dreamily, sliding from the winds, stepping lightly through the flower patch. At her approach, flower stalks leaned back, opening a path before her. Buds blossomed as Dana brushed past. She halted before a thick hedge of witch hazel. "I seem to recall . . . ," Dana mused, and kneeling before the hedge, she parted the lower branches. The fragrance of damp earth reached her nose and filled her memory, drawing her deeper into the thicket.

"Have you been here before?" asked Ibbur.

"Yes, I think, I must have." Dana pushed past leaves, bending back twigs.

"Careful, my queen—" but too late. A rebounding twig swept Ibbur's cap from his tiny head. There it dangled, red among the green, as Dana cried, "Here it is!"

"Well done," Ibbur said, glad but annoyed, taking back his jelly-cap.

What Dana found was a sheltered dugout in the high bank. Much like a cave, but of earth, not stone. A few steps in and Dana came against the back wall.

"I thought it led somewhere," she said, crawling back out through the hedge. With a heavy sigh she got to her feet, glancing anxiously about. The four colored winds hovered nearby stirring small breezes amid the moonflowers.

Among blades of grass, Dana sat down on the stream bank. She ran her fingers through the grass, then plucked a single blade and began nervously twisting it around her finger. She plucked another, delicately, then another. Ibbur watched as Dana picked blade after grassy blade, absently twisting them into a braid.

"But I know I've been here before," said Dana, fingers busy plaiting and tying off loose ends. She gathered more blades, braided them, and began weaving the braids together.

"Worlds before," said Ibbur, climbing to the ground. He sprang upon a blade, holding fast as it wobbled and swayed. "Each blade of grass—you were once fond of saying, my queen!—has an angel that tells it to grow."

Dana's woven braids began taking shape. They spiraled up in layers, gradually, to form a pouch. Ibbur watched Dana's hands growing quicker and more skillful with each twist. Then he swung out from his blade of grass and leaped, landing in the pouch.

Dana laughed, forgetting her troubles. "Well, Ibbur, how do you like it?" She looped one last grassy strand, tying it quickly and nimbly. "It seems I've made you a house!"

Ibbur smiled, shaking his head. He sprang from the pouch like a katydid to alight in the witch hazel. There standing on a branch, he pulled a tiny flint ax from his belt and sharpened the blade on his boot heel. Then he spat on his hands, gripped the handle, and began chopping at the stem of a leaf.

After a flurry of cuts, he called for Dana to come closer. He swiped his ax again and the leaf fell free. In a rush, the four colored winds caught it and floated the leaf to the pouch.

Dana was delighted. "Ibbur of many talents!" she cheered, recalling what Anavak had said.

Ibbur tipped his cap, then swung his ax into tree bark. Shavings flew and were carried by the winds to the pouch. "From the leaf and bark," he said, "I'll teach you to make medicines for bruises and burns, for bites and stings."

Dana poked a curious finger down into the pouch.

"No my queen!" cautioned Ibbur. "Please don't touch what you know nothing about!"

"But Ibbur, I'm the one who made the pouch," Dana insisted, lashing it to her belt with twined grass. "I must know something about this."

"About weaving strands together," said Ibbur hotly, "about moons and suns, bits and wholes, you once knew all there was! But about plants—their uses and dangers!—you never knew. How could you from where you stood in your castles? Only we who dwell among the green things know their properties, their tonics and poisons!" Ibbur's eyes narrowed and he chanted:

> *Beware the rose,*
> *its thorn and briar,*
> *Sweet petals protected*
> *to prick with fire!*
>
> *Or foxglove's peril,*
> *dead men's bells,*
> *By slightest touch,*
> *headaches and spells!*
>
> *Or sweet black elder*
> *or elder's berry,*
> *Poison before*
> *cooked down to jelly!*

Ibbur jumped to the back of the green wind and was carried to Dana. "I'll teach you, my queen, what you'll need to know about plants. But please be careful!" He pointed to a watery bog across the stream. "There! Fields of wild rosemary. Marsh tea. Makes a fine syrup for coughs. But if you take too much, it's poison! Remember and learn, dear queen. Seed and stalk, root and leaf, bud, flower and berry are like riddles. They hold clues to unmask and to know. They will teach you the nature of things. But they can also deceive and lead you astray!

"Know, my queen," warned Ibbur, "some plants contain seeds of treachery. Stinking nightshade! Henbane seeds! Tar would have you eat them and die!"

Dana's eyes opened wide. She turned abruptly, hurrying back to the dugout. The four winds followed, and Ibbur too, scurrying behind bewildered, calling, "What is it?!"

"Now I *do* remember this place!" said Dana excitedly. "I followed Tar here once before, long ago, when he'd taken the sparks of the Mountain of Wind." With haste and certainty, she pushed past the witch hazel, Ibbur scampering to catch up, hand on his jelly-cap. "He went through this hedge, then into the cave . . . and was gone—disappeared behind a shadow!"

"Good, my queen! Through here, then, lies our passage, through shadow behind shadow."

Ibbur groped the walls of the dugout, feeling among cracks and spider holes. Dana groped higher where Ibbur couldn't reach. In darkest shadow at the back of the dugout, Dana placed and replaced her hand. There beneath her palm, she felt a draft. "Ibbur, I've found something!"

Dana felt about until her fingertip dipped into a small hole. Wagging her finger above the hole, she felt wind rushing through it, as water down a drain. Ibbur jumped to Dana's sleeve and climbed along her arm to her hand. He observed the hole and nodded. "Through here we'll go, my queen, as through here went Tar with the last sparks of wind."

Brushing her finger above the hole, Dana made a whistling sound in the streaming wind. "You'll just about fit, Ibbur, and then my finger. But what about the rest of me?"

"Trust in a little glamour, my queen. The littlest, tiniest magic is at your fingertips, if you'll remember how to use it."

And Ibbur began:

> By whistle, by windsong,
> by thimble,
> by threading a needle
> with thistle,
> Down we by size,
> to Dana's surprise,
> How nimble, how skinny,
> how simple we shinny . . .

As he chanted, Dana felt a change in the wind at her fingertip. It seemed to no longer whistle past, but *through* her finger as if her finger, and then her whole body, were a whistling pipe. Ibbur's song too blew through her, sounding past her ears, vibrating in her head. . . . Down her arm it passed . . . sound flowing, sifting through her as through a flute, spiraling along her finger toward the hole in the dugout wall.

Ibbur now chanted words that held a charm:

> *Tulura Turia Tulu,*
> *by hollow,*
> *by bone*
> *blowing through.*
>
> *Turia Tulura Tuli,*
> *by breath*
> *of a pipe,*
> *through an eye. . . .*

Before he could finish, Ibbur's cap was sucked from his head toward the hole. He reached to grab it, and was pulled along behind like the tail of a comet. As he squeezed through the hole, Ibbur's last words made tiny echoes, "through an eye, eye, eye. . . ."

Now swept in the wind-stream went the four colored winds. In a blur, spinning color, they passed through the hole. Next was Dana. Like Ibbur, she too was pulled by her hand. Her whistling finger went first. . . .

Chapter Six

THE FLOOD OF WIND

Passing through the tiny hole, Dana thought, impossible! But her finger passed easily and then her hand collapsed and narrowed like wind winging through a tunnel. Dana shrank, squeezed, and funneled through the hole at furious speed.

She emerged into barren, dim twilight. Finger first, then hand and arm, then Dana's head, body and legs expanded as they came out. She resumed her usual shape.

In the gloom Dana saw Ibbur, only a few steps away. But looming behind him, something awesome. . . . Dana's heart beat faster. "Ibbur, what is it?"

For the first time since she'd met him, Ibbur appeared wonder-struck—eyes and mouth wide, green skin gone pale. His voice was smaller than ever and choked. "My queen, dear Dana, I—I've heard tales of this. Legends of old, told and retold. But I never thought, no I never. The Flood of Wind! Impossible to cross! Though beyond it, if legend holds true, the stolen sparks of wind!"

Dana bent low to hear Ibbur above the crashing flood. Before them, the Flood of Wind churned up a thick mist. Wind rose and fell and crashed in billowing waves.

"Impossible to cross, Ibbur? But we must! Tar went this way!"

Wind sprayed off the flood, pushing them back. The four colored winds, whipping like banners, clung to Dana's legs. "Anavak's winds!" she cried. "Can't they carry us over?" But even as she spoke, the winds retreated, slithering like snakes into Dana's shirt pocket.

With shaking fingers, Dana pulled at her pocket. "Come out,

please!" She then fumbled with the pouch on her belt. "Isn't there something in here that will help? Or maybe some words, some magic words. Ibbur, magic like before! What were those words? Oh, let me remember!"

Ibbur shook his head.

"But there must be a way!" Dana pressed. "Some way over or around." She called to the windy flood, "Tulura Turia Tu—"

"Know what you're saying, my queen!" shouted Ibbur. "A charm used wrongly may injure—!"

His words were drowned out by a foghorn's blast sounding over the Flood of Wind. The bow of a boat broke through the mist. A ferry appeared, gliding upon the flood. A voice came gliding too, throaty and blaring with song:

> *Blow high! Blow low! Ye gallant ship!*
> *A-shine-O through the dark,*
> *Braw lofty breezes haik ye up,*
> *Me ship, the Golden Spark!*

The boat came streaming to shore. At its tiller stood a ferryman, face wide and smiling. A single front tooth gleamed in his head, golden and sharp as reflected sun. Dana felt its sheen stab at her eyes.

As the ferryman tied to, Ibbur sprang for Dana's shoulder and slipping under her collar, whispered, "Be ever so careful, my queen. If he offers passage, be clear what the cost! Now, I'll keep out of sight and hearing. And I'll signal with signs. One poke in your arm for yes, two pokes for no," and he scampered down her sleeve.

When his boat had been lashed to a mighty stone, the ferryman turned to Dana. His eyes were deep and hooded. His nostrils flared like a bull's. "Oh! Hail her, oh! And who might ye be on the brae?"

"Who might I be on the what?" Dana asked as she curtsied.

The ferryman's eyes deepened, then he let out a laugh. "Queer speech ye haud. Aye, but ye bob an' bow laek a lass-bairn fair. And would ye be wanting to cross? Who are ye then?"

"A friend of Tar's."

The ferryman doubled over laughing. He coughed and choked and held his wide belly. "Aye, aye—" He arose gasping for air. "A foster o' Tar's then! I dinna ken he haud one. Grumly as he be. An' sich a one!"

"Then you know him? Can you take me to him?"

"Ken him? Aye, 'twas Tar alane wha geed me me tooth!" The ferryman smiled, flashing his grin. "I can taek ye across I can, for a price."

"How much?" Dana hesitated. "I have no money."

The ferryman eyed Dana's pouch. He reached out a grimy hand to squeeze it. "Then I'll taek wha'e'er ye haud in yere bag."

"But it's only twigs and leaves."

"Medicines then! So it's charms ye haud." He fingered the pouch again. "Aye, it's yere medicines I'll taek for pay."

Dana didn't know whether it was wise to agree. She needed to ask Ibbur, so she spoke aloud, as if to herself, "Hmm . . . should I give him what's in my pouch?"

Dana felt a single poke at her arm . . . yes.

"Yes," she said, "it's a deal."

"Hie hindy lass, aboard wie ye then. An' it's heave and awash for Tar's shore!"

Dana climbed on deck while the ferryman untied his boat. He pushed off, bare feet sloshing in the windy tide. With a grunt and great effort, he got aboard. Then he took up a long heavy oar and thrust it down through the windy waves. He twisted and worked the oar, sculling his boat across the Flood of Wind, a song blowing off his lips:

> *Look ahead, look a-weather,*
> *Look alert, me Flying Spark!*
> *Blaw ye strang an' awa-O,*
> *Aboon the blast o' raging flood,*
> *As winds do lift a wave-O,*
> *As winds do lift awa!*

The ferryman's boat pitched and teetered on cresting waves, then plunged down into windy swirls. With each rise and fall went Dana's stomach dancing like butter in a churn. Had her belly not been empty by this time, it shortly would have been. Dana wobbled so on her feet, she had to sit down. Even then, her head spun, and she felt like vomiting, but couldn't.

The ferryman cast a gleeful look upon her. "Wod ye be tossing up any bait lass? I wod fain ye tossed it o'er the side!" And he laughed, shaking his fat cheeks.

Dana felt too seasick to care. Black and white checks loomed before her eyes, wiping out her vision.

Sharp cries then came blowing on the wind, like the cawing of a thousand crows. Screeches descended from the sky and swam up swarming at the boat.

"Tar's welcoming brigade, ahoy!" called the ferryman.

As her vision was clouded by seasickness, Dana was spared their sight. But the sound of Tar's troops crashed on her ears like a tempest.

They were neither crows, nor any other bird. Neither were they bats, nor sharks, nor any fish. They were like reptiles, or legged serpents, wing-borne or swimming, scale-covered with sharp spikes down their backs. Like vultures they descended and surrounded like sharks, snapping and clawing in crowded frenzy.

"Hail their skriech and skreigh!" cried the ferryman.

Dana huddled over, drew up her legs, and ducked her head down between her knees. Through the deafening noise, she hardly noticed Ibbur's signal: no! Nor could she hear his muffled cry, "Move your knee! Don't crush me, my queen!" Ibbur had to wriggle himself to safety in a fold of sleeve.

"We're drawing nigh on Tar's shore!" bellowed the ferryman.

The boat neared land, an island shrouded in cloud and mist. Windy water oozed in the bay, inky thick as old grease. The ferryman pulled his boat up at a jetty of craggy gray rock and tied fast to the darkest stone.

The creatures dispersed into air and flood, flying or swimming away amid fading shrieks. All except one. The largest. It hovered on wing above the boat, jaws slack, tongue jutting, as a seabird hunting fish.

Dana rose shakily to her feet, grateful that the turbulent trip had ended. The checks before her eyes had gone. Looking back over the flood, she saw Tar's troops shrinking toward the edge of the horizon. Overhead, however, the largest one still circled like a vulture in reptile skin. Dana's own skin tingled with goose flesh as she walked with dizzy step to the boat's bow.

"Avast!" shouted the ferryman. "Wod ye jump ship withouten me pay?!"

"No—why no—" stammered Dana, fumbling with her pouch.

"Then gee it here!" he demanded and ripped the pouch from her belt. Then holding the pouch, he ordered her off.

"No!" yelled Dana. "I agreed to pay you with what's *in* the pouch!" She made a desperate grab for it.

The ferryman swung the pouch above his head, out of Dana's reach, and laughed.

"But the pouch is mine! It wasn't part of the deal!"

"What deal?" The ferryman sneered and smiled cruelly. Light glinted off his single golden tooth. "Ye expect fair play on Tar's shore, do ye?" Again he laughed. "Methinks there's more magic in the bag itself than in what's inside!"

Dana made another grab for the pouch, but the ferryman held it high above his head. He sniggered and smiled crookedly, and his gold tooth glistened.

Dana made a final leap, grabbing wildly for what she could reach—not the pouch, but the ferryman's tooth. She took hold of its golden shine and yanked. The ferryman cried out as the tooth came loose in Dana's hand. Surprised at her catch, Dana closed her hand tightly around it.

"Me tooth!" roared the ferryman. "Precious it be!" He swiped a hairy hand at Dana. She backed off quickly. "Ne'er shall ye taek it!"

"Then give me back my pouch!"

He threw it at her. Dana picked up the pouch and spoke out, as if to herself, "Should I give him back his tooth?"

Two pokes at her arm told her, no.

Dana thrust the tooth down into her pouch. The ferryman leaped for her throat. Before he could take hold, the hovering creature shot down like lightning. Sharp talons gripped the back of Dana's belt and snatched her from the deck.

"I'll ha back me tooth, I will . . . !"

Dana heard the ferryman's cry dwindle away as she was borne up through murky skies. It seemed to Dana that the ferryman and his boat just sank away below her. While above her head, a green reptile's chest heaved under giant flapping wings.

The creature rose through the murk, banked, and circled the island. It flew through a dark wind, veered, then sped down through layers of light and dark. Dana could see, then couldn't, then could, then couldn't again and again going down.

Down through the layers, the creature gained speed. In flashes of light, Dana tried to make things out. Something seemed to be spinning up toward her. It flickered into sight looming closer, larger. It came slicing through light and dark. To Dana it seemed like a giant sword coming to cleave her. Then it seemed like lightning ready to strike. In a final flash, it filled Dana's vision . . . Tar's Castle! Dana closed her eyes and screamed.

Chapter Seven

TAR'S CASTLE

When her scream had echoed and faded, the creature was gone. Dana found herself alone in a tower atop Tar's Castle. Alone but for Ibbur huddled deep in her sleeve and the four winds in her pocket.

Ibbur poked out his head. "You've certainly not forgotten how to scream, my queen," he said, straightening his cap.

"Ibbur, I thought I'd be cut into pieces!"

"Tar's trickery, my queen. His lies slice four ways! Always to deceive. He'll have you see what isn't there and blind you to what is. First black, then white, then black, then white again. One end, then the other, another and another. He'll pull you in all directions to keep you from the truth, to keep you from your sparks."

Ibbur's words puzzled Dana. But something troubled her more. "Do you know what this is—this place?"

"Tar's tower, my queen."

Dana's throat felt tight. She re-tied the pouch to her belt and held it, pensively. A new question formed in her mind.

"Yes, my queen, it is," said Ibbur.

"What is?" Dana wondered how he knew. "You mean the tooth?"

"Yes, the golden tooth. The first of your sparks! Taken from the mouth of Tar himself in one of his many guises. Well done, Queen Dana!"

Dana shuddered. "I didn't know it was him."

"And well you didn't. Had you known the ferryman was Tar, you might have panicked. Instead you've seized what is yours. Now you know you can face him, no matter his face."

Dana swallowed hard. Her brow knit in thought, then she spoke. "But if the ferryman was Tar as you say, why did his creature snatch me from his grasp?"

"Tar takes no chances, thoughtful queen. He wanted you in his cage. He never foresaw you'd take his tooth and was baffled when you did. You surprised him."

"I surprised myself," said Dana, now looking about the tower. It was round with curving stone walls. No doors. No windows. Only portholes built between stones—too narrow for Dana to fit through. Her eyes widened with fear. "Ibbur, how did that creature get us in here?"

"By some shadowy route of Tar's no doubt."

Dana peered out through a hole. "It's a long way down. And the sky is layered like a cake. Black and white, up and down." Dana lowered her head. "What do you suppose Tar plans to do? Leave us here forever?" Hot tears streamed down her face. "Ibbur, we'll starve!"

"Nonsense! Tar knows your powers better than you do! But he hopes you've forgotten. And now you've got something he wants—that single sparkling tooth. He'll not leave you till he gets it back."

"But Ibbur, don't you see? He has it back. I have the tooth, but Tar has me! We're trapped here in his tower!"

"If that's what you think, Queen Dana, then you don't know Tar and you don't remember yourself! Tar is greedy. For him to possess the spark, he must have it in his hand. Understand? Remember, you're trapped so long as you think you're trapped. Have you forgotten what Anavak told you? Each spark contains a charm, a key. Each will bestow a power and lead you forward. But only if you're wise enough to use it."

The golden tooth glowed faintly through the weave of Dana's pouch. Dana felt encouraged. Yes, perhaps there was a way out. If only she could find it. If only she knew how to use her charm. How might the spark help her?

She didn't have long to wonder. She heard the clank and turn of iron bolts and the creaking of old hinges. The largest of stones in the wall began to move. It groaned and slid heavily across the floor.

Dana stood frozen. The stone scraped to a halt. Her ears pricked and her eyes stared fixed. But her nose told her what had come: a spicy scent on the air. Whiffs of something savory and sweet. Dana's mouth watered. Her stomach grumbled. Food! She suddenly felt hungry. So hungry it hurt.

"Zoup!" announced a voice stepping from behind the stone. "Hot zoup! The hottezt! Pumpkin zoup. The pumpkiniezt!"

Dressed in white apron and chef's hat, the man behind the voice reminded Dana of a pumpkin himself. His flesh appeared orange and bulged like a pumpkin's. Fat ballooned out between folds.

At the first movement of the stone, Ibbur had quietly ducked from sight. He stood near Dana's ear, hidden behind her hair, whispering. "Queen Dana, please listen," he urged. "Don't eat it. Not a drop. I beg you! Not the tiniest slurp of that soup! For it's enchanted by Tar. By smell and look and taste it's food. But it isn't! No, it's the opposite of food. It's hunger itself. By eating it, you'll grow hungrier and emptier. A bowlful and you'll starve!"

Even as she heard Ibbur's warning, Dana's mouth watered. She hadn't eaten since when? Since Anavak's biscuits and tea. Her stomach ached. The smells teased her nose.

"Mmmmm . . . my yez, you have that hungry look, my zweet." The pumpkin-man waddled toward Dana offering a brimming bowl. "The zmell iz alluring, izn't it? But the flavor. Oh, the flavor iz divine! Here, here!" He pushed the bowl under Dana's nose. "Zuch zoup iz fit for a queen. Indeed, I've made it juzt for you!"

Dana stepped back. "I'm really not hungry. Thank you, no."

"Oh don't be shy. Pleaze don't. If only you knew how I've zlaved for you. To zatizfy your queenly tazte!"

Dana inched farther away. "For me? Why go to so much trouble for me? I don't even know you."

"Oh, but I know you!" The pumpkin-man held out a spoonful. "Who doezn't know Queen Dana? Who doezn't love our queen?"

He waddled closer holding the soup, spreading his pumpkin arms. The soupy aroma grew stronger. Spicier. Sweeter. It was on his very breath—an overpowering fragrance that came to enfold her. "A tazte. Juzt a tazte, my queen." His thick arms embraced her. "How can you rezizt my zoup? My labor of love for you. Zweet love and pumpkin zo pure."

He hugged her closer and his arms were like vines. They grew thicker and tighter around her. Pumpkin flesh pressed against her. Dana was smothering in his smells. Choking in his hold. Her ears pounded. She heard Ibbur's small voice, but couldn't make out what he said. "Let go!" she cried between breaths. "Please let go!" as she struggled for air.

"But I love you zo and I've waited zo long. And will you not try my zoup? Muzt you refuze my gift?"

"I have a gift for you too!" The words were out before Dana knew what she'd said.

"For me? Then you do love me!" The pumpkin-man loosened his grip. "What might it be? A queenly gift! It muzt be grand. It muzt be preciouz!"

"Yes!" said Dana desperately. "Precious." Again her words jumped out without thought. "It's here in my pouch."

"In your pouch? Oh, give it to me, then. Pleaze, pleaze!" He tightened his grip. His viney arms sent out tendrils that entwined and crept through the pouch. "Yez. What have we here? Twigz and leavez and oh! Feelz like a tooth!" The pumpkin-man's face lit up with a sinister jack-o'-lantern grin. "Zaving it for the tooth fairy?" He cackled as his tendrils exited the pouch wrapped around Dana's spark. "A queenly gift indeed! Zo fine it shinez!"

"No!" shouted Dana. "Not that! I didn't mean—"

"Yez you did!" The pumpkin-man let go his grip on Dana. His vines slipped away. "Zo great iz your love for me that it shinez!" Again he cackled. "Now I'll leave you to your zoup."

But as he backed off with the spark, there came a sizzling and the smell of burning wood. Smoke rose from the tendril that held the spark. The pumpkin-man cried out—and the golden tooth fell from his tendrilly fingers. He waddled quickly forward, tendrils flailing, while Ibbur, unseen, quietly retrieved the golden tooth.

"Where iz it?!" The jack-o'-lantern face burned brighter as once again the viney arms wrapped around Dana and squeezed. In his haste, however, the pumpkin-man pinned just one of Dana's arms. Dana struggled, smothering once more in fat pumpkin flesh. But now she felt a tingling in her hands, a rush of blood through her arms. Her free hand punched and scratched at the face and vines. Her nails seemed to sparkle, tearing wildly, gouging out pumpkin pulp.

From Dana's pocket emerged the four colored winds. They gathered as a flock and flew at the pumpkin face, beating the head as with wings. Again Dana heard Ibbur's tiny voice. What was he saying? She tried to listen as she fought for her life. One word. What was it? Over and again. . . . The viney arms tightened. Then she heard: "Eyes! Eyes!"

Boldly, Dana swiped at the pumpkin-man's shining eyes. Her heart pounded in her chest. Her fingers gripped and ripped at those triangular eyes. Still the jack-o'-lantern face burned brighter with evil.

Dana tore out chunks of pumpkin as the mouth wailed in pain. Something inside urged her on—a bravery she'd never known. In that moment, Dana felt no pity, no pause. Her fingers, then her whole hand entered the gourdy skull. Her nails gouged deeper into hot pumpkin flesh.

"Cruel queen!" cried the mouth.

As Dana clawed, she scraped some fragment from the pumpkin head walls. She felt it tumble and fall into her palm. In reflex her hand closed over it. Instantly, the light in the pumpkin face went out with a moan. The face caved in. The pumpkin-man crumpled to the floor.

Dana withdrew her tight-fisted hand, stepping from the limp twitching vines. The four tiny winds blew hollow through the pumpkin head.

"Hurrah! Queen Dana, you've done it!" cheered Ibbur.

Dana stood exhausted. Her hand hung clutched at her side. Sweet pumpkin smells dwindled, replaced by the odor of rot.

"What is your catch this time?" asked Ibbur.

"I—I don't know." Dana's hand remained clutched tight. Slowly she relaxed her fingers. Her hand opened like clouds passing to unveil a star. And there in Dana's palm, star-like, was the second shining spark.

"The second spark to be sure!" cried Ibbur. "Your powers do grow with your charms, my queen!"

Still breathing hard, Dana was bewildered. She felt grateful for the sparks, but confused as to their charms. "What charms, Ibbur, what magic do they hold?"

Ibbur held the tooth aloft. "This spark, the golden tooth, brought you bravery. It gave you a lion's heart and claws."

Dana stared at the tooth, eyes brimming with wonder, but flickering with doubt.

"Do you think you could have done what you did without it? The Dana who shivered in her bed could never!" Ibbur went on, "Anavak would say, ah, this first spark worked on you from within. It entered your heart and there worked its change."

Yes, Dana thought, she had felt something different as she'd torn at the pumpkin head. Her heart had pounded and welled in her chest. She'd felt blood pumping, hot, inflamed, like sparks to her fingertips. Dana clasped and unclasped the shining spark in her hand. "And what about this second one?" she asked.

"The second, I think, remains to be seen. We can't yet know what charm it holds. Though it was magic enough just to find it, was it not? Magic works in part by drawing you to it."

Dana took the second spark in her fingers and brought it to the lip of her pouch. "Then we'll see," she said to the spark, "what charm you have brought me." And she dropped it inside.

Ibbur handed her the golden tooth. This too she placed in the pouch and tied the grassy lips closed for safekeeping.

"Now then," said Ibbur, "two sparks and one more to go in Tar's shadow world behind the Mountain of Wind. And since you're still doubtful, Queen Dana, again I must warn you. Tar lies and tricks with his many masks. Good masking evil. Evil masking good. Four times over! He brings you hunger and calls it food. He harbors hate behind masks of love. His kind of love smothers and destroys!"

"But I didn't eat the soup, Ibbur. I didn't let him trick me!"

"No, you didn't. But you did offer him a gift from your pouch!"

"Just as we offered the ferryman!" Dana defended.

"That was before your pouch contained a spark!"

"But he was squeezing me to death!"

"And he would have. Had the first spark not worked a change in you!"

Dana grew silent. Ibbur climbed nimbly into her shirt pocket. When he was settled, Dana reached down and with a finger straightened his jelly-cap. Ibbur looked up smiling. "Thank you, my queen."

"Thank *you*, Ibbur."

Dana stepped past the rotting pumpkin-man where the heavy stone still stood ajar. The opening led to a passageway and as there was no other way to go, Dana stepped out into darkness.

Chapter Eight

ESCAPE . . . AND CAPTURE

A navak's winds led the way through the dark passage. Dana followed with rapid steps, until a crunching underfoot made her stop.

"What am I stepping on?"

There beneath her shoe was a white seed. "Pumpkin seeds, Ibbur." Several steps farther she found another. Then another. Farther and another.

"Save them, my queen," said Ibbur. "Keep them in your pouch."

"But how will they all fit? And why bother?"

"Queen Dana, you ought to know. The pouch itself is charmed. You wove magic into it yourself. Anything you place inside will fit, as if it were bottomless. Believe me, dear queen, the bother will be worth it. For the seeds will serve you, sooner than later."

Dana continued down the passageway stopping to gather pumpkin seeds as she went. Sometimes the passage narrowed and she could touch both walls with her palms. Other times it opened into large cave-like chambers. Though the passage was dim, Dana's way was lit by her two sparks shining through the weave of her pouch.

After much walking, bending and stooping, she came to a black rushing river. A golden bridge spanned its bank. Dana cautiously set one foot on the first golden plank of the bridge. The bridge neither creaked nor swayed. Another step forward and another and Dana was crossing the bridge.

When she'd gone halfway, suspended above midstream, she

heard a shuffling sound approaching. It grew louder, like the stomping of distant armies nearing. The bridge began to shake. Dana looked ahead and behind, and at first saw nothing. Then as she lowered her gaze to fix on the sound, she saw them. . . .

They came creeping up the thresholds at each end. In single files they came marching in step. Each as large as Dana. At first she was dumbstruck. Then terror overtook her and she screamed, "Ants!"

Giant ones. Like foot soldiers they advanced, distinct not only in size, but color. For those at one end had black heads, white middles, and black rumps. While the others were reversed—with white heads, black middles, and white rumps.

Dana ran in one direction, then the other. All in vain. Both ways were blocked. The ant armies pressed forward. White heads and mouths chomping from one direction, black from the other. And the black river rushed below.

The four winds rose in a flurry, quickly weaving into a blanket as they had done before. They swept beneath Dana, ready to fly her past. But the way was impassable. Ants had climbed upon each other's backs four high. The bridge was heaped and clogged with ants to the ceiling.

In a panic Dana leapt to the railing and was about to jump from the bridge, when Ibbur called out, "Wait! Tar's river is certain death. Know that! Queen Dana, you must stand your ground!"

Dana wavered. She could hear the raspy chomping of the ants' giant mouths and the eerie buzzing of antennae. Then a thought seized her and she remembered her first spark and its charm. Fear fled instantly as Dana took heart. She jumped back down to the golden planks of the bridge.

Dana took in a long and deep breath. She paused, holding her breath, then slowly exhaled. Now she felt ready.

Antennae buzzed closer. Soon they were touching. They felt about Dana's head exploring and searching, buzzing loudly. Dana felt them as light woolly fingers tickling her skin. Antennae prodded her pouch. Some tried to thrust through the weave, but those that did shrunk back. Dana could see the pouch grow brighter from within.

Then she thought she heard words amid the buzzing. Could the ants be speaking? Dana somehow understood them. A pair of black antennae flitted about her right ear. "She's ours!" they seemed to say.

"No, she's ours!" buzzed the white antennae at her other ear.

"I'm none of yours!" cried Dana, beating off their prodding.

Several hundred antennae buzzed with laughter. They crowded upon Dana, jeering her name, "Queen Dana, Queen Dana, you're no queen of ours!"

Dana lashed out bravely. But for each ant she swiped away, two more came climbing over its back. The ants quickly overwhelmed her. They seized her by her legs, white-headed ants to one side, black to the other. A tug of war began with Dana in the middle being tugged.

"Give her here!"

"No! Give her here!"

As Dana flailed with her arms, a thought flashed through her head. The pumpkin seeds! She brushed antennae away to get at her pouch. Bringing out a handful of seeds, she tossed them among the ants and reached for more.

Her hunch proved right, though only by half. The white-headed ants went greedily for the white bait. They scurried over each other and over the black in a frenzy for food. The ants broke ranks as Dana continued tossing seeds. The distracted white-headed ones quickly overwhelmed the black. Dana saw her chance. . . .

Past the confused swarm of ants she fled, stepping over their backs to cross the golden bridge. Gaining the new bank she raced down the passageway scattering seeds behind her.

The tangle of ants on the bridge soon sorted itself out. While white-headed ones remained greedily gathering seeds, the black-headed ants doubled back the way they'd come, pursuing Dana.

Dana could hear the hurried march of ants behind her. She rushed headlong through the passage seeking a way out. The passage stretched on, sloping and curving sharply down.

"Stir your tracks, my queen, make haste!" shouted Ibbur, popping his head up over the edge of Dana's pocket.

"Easy for you, Ibbur, easy for you," panted Dana, "hiding the way you do!"

"I have my place, Queen Dana. I do my part. Please hurry!"

Dana quickened her step. The ground underfoot became softer, the slope steeper. She was losing footing, slipping and sliding over earth and stones. The blanket of winds again swept beneath Dana, carrying her forward at greater speed.

The passage opened on chamber after chamber. One to the left. Another to the right. Another and another in a maze of tunnels and caves. Dana wasn't sure which way to turn or whether to continue on. She could hear the black ants' noisy approach from behind—the grating grinding of their jaws. Stale air rushed ahead of them.

"Turn here!" Dana called to the winds.

Into a chamber they ducked, hoping to lose the ants. The chamber went nowhere. Back they flew to the chamber entrance, but the sour breath of the ants was already upon them. Dana's escape was blocked. The four winds retreated to her pouch.

The black ant army buzzed shouts of victory, closing on Dana with open jaws. Dana struck back wildly. But her efforts were useless. The ant army hoisted her wriggling upon their backs and carried her off. Down the passageway they went, antennae buzzing a chorus of cheers:

> *We've nabbed her,*
> *we've grabbed her,*
> *guffaw!*
> *We bear her,*
> *we'll tear her,*
> *haw, haw!*
> *Down to our nest,*
> *this hideous pest,*
> *ha-ha, tee-hee,*
> *and hee-haw!*
> *We'll gash her,*
> *and mash her,*
> *and more!*

Past chambers they bore her raising shouts, chortles, and chirps. Dana struggled bravely, but vainly. Near the end of the passageway they entered the largest chamber. There they spun her on their backs romping and kicking up dust.

Then through their uproar, Dana heard a single, piercing voice, "Enough! Quite enough!"

The cheering ended with a hush. Dana was set down. The ant army bowed low all as one. The silence was deep with respect.

"A task well executed," boomed the voice. "Now rise and go to your rest. Guards! Bring her to me!"

A dozen of the largest ants pushed Dana forward. There before her, sitting high on a nest of jewels, loomed the largest, fattest ant of all. A guard poked Dana at the back of her knees. "Bow in the presence of the queen!"

"Oh!" Dana started and quickly curtsied. "I meant no disrespect."

"No disrespect indeed!" The ant queen spoke from her nest. "Why your very presence is disrespectful!"

The guards buzzed in agreement. "Silence!" commanded the ant queen. Then to Dana, "You seem to understand our language. Is that so?"

"I guess . . . yes, I guess I do!" said Dana.

"How is that?" buzzed the ant queen. "Have you always?"

"No, I don't think so. I mean, I never tried. I never knew I could before!"

"Ha! How you lie! Oh you're a sly one you are. A sorceress, no doubt. How else could one such as you know our speech?"

"I—I truly don't—"

"Truly!" The ant queen shifted sluggishly on her nest of jewels. "Truly you're a sorceress and a witch! What brings you here, witch?"

"I—" Dana hesitated. "Tar! I came to see Tar."

"By invitation?" asked the ant queen in a mocking tone. The company of guards tittered with scorn. "You're an invader!" continued the queen.

"No, I—I'm Dana . . . just a girl."

"Dana then? Guffaw, guffaw, and guffaw! Oh, we know all about you, Dana!" The ant queen spat out the name. "Dana the witch who pretends she's a queen! How could a creature ugly as you claim queenhood? Seize the witch!" the ant queen called to her guards. "For invading my nest," the ant queen rasped. "For interrupting the hatching of my wealth. For getting in the way of our war on the bridge. For spoiling our fun! I condemn you to death. Away with her!"

Though she resisted, the ant-guard began hauling Dana off. In the short scuffle that ensued none saw tiny Ibbur leap and secretly creep along Dana's shoulder. Hidden behind her ear, he whispered, "Dear Dana, for all you're worth, flatter her. Appeal to her mercy. Appeal to her greed. If none of that works, threaten her. For surely if you don't we'll be ant food!"

Dana stopped struggling and dropped to her knees. "Oh queen, dear queen, I beg you!" she pleaded. "Darling queen! Generous queen! Lovely queen, have mercy! By your beauty, by your grace, please spare me!" she cried.

The ant queen smiled vainly. She puffed up her fat belly and chest. "Now, now. That's the proper tone. And conduct more befitting your place! But I wonder, witch . . . if I do spare you, what do you offer in return?"

"In return . . . in return—" Dana stammered, not knowing what to say. She wouldn't offer the contents of her pouch, not again! But it was all she had. Or was it? A new thought entered Dana's head and she seized it. Simple, she reasoned, I'll offer myself.

"Dear queen, darling queen," Dana spoke outright. "I'll be your servant, your handmaiden. I'll wait on you, bathe you, shampoo your fine furry legs. I'll massage your royal back and shine your regal skin!"

"Ha!" rebuffed the ant queen. "I have maidservants aplenty. Ten thousand to be sure. I do not need one more as awfully hideous as you!"

"Then—then—" Sudden thoughts all new and clever crowded Dana's mind. She wondered at her own thinking: so quick, so fast, so cunning! But I've never thought like this before, she considered with amazement. All at once she knew what to say.

"I offer you magic!"

Dana felt a sharp pinch at her ear. "Not your pouch! Not again!" warned Ibbur.

"Hmm. Magic then?" buzzed the ant queen. "What witchy magic could you bestow?"

Dana spoke with quick assurance. "The kind to increase your wealth, sweet queen. Riches to double, no, triple your nest!"

The ant queen's antennae buzzed with greedy interest. "Riches you say? Gems and jewels? Hmm. Hmm. Come forward witch. Release her! Come sit with me here, witch. How might this magic of yours work?" Dana stepped closer to the nest. "A ladder!" ordered the queen. "A ladder for the witch!"

On command the ant-guard formed a chain, head to tail, twelve ants long. Dana climbed along their backs up the ant-chain to the shining nest of jewels.

"Offer to change her crumbs into jewels!" whispered Ibbur urgently, dangling at the back of Dana's ear.

"Can I do it?"

"You can do it!"

"Are you asking or answering me, witch?" The ant queen was annoyed. "Which is it?"

"Magic, most beautiful queen. Magic to turn your crumbs into riches!"

"Crumbs into riches, indeed," sneered the ant queen and licked her lips. "Pray for your own sake you can do it!" She laughed through her ant nose and called to her guard, "Stir my army! Bring all crumbs of food here to my chamber! Leave them for the witch to worry over with her spells." She set her vast ant eyes on Dana. "And as you're so sure of yourself, witch, I'll leave you another task as well. Find my priceless diamond pin lost deep in my nest. Find it," the ant queen cruelly threatened, "or you'll be changed to crumbs yourself!"

The chamber resounded with the raspy laughs of ant legions. "Guffaw and guffaw!" They were filing in bearing crumbs and marching out for more.

The ant queen glowered at Dana. "And no witchy tricks!" Then she turned her fat back and lazily crept from her nest.

The ants bent to their task. Piles of crumbs grew around Dana, mounds upon mounds of ant morsels. Mountains of crumbs rose and dwarfed the nest of jewels where Dana stood.

When the last crumb was carefully packed in place and the last ant was out, the chamber was sealed. Dirt-moving ants buried Dana inside. In the silence of the chamber, Dana wondered, how long would the air hold out?

Chapter Nine

MASHIRE

L ooking down from the nest at the heaps of crumbs, Dana was weary and doubtful. How could she ever do it, even with Ibbur's help? Change crumbs into gems and jewels? Find the ant queen's diamond pin? As the ants were so fond of saying, guffaw!

"Most hospitable company, ants." Ibbur walked along Dana's collar bone. "Chin up, my queen," he said poking a tiny finger under Dana's jaw.

"But how will I do it, Ibbur? We'll smother or become ant snacks!"

"Then perhaps you should think, Queen Dana. What were you thinking when you offered magic to the ant queen? Was it again your pouch?"

"No, Ibbur, no! Never again! Not the pouch, something else. But I don't know. . . . I felt so certain. And I knew what to say. My thoughts were so clear. Like understanding the ants. Their buzzing became words in my head! Words and ideas going around. And I knew how to pick out the right ones. Magic, I was certain. Was I wrong, Ibbur?"

"Far from it, fair queen!" Ibbur was beaming. "Within you again there were changes. Charms brought by the second spark to be sure! That one taken from the pumpkin head. It carries a headful of cunning, yes? Cleverness! And another gift too, a boon, the speech of animals."

"So that's how I understood the ants. But think as I may, I still don't know what magic turns crumbs into riches."

"My queen, there was a time when changing crumbs to riches was but a boring game to you."

Dana became quiet, thoughtful. . . . "Did you know me then, Ibbur?"

"Forever watchful I've been, Queen Dana." Ibbur bowed deeply, and rose excitedly. "Now for some magic!" He tossed his red jelly-cap out over the teeming crumbs. "You see it? It's there!"

The cap flew around the room spilling color as it went. Where it passed, the crumbs below bloomed into gems, gold, silver, and jewels. Green emeralds poured down over topaz and blue sapphire. Diamonds cascaded like waterfalling rainbows. Opal avalanches tumbled. Rubies hatched from crumbs. Golden beads and bracelets glittered spangled color.

The cap returned to Ibbur's hand like a cardinal to her nest. But before its flight was done, not a crumb had been left a crumb. The chamber shone like a galaxy of stars, sparkling in Dana's eyes.

Ibbur set his cap back on his head. "Splendor . . . say it."

"Say it, but why, what is it?" asked Dana.

"Splendor? Why it's before you! Magic and more. Majesty, radiance, beauty! Splendor, say it."

Dana gazed about the chamber, dazzled by its glow. Jewels shimmered in heaps, almost afire, pulsing with color. "Yes," she said, "splendor." And again, more certain, "Splendor!"

The nest of jewels began to rumble beneath Dana's feet. The heaps of royal gems shifted and swirled. Riches gushed and spewed about the chamber like rocks from the mouth of a volcano. Dana lost her footing, slipping over rubies and jade, while Ibbur held fast to her hair.

"Ibbur, it's an earthquake!"

"Not exactly!"

A gap opened in the nest and down they plunged, swallowed through the jeweled hole. When they reached bottom, the quaking stopped. So quiet, thought Dana, she could hear—but before she finished her thought . . . Dana felt herself hurled back up through the nest. Now she was standing on top where she'd been. The chamber once again grew quiet and still.

"Splendid!" hailed Ibbur. "Splendor does, splendor did!"

"It certainly did!" said Dana, picking jewels from her hair, pulling opal from her pockets, brushing gold dust from her pouch. "Ouch!" Dana's finger pricked on a jutting jewel.

"The pin!" she cried. "The diamond pin!"

Ibbur lowered himself to the lip of the pouch and examined the pin. His eyes shone like beads of black onyx. Softly, reverently he spoke, "Mashire," and knelt devoutly on one knee. The diamond pin glistened.

"You know it? You've seen it before?" Dana was bewildered.

"I've only heard tell of it. Mashire. A gracious gift, my queen. The third of your sparks! Take it now."

Dana withdrew the pin from where it stuck in her pouch. It glinted between her fingers like a tiny sword drawn from a scabbard. Dana saw how the pin was jagged, formed in a zigzagging shape, angle after angle tapering to a point. It was wrought of rare and noble metals honed to a razor's edge, with a slender handle of gold. At its tip was a tiny diamond, the hardest of all and any, cut and polished to the sharpest of points.

"Mashire the Thunderbolt, my queen." Ibbur's voice was hushed. "With it you may cut through anything. Shield, fortress, and castle yield to it. No mountain stands against it. But know this: The Thunderbolt grows in power and size with the skills of its user. In unskilled hands Mashire may still be defeated. In the right hands, however, Mashire is invincible."

Dana turned the tiny shimmering sword in her fingers. "Are mine the right hands, Ibbur?"

"Yes, my queen, they are. But you'll still have to learn. And the learning isn't just in your hands."

Dana gripped the sword. So much power in such a small thing, she marveled. "How will I learn to use it?"

"You'll teach yourself, my queen, by feel, by remembering what you know."

Dana gazed intently at the tiny diamond-tipped sword. "Mashire." Shine glinted off the crooked blade and cast a tiny glow across Dana's cheek.

There came a trembling at the chamber entrance. The buried earth shuddered with movement. Dana could hear the muffled sounds of digging, scraping, and a thousand voices raspy with song:

> *Dig a-dig dig,*
> *while yet she breathes,*
> *Dana the witch,*
> *to squeeze and tease . . .*

Now the four winds, which had remained well hidden in Dana's pouch, flew to her side. Ibbur jumped into her pocket. As the first ant broke through to the chamber, the winds gathered and swirled at the entrance.

"The winds will delay them, my queen," said Ibbur, "but they can't stop an army!"

"Then what, Ibbur, what?!" cried Dana.

"Your charms, dear queen! Your lion's heart, your cunning, and the Thunderbolt, Mashire!" As he spoke, ants poured into the chamber overwhelming the winds.

Dana closed her eyes and gripped the sword in her fingertips. She breathed deeply, focusing her attention on her heart, her mind, and the tiny sword in her hand.

Into the chamber swarmed the ants bearing their queen upon their backs. At first sight of the jeweled mounds, the ant-queen rasped, "Halt!" All became hushed.

"Guffaw and guffaw!" The ant queen burst out laughing. "Crumbs to jewels? You've proven yourself, indeed. Witch then you must be! And my diamond pin? Why it's there in your hand, witch. Seize her!"

The guards rushed forward. Before they reached Dana, the four winds encircled her arm, spiraling down to her hand. In Dana's heart pulsed bravery. In her mind, cleverness. And in her arm, with the tiny sword at her fingertips, flexed new strength, new power and force.

The winds swept beneath Dana, lifting her above the ants.

"Your sorcery will get you nowhere, witch!" the ant queen shrieked. "Legions!"

All as one, the ant colony swarmed. As before, they piled

upon backs, four high and farther to the chamber ceiling. The winds had no way through.

Quick as thought, the words were upon Dana's lips, "Here's off!"

"Here's after!" replied Ibbur from her pocket.

"I'm off!"

"I'm after!"

Straight up they rose, Dana upon the winds, arm extended above her head. In her hand, the sword Mashire glinted sharpest light. Past ant upon ant, they gained speed, jaws snapping as Dana sped by.

"Fool witch!" taunted the ant queen. "You'll be crushed!"

Dana sped on and up to the vaulted ceiling above. Mind, heart, and hand were fixed, unswerving.

On impact the ant legions roared with one laugh, but in the next instant they gasped and fell silent. For as Dana reached the ceiling, Mashire pierced its boundary. Earth and stone cleaved before her. Through rock-hard shadow, Dana drilled wielding her tiny thunderbolt. Stone melted like butter before Mashire's diamond-tipped blade. And the four colored winds whirred, sweeping away the debris.

Higher they tunneled at furious speed. Dense dry rock gave way to moist porous sandstone. Debris mixed with mist as Dana broke through layers of gravel. Water trickled down her arm. With a rush then, rock fell away and Dana entered an underground stream.

Through a whirlpool they spun rising. More gravel above, then sediment, and other streams. Each flowed colder than the one before it. Dana had begun to shiver. With chattering teeth she called out, "Ib-bur! I'm freezing!"

"Please endure it, my queen, you must!"

Just as he spoke, Mashire pierced thick solid cold. Icy chill stiffened Dana's arm. Her hand froze fast to the tiny sword.

"Through the Pillar of Ice!" called Ibbur. "To the world before the one left behind! To the Mountain of Water, Queen Dana!"

Chapter Ten

THE MOUNTAIN OF WATER

Cold bored through Dana as Mashire chipped through the Pillar of Ice. Great chunks crunched and broke away, falling in icy sheets. While around her, suspended in the column of ice, Dana saw fish and birds and other creatures frozen solid.

Will that happen to me? Dana worried to herself, anxious and bitten with frost. There came a final crunch as Mashire broke past the Pillar of Ice and splashed into the Mountain of Water. Dana gushed through the curving crest of a giant wave. Crashing waters roiled around her as she tumbled through the wave's hollow.

"Ibbur . . . !" she screamed, head over heel.

At the end of the watery flume a shadow gaped. Dana hurtled through sea-spray toward the yawning dark. At its threshold, darkness closed about her. She spun through murky shadow, Mashire in hand. Dark waves buffeted, recoiled, and with one final heave spewed her out.

Dana emerged, dripping and drained, in a thick forest, shivering where she stood on the bank of a boggy pond. The sword, Mashire, was still in her hand, but doubled in size. Her hand opened and closed in wonder. "Mashire has grown, Ibbur, just as you said."

Ibbur's head poked above Dana's shirt pocket. "Yes, my queen, expanding in power and size with your skill."

Dana tucked Mashire into her pouch, then peered into the dank pond. Again she saw checks, black and white before her eyes, as in Tar's world. But these checks appeared larger as if she were looking through square-lensed glasses, one lens black, the other white.

"Another checkerboard, Ibbur. Big and square!"

"Yes, Queen Dana. And again your eyes will adjust. But again I say, don't be fooled! This is Zar's shadow world, behind the Mountain of Water, where good masks evil, and evil masks good. Where every smile is crooked!"

"Yes, I know, as Anavak said. But Tar was worse—she said that too. And I overcame him, didn't I?"

"Worse for his tricks, yes, my queen. Yet Zar's evil is richer than Tar's. He's twice more cruel and vile. Do not let down your guard, or permit yourself to think the struggle will be easier. I give you warning, my queen."

Dana heard Ibbur's words and took them to heart as again she looked into the pond. Odd, she thought, shouldn't I see my reflection? A foul stink suddenly filled her nose, driving her back.

"Blank is Zar's pool," advised Ibbur, "lifeless and reeking of death!"

Dana shuddered. A fresh chill spread over her skin. As one, the four winds darted and whirled in great speed around her. Their colors flashed heat drying Dana and Ibbur both. Then they slowed, sagged, and with colors fading dropped at Dana's feet.

"What's wrong?" Dana cried, stooping to the winds.

"This world is not their place," explained Ibbur. "They knew to stay behind and should have! Instead, they've clung to you, their queen." Ibbur shook his head. "It's best they were gone, if that's still possible."

Dana knelt among the winds, gathering them in her arms. At her touch they brightened, but slightly. "Poor things, what have you done?" A thought then gleamed in Dana's mind. . . . It's air they need, not water! With that, she breathed deeply and blew. And as air passed her lips, each wind swelled, puffing with color.

The winds rose renewed as there came a crashing off in the woods. "Go now!" insisted Ibbur. "Quickly!" The crashing approached as thunder on a storm. "Ho! And away for Anavak!"

The four winds spiraled into a shining ball hovering before Dana. With deep breath she blew . . . and the winds bounded off, plunking down into the pond through which they'd come to vanish beneath the dark waters.

From out of the thicket came a call, "Hey!" And another, "Hey!" Dana started, her ears pricked. There came a rustling, rumbling across the forest floor. Ibbur hunched down. Only his eyes and cap showed above Dana's shirt pocket.

Thwack! Two figures jumped out from behind the trees. . . . "Hey!" "Hey!" Dana turned to run, but one was behind her, the other before her. . . . "Hey!" "Hey!"

Dana spun in her tracks. "Who—what are you?!"

They were three feet tall and wide, standing upright like people. Upon their shoulders sat horrible heads, snouts and tusks like wild boars. Their hands and feet looked human, though fixed to the bodies of dogs. One was white with pitch-black eyes. The other black with eyes of pearl white.

With hairy snouts they began sniffing at Dana, snorting foul air. Ibbur ducked down. Their sniffing was intent and fussy. Upon reaching Dana's shirt, the creatures grew excited. One sniffed her sleeve, the other her collar. They reached her pocket, rooting wildly to get inside. A tiny voice cried out, "Hey!" Surprised and delighted, they answered, "Hey!" "Hey!"

"Keep your noses to yourselves!" shouted Ibbur.

"Then out with you!" said one.

"All right then, stand back!" Ibbur climbed out slowly. He sprang to Dana's shoulder, half-hiding behind her hair.

"Why, Rumble, I believe it's a hob!" The creature peered closely at Ibbur.

"No, Grumble, would you look at those eyes. I'd bet a tusk he's a pook—and up to no good."

"A pook? Bah! Can't you see, dear brother, that cap? A hob, I say. And if not a hob, then a bobble. Yes, I believe he's a bobble. I'd swear it!"

"A bobble? Pah! Dear brother, he's a pook. A pook, dear Grumble. And if he isn't, he's a tig. A tig, do you hear?"

"By your boorish head perhaps!"

"May your tusks fall out, my brother. Why don't you ask what he is and settle it!"

"I? Why Rumble, you'll do it!"

Dana was slowly backing away, hoping that the creatures, busy with themselves, wouldn't notice. Several steps back, she tripped over a root. The creatures were upon her in an instant, each grabbing an arm and a leg.

"Hey! You'll pull me apart!" Dana screamed.

"Hey!" "Hey!" they replied.

"Let go, Rumble!"

"Let go first, Grumble!"

"Let go, the both of you!" shouted Ibbur.

"Then out with it, who are you?" said one.

Ibbur spoke in hushed tones at Dana's ear.

"Why Rumble, they're rude, whatever they are."

"What more to expect of a tig."

"Tie them up!"

"Yes, tie them up!"

One held Dana as the other climbed a tree, pulling down vines. Dana squirmed uselessly. The creature tightened his grip, half-choking her air.

Ibbur had meanwhile dropped to the pouch to retrieve Mashire, when the white creature returned trailing vines. "Up to no good, hey tig?" he snorted and clasped Ibbur's head between two hairy fingers.

"No!" cried Dana.

The creatures laughed uproariously, stomping their feet.

"Shall I pinch him, Grumble?"

"Oh, yes do! Crack his head like an acorn! Squeeze the brains from him like water from a stone!"

"U-mmm! Then we'll suck his skull, like marrow from bone!" Again they laughed and the fingers tightened against Ibbur's head. "On second thought, Grumble . . . too quick." The fingers loosened. "We'll roast them!"

"A slow roast, dear Rumble, please. May they baste in their own tears." And they both doubled over laughing.

The white creature lifted Ibbur by his head, tiny legs and arms flailing, to deposit him back in Dana's pocket. "There you'll keep, tig. To bake like a pig in a blanket!"

Sniggering they wound vines around Dana, twist after tightening twist. Like a mummy they bound her, muffling her cries. Then tossing a vine over a limb, they hoisted her up in her basket-like tomb.

Dana dangled helplessly as the creatures gathered wood for a fire. They snorted and snickered, heaping leaves and twigs beneath her.

"Now, Rumble, for the roast!"

"Hey yes! Have you the spark?"

"The spark? Hey no! You have it."

"I, Grumble?" Each narrowed his eyes, flashing his tusks. Sharp accusing snorts passed between them. Then all at once they stopped—"Hey!" "Hey!"—and slapping each other's backs, broke into a riddle:

> *Sniff it where it is,*
>   *Hey! Or where it isn't,*
> *Root it where it used to be,*
>   *Grope it where it wasn't!*
> *Track it where you start,*
>   *Hey! Or where you stop,*
> *Grub it at the bottom,*
>   *Nose it at the top!*
> *Trace it to the kindly,*
>   *Hey! Or to the cruel,*
> *Find it on the surface,*
>   *Down beneath Zar's pool!*

"Hey!" "Hey!" Together they flopped into the dark pond, disappearing from sight. Dana hung waiting anxiously, arms pinned in pain. Ibbur too was fully ensnared, unable to slip free to reach Mashire.

Splosh! The creatures spouted back out of the pond. Giggling they rolled on the bank, scratching each other's hides.

"Well done, Rumble."

"Then give it here, Grumble. I'll do it."

"You! Always you. No! I'll set the spark."

Tumbling one upon the other they reached the pile of twigs. Hand clawed hand tussling the sparkling glow. They fumbled. . . . The spark fell with a flash and ignited leaves and twigs.

The creatures fed wood to the fire. "Not too much, Rumble. Cook them ever so slowly. A tender, tormented melt!"

Flames licked at Dana's feet. Her cage of vines scorched and began to burn. While round the fire danced the creatures, stomping, voices raucous with song:

> *Hey, Dana, we know who you are!*
> *Now roast, toast, and fry before Zar!*
> *Your powers now melt,*
> *Ibbur can't help,*
> *So yelp, as you'll never restore,*
> *Worlds lost forever and more!*

Teasing song mixed with muffled cries and crackling blaze. Fiery heat seared Dana's jeans and blistered her sneakers. Smoke filled her face.

"Do not forsake hope—my queen," Ibbur wheezed. But Dana never heard him. Her head lolled in a swoon.

The creatures danced with abandon, white eyes and black aglow with red fire. "Another log to the flame, dear Rumble. Zar's spark must be fed." Flames leapt with new fuel to engulf Dana's cage. "Bake her good, Rumble, but tender I say, not to a crisp."

"And the tidbit of a tig?"

"You mean her shrimp of an angel. Fry him to a goodly crunch!"

Flame jumped higher to quicken their frenzy. "Hey!" "Hey!" But as their fevered squall grew to a hellish roar, the creatures did not notice Zar's pool bubbling over. Nor did they see how the waters had begun to surge. From behind their backs there burst forth a wave. It crashed upon them . . . "He—!" "He—!" sinking their calls in a gurgle and swallowing their fire.

Four crests billowed from the wave. Like fingers, they reached for Dana's cage and with a thunderous clap tore the vines from the tree. On rolling surf Dana was carried, free as a boat set adrift in wide sea.

Chapter Eleven

CASTAWAY

In a rushing spray, Dana awoke, her baskety cage bobbing like driftwood. Still bound by vines, she strained to look about, able only to move her eyes.

"Ib-bur . . . ," she muttered, vines pressed to her lips.

"At—your service, my queen," the small voice stammered.

Across the dark tossing sea, Dana saw distant waves breaking upon a beach. Her basket skimmed the waters as a seal making for shore. The beach seemed to rush forward. Swiftly the shoreline was reached. Surf pounded the baskety cage, smashing it to pieces as an ocean wrecks ships. And so Dana hatched free, bruised and burned, sprawled on the sandy shore.

Ibbur crawled from her pocket, surveying the beach—a small barren island, solitary in the vast sea. In the surf, four waves rose as watery shafts. Ibbur grinned, and his eyes, which had dimmed, now brightened. "Ho! You've returned and I thank you!"

Dana raised her head, shaking away dizziness and pained wounds to focus her eyes. Colors swirled in a tangle, separating slowly, drop by drop. Red split from yellow, divided from blue, sifted from green.

"The winds!" cried Dana, bedazzled.

"Not winds, my queen, but waves!" corrected Ibbur.

"Waves? How?"

"As winds they returned to Anavak. But she sent them back—transformed!—knowing they'd be needed. As waves they snatched us from Zar and put us to sea." Ibbur swept his arm toward the beach. "Behold, Queen Dana, your waves!"

Dana staggered to her feet and into the surf, arms spread in embrace. Four colors of spray fell upon her, then merged in a watery blend shining light from its midst. Dana reached into the light . . . and withdrawing her hand, held a spark.

"The first spark in the Mountain of Water!" cheered Ibbur. "Snatched from the fire of those beasts. No longer is it Zar's!"

Dana bowed her head, shedding tears. The waves rose as one, billowing, then settled down to roll in the surf. Dana eased the spark deep into her pouch, and walked up the beach to Ibbur. "What charm, Ibbur—what charm might this one hold?"

"We shall see, my queen. Without doubt, we shall see. For now, let us tend to your wounds." Ibbur knelt in the sand. "We'll need the witch hazel leaves and bark together with your pouch." Dana untied the pouch and set it in the sand next to Ibbur. "Good. And we must have water."

"There's plenty in this world, Ibbur."

"Fresh water, my queen, not briny sea." Ibbur frowned. "A river or a spring."

Now the charm of Dana's second spark, cleverness, took hold in her mind. From her pouch she withdrew the third spark, Mashire the Thunderbolt. "Right here, Ibbur, this is the spot," she said thrusting the sword into the sand. Mashire drilled down the length of Dana's arm, then deeper, twisting from her hand to tap a stream far below. In an instant, Mashire returned bearing water pouring up in a well.

"Praises, Queen Dana! Not only your sword, but likewise your cleverness—it penetrates and grows!"

Dana regarded Mashire, now grown larger than her hand, and hitched the sword in her belt. She saw a shimmer run down the edge of the blade to its diamond tip. The shimmer seemed to jump and glisten off the surface of the well, before diving below. Water flashed golden in Dana's face . . . and she followed the shimmer with her eyes down through the well's shining depths. . . .

Her eyes sank like weights . . . through warm, then cold, then warm again, cold again waters, sinking down without end . . . until Dana saw her own face shining up from the deep. It seemed as if she were looking down and up both at once. Face gazed upon face. A reflection? Dana wondered. She touched the top of her own head. Nothing, just hair. But far below, her head wore a crown. And from ten points of the crown glanced lights . . . like stars, thought Dana—or sparks!—dancing, spinning delight. But as Dana looked on, each sparkling point in turn spun free and vanished. Then too, the crown. Then too, the face.

Dana started from her stare with a shiver. Ibbur was carefully emptying the pouch, gathering the sparks in one place. "You'll first dip your hands, my queen, then"—and he passed her the pouch—"scoop water from the well with your pouch." Dana did as he asked, half-anxious she'd scoop the crown and face along with the water. But though she held them in mind, they were gone.

Dana offered the water-full pouch to Ibbur. "Place it here over the sparks, my queen." To Dana's amazement, the pouch hovered where she set it just above the sparks, spilling not a drop.

"Won't the pouch burn, Ibbur?"

"It would but for the magic it contains."

When the water had begun to boil, Ibbur motioned to Dana. "Slip the leaves and bark into the boiling froth, my queen, to brew like a tea." The witch hazel plunged in and seethed. "Ho! And lift!" The pouch rose higher. The boiling ceased. "They'll steep as the water draws medicine to itself."

Ibbur then pulled the tiniest of bundles from beneath his coat. He untied it and unwrapped a small cloth held inside. Within was a paste, thinner than beeswax, thicker than oil. He set it aside and removed his cap. "Now we'll strain our brew and keep only the liquid." Ibbur spun his cap. It stretched and widened beneath the pouch. "Pour the tea through, Queen Dana."

"But what will catch the tea, Ibbur?"

"Glamour, my queen. Your own magic."

Dana poured. No sooner had the pouch emptied, than it vanished from her hand. She found it again below the cap, tea pouring down to it. Dana's hand tingled.

Ibbur dropped a portion of his paste into the tea. By the heat of the sparks, water boiled out. Left behind was a thick healing balm—yellow and green, brown and red all at once.

The pouch floated down to the sand. "Your witch hazel ointment, Queen Dana," said Ibbur scooping out a tiny handful. "Now where are your wounds?"

With the slightest touch, Ibbur tended Dana's bruises and burns. The balm soothed her, taking away pain. "Learn and remember, Queen Dana."

Dana relaxed, breathing deeply. She began to doze, but shortly trembled and jolted awake. "They were Zar! Weren't they? Those two beasts, so confusing and cruel! And their riddle: is and isn't, was and wasn't! How strange. Everything was reversed!"

Cold fog blew off the sea spreading a dark blanket of haze over the beach. Near the shore, seagulls dropped clams from the sky smashing the shells on rocks below. Ibbur scowled looking out to sea, his eyes fixed on rising waters. "You are wise to ask, my queen. More clever than I! For I should have foreseen. Zar would try to break you with riddles as a gull breaks clams upon stone!"

He spun to face her. "Zar weaves a web of lies and twisted truths, Queen Dana. He is everything and its opposite. Only to confuse. Don't let him. Take heed. Most riddles mislead but contain seeds of truth. Zar's riddles mislead with the seeds of lies!"

Ibbur dabbed Dana's last bruise and quickly repacked the pouch counting each of the sparks. He shook out his shrinking cap and returned it to his head. "Not a moment to lose." He rubbed his tiny palms together, and clasped his hands. "A lesson in riddles. Ready?"

"Yes—I guess," Dana hesitated, irked by Ibbur's urgency. She tied the pouch to her belt.

"Good, now be mindful. Look between and around and through the words of a riddle for the nature of the thing. And remember, things are not often what they seem. Here's one. Try it. . . .

"A white horse swims in a lake by night, yet she never grows wet. Who is she?"

Dana thought and pictured the horse. In her mind it rippled like moonlight across the water. Then she knew. . . . "Who else could the horse be, dear Ibbur, but the moon reflected in the lake!"

"Fine, Queen Dana, now another: A little lady sweeps a path, yet she holds neither broom nor brush. Who is she?"

Dana knew in an instant. "Who else but the wind!"

"Excellent, my queen! Then another: In my flock I've countless lambs, but a single sheep to lead them."

Dana thought. At first she pictured lambs in her head, a huge grazing flock. But the picture quickly changed to the night sky. Then Dana knew. She spoke with assurance. "The lambs are stars and the sheep is the moon!"

"Exactly! A charm lights your mind, my queen! One riddle more: I see it, but I do not see it. It lies down in the dew, yet does not get wet. It is never alone. There it waits upon a wall. It lurks in my holly bush, a bird without skin."

Dana thought and tried to see it. The many clues confused her with different pictures, pulling her mind in crisscrossing ways. She was about to give up when a flock of seabirds flew overhead. Beneath them, upon the sand, flew their faintest shadows.

"The answer is . . . ," cried Dana, "a shadow!"

"And nothing else!" Ibbur jumped to his feet. "And what's behind the shadow?"

"Zar!"

From the winged throats above broke terrified squawks. Along the beach, shorebirds clamored into flight, swelling the skies like clouds, fleeing before a peril. A riptide rent the surf. Waters clashed exploding from the sea, wave dashing wave, current crashing current.

"Run, Queen Dana!" shouted Ibbur. "Quickly, for higher ground!" and he scrambled up Dana's shirt sleeve as whitecaps surged ashore, charging at Dana's heels.

Chapter Twelve

To Hold a Stare

D ana fled up the beach slipping in sea foam. Behind her, waters boomed and broke upon waters, tearing at the shore. As she ran amid the fray, one thought troubled her more than the breakers rushing at her feet . . . and she lifted her voice, "The four waves, they'll be lost!" But the tempest tattered her call, thrashing her words into mist.

Dana scrambled to a dune and clambered to the top where the waters had not reached. There she stood whipped in wet wind, shielding her eyes, looking to shore. The four waves pitched and plunged in the surf, colors running together. Dana saw the sea part beneath them and erupt, waters gushing from their midst. And as a whale leaps from the sea; as an island births from ocean bottom, a monstrous head breached the waves, rising gigantic and terrible.

It surfaced shedding sea and sea stuff. Sand, shell, and coral cascaded from hair tangled with seaweed. The head reared on a neck thicker than any tree, planted upon mountainous shoulders, gushing forth from a chest broad as a ship.

While Dana stared stark still, a giant rose to its waist. It rose higher and strode through the surf crushing waves beneath its feet. Laughter roared from its head, resounding with more than one voice.

The giant gained the beach and in two strides stood before Dana. "What's this, a child, a twerp?" it thundered and again laughed with more than one voice. Then it crouched in the sand and lowered its ghastly head for a better look.

With red-rimmed eyes, big and sunken as craters, the giant

eyed Dana. Hot breath steamed from cave-like nostrils blowing gusts through her hair. Then the great head turned as if seeking another angle, but oddly kept turning. As Dana looked on, the face gave way to another at the back of its head. Dana flinched, her knees buckled, but something supported her . . . a voice in her head—Anavak's. "When the time comes and you must hold a stare, don't falter! Or you'll lose everything!" And Dana knew, that time had come.

Encouraged, Dana gazed resolutely as the second face—the one at the back, now the front!—rolled around to face her. While the eyes before had been sunken, these jutted out, great round orbs like the eyes of a fish. And while the face before had been a man's, this one appeared to be a woman's, lighter in complexion, and equally fearsome. The huge eyes bulged and peered at Dana from the depths of dark oceans, oozing slime. Massive lips then parted the face as a ship parts the sea, unveiling teeth like jagged ice floes.

"One hot, one cold!" the mouth bellowed spitting forth foam. "Each flees the other. Each follows the other. Beneath the same roof live they." The giant's eyes bulged wider in challenge. "Riddle me that, Dana whom time has forgot!"

Dana held the bulging stare, not daring to falter. Now she understood Ibbur's urgency about riddles. Zar would beat her with warped games if he could. And then what? She didn't want to think about it. Instead she focused her mind on the clues, puzzling them out. Which were truths? Which were lies? Or were they all lies?

One hot, one cold. Opposites, she thought. The first twist. Each flees, each follows. Opposites again. Another twist. Yet under the same roof. The opposites twisted together. Dana worked to think it through, carefully unraveling each twist.

"Riddle it!" shrieked the giant.

"Why should I?" countered Dana, biding time.

"Pshaw!" Laughter burst from the beast's lips in a spray. "Why, I'll chew you to a pulp, then chew you again, my cud!"

Dana didn't waver. She sorted and divided clues in her head. Opposites confused and collided, lies bumping against truths, truths bouncing off lies, while those monstrous eyes loomed.

Dana's mind began to reel and plunged down through memory to her own shining face and crown. To before all befores as Anavak had told . . . among her sparks, where worlds split from worlds and from no place. There Dana found an answer—and another. . . .

"One is night. The other is day, but—"

"Wrong!" The mouth opened like a trap.

"Let me finish!" Dana shouted, eyes fixed and sharp. "One is night. The other is day, but they are also two faces. Two faces in one head! You!"

The giant's head spun furiously, revolving back to the first face, the man's. The sunken eyes looked out from dark, hooded sockets. "Clever! So very cunning is she!" spat the gruesome man's lips. "But you don't remember all. I'll gnaw your bones yet!" The sunken eyes widened into gaping black wells. "Riddle me complete! Which face is night and which is day?"

Again Dana sifted the clues, lie from truth, lie from lie, searching among the sparks and through Anavak's tale. Before and before and before, she thought. Again Anavak's words spoke in her head. . . . "That moon and sun were the first—and one! One shone within the other and the other within one."

Now the answer came clear, but Dana weighed it and weighed it again, and sought after more. For Zar dealt in tricks, this she knew. Moreover she knew Zar was selfish—and this was the surest clue. For as Zar thought only of himself, each of his riddles, every tiny twist must point to himself.

Which face is night and which is day? As before, Dana found not one answer, but two. She was certain. "Moon is night and sun is day—"

"Pshaw—!"

"—but also," Dana continued unblinking, "the face that looks up is day, while the one behind, looking down in shadow, is night."

"One answer, one answer only!" the giant bellowed. Again the head spun around enraged, back to the woman's face with bulging eyes. "One is all you get!"

"Then you'd cheat me—you would!—and say it's the other!" Dana stood firm, eyes open and clear.

"Cheat you? I? I'd crush you before I'd cheat you!" The bulbous eyes flashed bearing down on Dana. Dana's eyes strained and stung, but held firm. "Dash the riddles!" roared the blubbery lips. "I'll bite off your head and end it!"

The great mouth descended. "Defeat, then devour!" it shrieked. "First I'll crush your mind, then I'll crush your bones!" The lips hung open dripping slime, gnashing teeth. But the voice from behind called out, "Not so fast!" and again the head spun around. "First your cleverness must fail you!" The sunken eyes glowered. "You will taste defeat and your tortures will linger! Then I'll eat."

A huge hand swiped down like a boulder with claws seizing Dana in its grip. There wasn't time to draw Mashire and now Dana couldn't move. Only her head showed above the locked fist.

As the giant strode off roaring laughter from two mouths, Dana fretted over Ibbur, shut in the fist . . . hidden in the folds of her sleeve, now only to be crushed in the dark?!

The giant trudged the beach trampling dunes. Salt grasses and shrubs, bayberry and myrtle flattened underfoot. Through a thicket of stunted hemlocks and pines, the giant clomped kicking down trees. But amid the booming tread, crunch and snap of wood, a seeping murmur followed. . . . It dogged the giant's heels, subtle as a tide, unnoticed and unheard.

Dana neither struggled nor screamed. To squirm could only injure Ibbur, if he still breathed. And to scream above the clomping din was impossible. Besides, who was there to hear? Dana saved her strength and steeled herself for whatever was to come.

The giant stomped the scarred path to a clearing. There at the center of trampled grasses, sands, and uprooted pines rose a single towering tree. Dana gawked at its size—big around as a castle, piercing the sky. Its limbs spread like a forest while clouds hung upon its branches, clinging like snow.

Still more marvelous than the tree's size was its fruit. Each twig bore a single kind: pear, apple, or apricot, plum or cherry, pineapple, peach, the fattest of figs, grapefruits, breadfruits, litchi and loganberry, citron and candleberry. Fruits of every and any description, common and never before seen; each one large and heavy as a boulder, dangling from stems thick as trees themselves.

At the base of the tree, the giant pawed a deep rut with its feet and sat down with two grunts. The clenched fist began to open upon the ground, slowly, finger by finger. When the giant's thumb and two fingers had opened, Dana was freed to the waist, but still trapped.

Now the other huge hand swooped down like a hawk to snatch the sword from Dana's belt. The giant sniggered and the fist opened fully. Dana stood upon the ground watching her captor begin a beastly manicure with Mashire. Great gobs of grime fell about her as the giant spitefully dug dirt from finger and toenails. One face eyed Dana while the other attended to its mock grooming.

Dana nearly sickened to see it, but her mind was absorbed with escape and regaining her sword. Also, she was listening for any sound, any movement of Ibbur to know that he lived. For she dared not look down or feel at her sleeve lest the giant squash Ibbur like a bug.

"There, that's better," spoke the popeyed face when the nail cleaning was done. "Lucky for you! I'm in a more generous mood, here beneath the tree that sustains me. Two more games you shall have. Two more plays to your death! One for you . . . and one for that pip-squeak up your sleeve!"

Dana's heart jumped and so did Ibbur's, she could feel it. Relief and uncertainty both at once. The giant laughed cruelly. "Yes, yes, your hidden angel. Don't look so surprised. Did you doubt my two grand noses would sniff him out? That eternal reeking pest! Out with you, Ibbur. I know your name."

The red jelly-cap peeked from Dana's sleeve. The black peeping eyes next, looking up at Dana grinning with relief. Emboldened, Ibbur sprang to Dana's shoulder. The giant grinned menacingly with two faces. The head then turned bringing the sunken eyes forward. "Now your wits shall fail you, Dana, Queen of Nothing!

"My first game stakes your pest. If you fail, I snuff him out before you. You'll see!" The hooded eyes fixed on Ibbur. "And don't think I can't do it, angel though you be. For I know the secrets and hidden names, I do!" Again the giant grinned. "So, let's play! . . . I'm thinking of a name. Not yours. Not the pest's. What name is it?"

Dana thought to herself . . . another riddle. And as before, she reasoned Zar must mean himself. Could it be that easy? No, it's a trick. Zar is Tar and also Var and the many names Anavak told he has in the Mountain of Dust. What were they? Zat! Vat! Others and worse! Masks and veils and disguises, too many to name. So which should I choose? It came to her as moonlight parts a cloud: The giant's own name and no other! The mask Zar is wearing right now! But which is it, who is it? The woman's face or the man's? Not only she. Not only he. Dana felt her thoughts reaching down . . . then up into dizzying heights for an answer where the moonlight brightened. . . .

"The name you mean"—Dana finally knew—"is yours alone. But you're never alone are you?" Dana spoke with force. "You can't be called He and you can't be called She. Then you must be—Sh-he!"

"Psh—" The giant began to scoff, but then couldn't. The head spun around, eyes red, bulging with fury. "So be it! Ibbur squirms free, the worm. Only to watch you die, painfully, slowly, coughing up your innards, do you hear?!" A great hand plunged and grabbed her. Ibbur held on by Dana's hair as she was swept to the tree, plunked down on a limb and left there.

The giant snickered, the sound of thunder rolling in its breast. "Have you an appetite yet, lost queen? Does hunger gnaw at your royal gut? Then stay for a bite, please do! All fruits of all worlds are here at your grasp. The sweetest, the finest, ripened for your imperial lips." The two voices rasped at once. "I offer a game of choosing. Any fruit, your choice. But here's the fun, here's the challenge: All are poison, but one! A single bite of any, but the one, kills you slowly from the inside out. Spasm upon spasm to wrench up your guts!"

"I won't!" Dana shouted.

"You won't? But you must! One bite, that's all." The giant smiled two sinister smiles. "Oh, but you need encouragement. Well then . . . if you refuse, I'll dismember your angel, then you!

I'll rip out your arms, tear off your legs, twist off your heads like lobsters! So choose!" The giant sat down with self-satisfied grunts and began cleaning its teeth using Mashire as a toothpick.

Dana gazed up through the tangle of branches at a jungle of tantalizing fruit. Each shone with readiness, dripping misty droplets. Dana was confounded. Choose one? An impossible task! "Ibbur, how can I choose from among so many?"

"I don't know, my queen. Yet I believe you can, and I know you must!" Ibbur slid down hair strands to her pocket.

"Let's climb up then and see."

Dana used spaces in the great rough bark as footholds and handholds to hoist herself up. She shinnied from limbs to branches and along branches to twigs eyeing each giant fruit. From under each peel, juice and pulp seemed to call out, "Taste me!"

"No, not you," Dana would say and move on, not knowing for sure, but trusting her feeling. I'll climb out of the giant's reach, she thought, seeking a way out of the cruel game. Before long she realized, however, that the giant would only climb after her.

When fatigue overcame her, Dana rested in the crook of a bough. Catching her breath, she looked around from her perch.

The tree enveloped her, a web of branches and fruit. Far below and away was the ocean. She could hear it, surf rolling and crashing on the beach. She tried to see out to her four waves—were they still there?—but the tree blocked her view. Dana's heart sank.

To her ears, then, another sound came. First a rustling in the branches above, then chitters and chirrs. Trilling song floated down to Dana, stirring and rousing her attention. A bird, she thought, climbing after the sound . . . and as it came clearer, the chitters took on meaning—a whistling of words.

Dana came to a nest upon which sat the rarest of birds, its feathers swirled in black and white spirals. The bird fluttered and whistled a greeting to which Dana responded with a chirp. She clasped her throat, eyes wide and astounded. Ibbur laughed. "Have you forgotten your second spark, my queen? Part of your cleverness—the tongues of all creatures!"

With chirping words the bird asked Dana a flurry of questions. Who was she? Why was she here? Dana explained quickly with chirrups and chitters.

"Queen Dana, truly?" The bird bowed its head, then ruffled its neck. "That miserable Sh-he! A maniac to be sure. To think it'd poison our queen. Ffsssah! Not as I've a feather on my back. Come, I know every fruit on this tree."

The bird led Dana into higher branches past the fruits that called, "Taste me!" to where there grew a single silvery twig. At its tip hung the fairest of fruits, moonlight pink and perfectly round. Its fragrance was calming—lavender, sandalwood, and rose all in one. Unlike the others, it dangled in silence, modest and poised.

Dana reached out with delicate touch, then drew back her hand. "Dare I eat it, Ibbur, and destroy it?"

"What choice have you, my queen? We'll be lobsters!"

"Eat it, Queen Dana, it's yours," chirped the bird. "Down through the ages it's waited whispering for you. I know for I've heard."

"All right then," said Dana. Defiantly she called to the giant, "I've made my choice, come look!"

A deep grumble belched far below. Up came the head as the giant stood to its feet.

"May you fare well, Queen Dana," called the bird, scattering to its nest.

The head with two faces rose to meet Dana, bulging eyes gloating between boughs. "Very well, Queen of No Place, taste your death!" Through the jungle of fruit, Dana spied Mashire gleaming. Its blade had been thrust through a giant earlobe, dripping black blood. The bug-eyed face smirked. "Oh yes, your sword. As you'll not be needing it, I've taken it for an earring."

Dana heard Ibbur mutter under his breath. She held her own anger and pointed to the pink fruit. "This is the one I've chosen. Now watch!" Dana sniffed the perfect peel and bit into it. Her nose, then her mouth filled with delight. Glowing juices spilled from her lips. Golden light streamed down her chin. Enraptured, she smiled and laughed.

The giant's jaw dropped. The head spun around and the second jaw dropped.

"Care for a bite?" Dana asked. "It's yummy!"

The sunken black eyes glowed like fire pots of hate. The blubbery lips drooled and smacked with craving. "A bite, yes," the two mouths bellowed. "And a crunch of your skull, a sup of your brains, a sip of your gall!" One giant hand ripped away branches as the other reached in after Dana. Dana retreated to the far side of the tree where the hand couldn't reach.

The giant raved crazily clawing fruit, snapping branches and limbs. One hand withdrew and returned brandishing Mashire. Swiping and slashing, the giant whittled at the tree. Bark flew and fell in great chunks. Like a hacked wooden shield, the trunk began to splinter. Then Dana heard a rush from below. . . .

Charging through the boughs came a flood, a wayward waterfall plunging upward. The giant's eyes bugged in surprise, but the hacking blows redoubled, striking fury. The flood climbed faster and lunged. The giant was swamped in a watery snare, floundering, flailing for a hold.

Dana looked on as the flood passed her by. In the rush she saw . . . four colors entwined. Dana's waves! The giant's hands punched through the surge, one wielding Mashire, the other swiping wildly. It clutched at Dana but missed, grabbing hold of the savory fruit. The giant held the fruit like an anchor, squeezing juice through fat fingers. Tighter it held, squeezing to the fruit's core. Golden light dripped, then exploded.

From the shattered fruit there streamed forth a seed, shining, sailing on spray. It loomed at Dana and expanded as light fills a room. Before her eyes, Dana saw a glowing ship grow in full sail. "Step aboard, Queen Dana!" called Ibbur. "Your second spark in the Mountain of Water awaits its captain!"

Dana's waves bore the giant to the nether side of the island. There the heaving hulk was left awash on the beach. One face then the other lolled in the sand sputtering water, cursing Dana's name.

Dana boarded her ship where it rested on a bough of the tree. She strode the decks and made ready to sail, tightening lines with Ibbur. Overjoyed though she was with her ship, Dana fretted deeply over Mashire.

"Your waves will retrieve your sword," Ibbur assured her.

Dana wasn't so sure. She was coiling a rope on the afterdeck when a glint caught her eye. Jutting from the tree like a dagger was a golden handle. Mashire! The blade had been thrust with such force, it had sunk to the hilt. Dana grasped the handle and pulled, and with two hands pulled again. No movement. Again she yanked, straining . . . and let go. "Impossible!" Mashire was stuck fast.

"You'll not succeed that way, my queen," said Ibbur. "Not with muscle alone. Your hand takes strength from your heart and mind, from what you know and understand."

Dana listened and re-grasped the sword.

"Close your eyes," continued Ibbur. "Remember and see who you are. Queen Dana, none other. From before all befores. Know it. Understand it. You'll find that Mashire is already in your hands. Seize what is yours, Queen of Worlds. Take it now!"

Dana strained again, eyes clenched, muscles tightening to free her sword. She held a foot against the tree for leverage and pulled not only with her hands, but with the grasp of her heart. With mind too she envisioned Mashire free and in that instant, as a needle slips from a pincushion, Mashire slipped from the tree. Dana opened her eyes to behold the sword gleaming in her hands.

Just then the deck lurched. Dana's waves had returned and now buffeted the ship.

"Aloft and away!" cried Ibbur.

"Away and aloft!" sang out Dana.

The ship pitched, swayed, and pushed off. Dana was borne on crests of four colors over the Sea of Water, leaving the giant's island far behind.

Chapter Thirteen

BATTLE ON HIGH SEAS

As a half-moon riding on open sea, Dana's ship skimmed the waters. Lapping alongside were her waves, driving her on, setting her course. The spray of the sea renewed her, sprinkling her face with ocean dew, and the sway beneath her feet eased her troubles.

Dana stood balanced at the tiller, one hand upon Mashire in her belt, chin to the surge, eyes ahead, relaxed, almost dreamy. Her thoughts seemed to soar and to catch in the sails. Then off they bounded to dive into the sea . . . and to come up bobbing. Then back upon ship, gently lulled by her waves in a cradle softly rocking.

Ibbur looked out from a crow's-nest high in the crosstrees, hand on his jelly-cap, coattails luffing in the wind. He too felt light and enlivened, hopeful, and pleased with his queen. And so he rejoiced with song, voice rising and falling with the toss and tumble of the ship, keeping his thoughts from the dangers ahead:

> *First spark's charm on boundless sea,*
> *Lion's heart formed in bravery,*
> *Hark I-iddle-du, lily Lu-lee,*
> *Queen of Hearts all kinds is she!*
>
> *Second spark's charm on endless sea,*
> *Clever in mind and cunning is she,*
> *Ark I-iddle-du, lily Lu-lee,*
> *Chirp and chitter, all tongues has she!*

Third spark's charm on ageless sea,
Sword in hand and mastery,
Bark I-iddle-du, lily Lu-lee,
Blaze her path of destiny!

Fourth spark's charm on timeless sea,
Puzzler's knack and riddler's key,
Lark I-iddle-du, lily Lu-lee,
Truth from lies and tricks knows she!

Fifth spark's charm on spaceless sea,
Ship from seed from fruit from tree,
Mark I-iddle-du, lily Lu-lee,
Queen of Worlds—Moons—and . . .

Ibbur faltered and trailed off. He'd been keeping keen watch as he sang for any disturbance upon the waters. Now in the distance from which they'd come, he spied a break in otherwise calm seas. It appeared as a dark churning wave or a ship cutting deeply through the wake. It was coming on fast.

Ibbur jumped to the shrouds, sliding down along rigging, rope to rope to the deck. "Queen Dana!" he cried running toward her. "Gather your sword and your wits for battle!"

Dana broke from her reverie to see a great wall of black froth rushing toward them. As it neared, she could see above the froth, jutting . . . that huge horrific head—Sh-he! Ibbur sprang to Dana's arm and disappeared up her sleeve.

Dana thrust Mashire high. "Waves!" she called. "Away!"

At her command, the waves billowed and quickened. Like horses they reared and broke into gallop, pulling together, yoked in a team. Waters churned and leapt from their path.

Still the giant made headway, rushing forward . . . closer, and Dana saw poking from the froth, seven long twisted necks. Astride a seven-headed beast guided with bridles of eels, the giant rode thundering, "Faster, my furies!" And the beast pawed the sea to a boil.

Dana's waves gathered speed; four painted steeds foaming at the mouth. Her ship cleaved the sea as a plow breaks a field digging furrows. Down this track raced the waves in a straining rush of lather.

The seven beastly heads, each one large as the ship, lurched forward on seven necks. Along the thickest and most twisted neck climbed the giant.

"Hurry, please!" called Dana to her waves. They could go no faster. Dana looked to the sails above, thinking, please blow quicker! But they were already straining their seams. To Dana's ears, then, there came a laugh—a scoffing, mocking roar. Close upon the ship stretched the thickest neck. At its end, straddling the biggest head, sat the giant.

"Dana, Queen of Sunken Ships!" the bug-eyed face teased. "I almost forgot. One final riddle!" The eyes bugged wider. "Riddle this: What am I thinking?"

Upon its terrible perch, the giant stretched nearer the deck. Dana stood firm, Mashire in hand. "If I answer correctly, will you leave?"

The giant spat. A great black bloody gob crashed to the deck. "If you answer correctly, I'll devour you in one bite, instead of two! A little less painful." The giant laughed insanely, leaning closer. "Where is your angel, I wonder?" Ibbur squirmed deeper into Dana's sleeve. "Hidden somewhere on your person, no doubt. I know his tricks, the coward! Then I'll munch him too, though sour he be. And just as well, for you're too sweet, I wager."

The giant's head spun around. The sunken eyes screwed closer, glowering from their depths. "Now riddle me, Dana, Queen of Defeat! And riddle your last! Again . . . what am I thinking?"

"What are you thinking?" Dana repeated slowly, stepping closer to one side of the face. The sea beast's jaws gnashed, drooling venom. "I wonder . . . ," Dana continued, gauging her position.

When again she spoke, her tone was assured and final. "I have two answers, giant, for your two faces." Dana pressed her palm against Mashire's handle. "First, you're thinking only of yourself, as always. And second, you're thinking"—Dana lunged wielding Mashire—"your last thoughts!—" and swiped her blade through the giant's own neck. Mashire sliced clean. Before the giant could finish, "Psh—" the great bulbous head rolled from its neck, face spinning after face, eyes bulging then sunken, then bulging, then rolling from the deck—splash!—to sink in the sea.

The sea beast's seven necks recoiled and attacked all as one. As arrows they descended, tipped with dragon-toothed heads. Dana brandished Mashire—grown larger still!—sweeping her blade ably, severing one head then two. The beast shrieked wildly spurting black blood. Neck stumps writhed. Five maddened heads opened upon Dana, but deftly she swiped, slashing wound upon wound. And with each slash Mashire gleamed sharper.

A third head fell away coughing blood. Necks pulled back, deployed, then swooped, teeth flashing. Dana severed jaws and pieces of jaws, brackish green scaly flesh, and vile wagging tongues. Swipe upon swipe. Yet four heads remained, and these the most fearful. Their eyes shot fire like darts, red and black. They screeched fiendish sounds to shatter courage. Still Dana was unmoved. The four heads rose and hovered. . . .

"Now who tastes death?" Dana shouted, panting for breath. "Who, Zar, is it you?" The four beastly throats shrieked, spitting venom. "How many of your masks must I cut away?!"

The heads dove at Dana from four sides at once. She slashed and spun taking two, then three . . . but before her next blow fell, the last and quickest of heads snatched her up. Dana stood between wet closing jaws, covered in throaty slime, Mashire slipping from her grasp. On the tossing black tongue, she quickly lost her footing. She was thrown back and away from her sword, sliding farther toward the throat . . . angry teeth closing to trap her.

Chapter Fourteen

BELLY OF THE SEA BEAST

Plunging through shadow down waving tubes and gurgling black cave, Dana was swallowed whole. Bouncing and rebounding she came to rest amid rubbery walls—the beast's belly. She stood shakily to her feet, ankle-deep in ooze, peering into dripping cold dark. Far above her head a roar echoed as through the depths of mountains lost undersea. A shudder ran through her bones.

"Ugh—!" Ibbur burst from Dana's sleeve. "Like as I'd been bounced through a hurly match!" He straightened his jelly-cap, looking up at Dana. "Six heads, my queen! Seven with the giant's. You've come far, indeed!"

Yet Dana didn't feel triumphant. A chill crept over her skin draining the flush of battle. She looked pale and shaken.

Ibbur jumped to her shoulder. "There now, there, dear queen," he soothed. "You must be exhausted. Rest yourself, please do."

Dana sat down heavily on a bump in the belly wall. Her limbs were weak, her head dizzy. A faint whistling sound piped in her ears. Her stomach ached with hunger—and seasickness.

"You'll rest and revive, Queen Dana." But even as he spoke, Ibbur was distracted, ears cocked, listening past the roar. For he too heard the piping whistle. It faded and stopped. "Have no fear," he comforted.

"But that's just it—" Dana's voice choked. "I *am* afraid! One horrible head, then another, another and another . . . and black blood! Fighting for my life. Fighting and fighting! I can't stand it anymore! I'm terrified! I'm not your queen!" A cry fled Dana's throat like a lost, frantic bird.

"Ease yourself," hushed Ibbur. Sobs tore from Dana's chest. "Of course you're afraid," he cooed with a soft, tiny touch upon her shoulder. "Unburden your heart as you will, as you need. Such suffering as yours—the worlds' troubles. You're Queen Dana after all, not a stone." Through the weave of her pouch, Dana's sparks softly glowed. "Queen Dana would never draw blood without conscience, not even Zar's. So feel."

As Ibbur spoke, sobs racked Dana's frame in great heaves. Heartsick wounds. Seas of grief. She drew breath, choked, and poured sorrow.

"Your tears run deep, my queen, as they should. Back to the Spring of Beginning. Out with them then, as a river fills the sea."

Dana wailed, "Where's Mashire? Lost! And my waves? My ship? And where am I? Lost too! In the dark. Down inside a monster—a dragon—a—I don't know what!" Her confusion spilled out. "I don't even know who I am anymore! Or—or what will become of me!"

"Queen Dana. That's who you are, and it becomes you."

"Ibbur, you don't understand. I feel alone. Smothered and alone!"

"You think I don't know what you feel?" Ibbur's black mustard seed eyes became wells of despair down which Dana now gazed. Slowly, he spoke, "You're thinking of the closet, are you not?"

"The closet!" Dana felt herself rise through the wells to the surface, startled, panting for breath. "How do you know, how could you?!" Surprise stopped her tears.

"As I've told you, my queen—forever watchful I've been." Ibbur's eyes pierced the dark. "The bedroom closet, yes, Queen Dana . . . when your brother locked you inside. A prank. But he forgot and left you there."

"Alone, I remember . . . I could hardly breathe! I pounded and called. I screamed! Where was he? Then the dark got smaller—the walls moving in! I tucked my head down to shrink and shrink . . . so tiny and alone!"

"But you weren't alone."

"I was!"

"How did you get out? Who opened the door?"

"I don't know. No one. I was crunched into a ball, then—I never knew how. Suddenly I was on the other side!"

"And the door, my queen?"

"It was still locked!"

"Indeed!" Ibbur smiled. The faint glow of sparks shone pink on his teeth. "And after a while you forgot all about it. Who'd want to remember? But deep in your belly and dark corners of mind the fear stayed with you." Dana stared amazed. "What you hide away, my queen, comes back to haunt you."

"You let me out! Ibbur, it was you!"

"No one is alone, ever. Not the slightest blade of grass. Remember? And certainly not a queen!"

"So there's nothing to fear? But I'm still afraid!"

"In the end, you'll find, there's no cause for fear. Only wonder and awe. But for now, be mindful. Even the lion knows fear. He fights or he runs. He acts to possess it. The trick is to never let fear possess you. To never let fear devour you!"

"But what if I can't act, Ibbur? What if I can't even move, like when those beasts tied me with vines?"

"Action occurs first in thought, then in the hand. Mind first, my queen. How did you exit the locked closet?"

"You!"

"I was only there to remind you. Think. . . . You did it yourself."

An image skipped across Dana's mind as a spark jumps from struck stones, igniting memory . . . to that time, when huddled in a ball in the closet, she'd scrunched her eyes tightly and wished . . . and wished she were out . . . till finally, like magic, she was. This too she'd forgotten.

"I wished my way out!"

"With thought!"

Dana's sparks glowed brighter within her pouch, reflecting moon-pink in her eyes. Ibbur's face gleamed. "Another puzzle solved, Dana, Queen of Riddles?"

Dana smiled. "By my fourth spark, to be sure." A laugh escaped her lips. "I'm beginning to sound like you, Ibbur."

"I'm honored, my queen." Ibbur bowed, sweeping his cap. "Now how shall we exit this belly-trap, this closet of Zar's?"

Above the beast's rumbling roar, the whistling heard earlier piped again. "Listen . . . do you hear it, my queen?"

"Yes, and I heard it before." Dana stood abruptly to her feet—almost jarring Ibbur from her shoulder. "It's a spark! I know it!"

Ibbur righted himself. "To be sure?"

"To be sure!" Dana untied her pouch and held it out in her hand, a lantern to light her way. With each step, the belly squished like a sponge. The piping echoed as through a cavern.

This way, Dana thought, but after several steps . . . no there! . . . and she changed direction, bumping into walls, brushing against slime. Her light fell upon food scraps, broken shells, shipwrecks, undigested fish heads and bones. Dana stepped around and over the mess in ooze-filled sneakers, sloshing one way, then another.

"Impossible, Ibbur! The belly goes on and on and so does the sound. First here, then there. I may be walking in circles and not know it. Yes, I think I passed this wrecked ship before."

The piping grew louder. A shiver ran up Dana's spine.

"Walking in circles can have a charm of its own," said Ibbur, "or it can bring a charm out. Go around this ship with careful eye. We shall see, my queen—and hear."

The wreck was rotted and ancient, moldy and covered with barnacles. Dana walked around it, crunching clam shells and fish skulls underfoot. Once around, and twice. The piping whistle rose and fell like waves. On her third pass, something did catch her eye: jutting from among the fish bones were bones of another sort. Dana peered closer casting her light . . . closer, heart pounding . . . as the whistling rose higher. There! In the company of fish heads—Dana's own bones chilled, her lips numbed and fumbled to cry out, "A hand!"

Five skeletal fingers seemed to reach out from the bed of fish bones. The hand had been severed at the wrist. Each bony digit shone with a coral-colored glow and whistled like a flute.

Dana shrank back.

"Do not fear it," encouraged Ibbur, but his own skin had turned ashen-green.

Dana whispered, breathless, "It's Anavak's!" and forced herself closer, inching through the bone bed. As she neared, her sparks glowed brighter. The bony fingers sounded long airy tones, like the pipes of an organ. A melody played, rising and falling with five different sounds. Tone followed tone, resounding in Dana's head, inviting and oddly familiar, easing her fears. Part of an old song, she thought, but I knew it when it was new!

Now as Dana looked upon the hand of bone and listened, shedding fear, she saw with amazement what she couldn't see before. From finger to finger leaped a ring, flashing, spinning light. It rose and fell with each piping tone, shining, gyrating color.

"My sixth spark."

"Your last in the Mountain of Water, dear queen."

Cautiously, Dana reached out her hand, but before she could grasp it, the ring leaped to settle around her smallest finger. A perfect fit. "It *is* mine, Ibbur."

As Dana marveled, the severed hand crumbled to dust. Ibbur looked away, downcast. A hollow feeling seized Dana. "Zar took that hand from her, Ibbur."

"Yes, my queen." Ibbur labored to speak. "Long ago . . . very old. Let it go," and he climbed slowly into Dana's pocket.

Dana shook her eyes from the pile of bone dust to gaze at the ring on her finger. "What charm does it hold, I—"

The roaring of the beast drowned out her words. The belly lurched. Bones and wrecks and fish heads churned like a roiling sea. Dana was pitched from her feet, tumbling in turbulent slime. The belly walls quaked and pressed, shrinking like a deflating blowfish. Dana was squeezed between fleshy folds. Rotting fish tails whipped her face. Blubbery walls pressed her cheeks.

"Ib-bur—!" But through deafening roar and muffling ooze Dana heard no reply.

The belly walls rippled and squished. Beastly muscle squeezed at Dana's chest. Her breath came in fits. I'm smothering! she thought . . . smothering . . . and her vision blurred. Dizzy thoughts filled her head: trapped in Zar's closet, gasping for air—a stolen breath. Mashire! Where? The closet door . . . and I wished . . . Think! Mind first. The door was locked. I thought my way out . . . from smothering dark. Winds! No—waves! Waves, I'm dying!

Down the throat of the beast came a thundering surge. It burst the gullet and rushed in. Water and streaking stars! Now the belly flooded with new strife swelling and thrashing its walls. Gushing around Dana came curving crests, enfolding like arms, lifting, freeing, reviving . . . Waves! And billowing from their midst, sparkling sails, a shimmering deck, a ship alike no other. Dana's! Dana was swept aboard breathless, shaking and stunned, struggling to her feet . . . hand reaching out for Mashire, blade jabbed in the deck.

Dana's eyes shone. She grasped the sword and yanked the blade free. "Aloft and away!" she cried, thrusting Mashire high.

"Away and aloft!" called Ibbur, head popping from Dana's pocket. The ship glistened, rolling on four teeming waves. Dana grinned and hurried to the bow, as ahead they rushed through the belly of the beast. She stood on the foredeck, sword pointed over the bow. The belly wall sped closer. Shipwrecks and bones were a blur. The slimy flesh loomed, a hair's-breadth from Mashire's diamond-tipped point.

"To the Mountain of Light!" Dana cried, and Mashire pierced the belly. Wicked fury! The gutted beast exploded! Black blood sprayed the seas. Frenzied shrieks tore from the last beastly head and quickly faded—to nothing.

For now the ship sailed on rising waves, shooting from the sea into skies of mist. And the great waters below shrank to droplets—then were gone.

Chapter Fifteen

THE MOUNTAIN OF LIGHT

Through drizzling mist, Dana's four waves rolled as they flew. In their swell rode the ship, gliding like a golden gull. Sails bent like sunlight in wet skies—red and yellow, blue and green upon the waves. Four waves, four colors of glow.

Dana rejoiced watching clouds part before her ship. Ibbur too took delight. He clambered out upon the jutting bowsprit and danced along its length like a tightrope acrobat. As always when pleased and journeying, Ibbur sang, now continuing his song of before:

> *Sixth spark's charm on flying sea,*
> *Ring of sound, song to free,*
> *Arc I-iddle-du, lily Lu-lee,*
> *Nature's round in light she'll see!*

Dana musefully turned the ring on her finger, delighting in Ibbur's dance, and wondering over his words. She called over the bow, "Ibbur!" pointing to her ring. "What charm does it hold?"

Ibbur slid down the bowsprit on the seat of his pants, tipped his cap, and again sang the verse for Dana.

"Yes, I heard you, Ibbur. But what do you mean?"

"Only this: Your sixth spark, the ring, contains the power of song. More I can't say, not now. You'll learn its uses as you have the others'."

Dana nodded. "I see . . ." and regarded her ring.

Her ship sailed on through watery skies. Mist cleared and the drizzle stopped. The four waves grew quiet, rolling softly. The ship seemed lighter, swaying slightly, then not at all.

A golden glow edged the clouds. Cloudlets gathered in tufts, clinging like feathery seeds. Dana watched them form into a single cloud, drifting around a darkened hole. Through this hole passed her ship. Skies opened wide and black, studded with faded stars. Dana's ship sped on, but no longer upon waves. For now four beaming rays of light—red, yellow, blue, and green—streaked below the gleaming hull.

The dark was smoky and vast. The shining ship was little more than a flare in a sea of fog. And the air was hot, fiery hot. Sweat dripped from Dana's brow stinging her eyes. "Are you sure this is the way, Ibbur? I can hardly see!"

"It's Var's black fire, my queen. His darkness burns at the rim of the Mountain of Light. But you'll see, just as in the checkered worlds below, your eyes will adjust. So again I say, don't be fooled. Var's evil is the most wicked of all. Four times cruel and vile. For Var wears no masks. He knows no riddles. He plays no games. Beware, I say! Nothing, Queen Dana, nothing you've seen matches Var!"

Dana heeded Ibbur's words without question. In mind and heart she knew he was right. There was nothing to doubt, this much she'd learned. Except, perhaps—and she shuddered to think it: she doubted herself.

The ship streaked forward, gathering speed. Just as Ibbur had said, Dana's eyes began to adjust to the smoky dark. The skies brightened to deepest purple with a hint of daybreak. Into the crack of dawn Dana's ship now passed.

"Through the Pillar of Light!" called Ibbur.

Flickering twilight wreathed Dana's streaking ship. And tumbling out of twilight came sound. It pealed with a noise of great rushing. Dana listened, trying to make it out. There was music, and talk, jumbled words, whispers, claps and stomps, drums, pipes, strings, and wordless song. A blizzard of noise. It seemed to fall from great heights. Soft out of silence and louder as it neared. It reached her ears, then melted . . . snowfalling sound.

A shiver ran up Dana's spine to the base of her head. She

closed her eyes. Sound seemed to dance behind her eyelids, flickering tones and tints; a kaleidoscope of color. Dana's head filled with light, jumbled with sound, scrambled with motion. Somewhere faintly, she heard Ibbur call, "To the diamond world, pressed of a trillion stars!" Behind her eyes, light showered Dana and bathed her with diamond dust. As upon speeding light, through the Pillar of Light, Dana entered the Mountain of Light.

When the rushing stopped, she opened her eyes. Her ship had come aground in a glade of clover. "Step lively, my queen," coaxed Ibbur as beneath Dana's feet the sparkling ship shrank . . . and shrank . . . to the size of a rowboat.

"Ohhh!" Dana jumped out, followed by Ibbur. The ship kept shrinking. Smaller to the size of a bath toy . . . smaller till it was a sparkling seed at rest in the glade.

Dana knelt in clover taking the seed in her hand. "Now into the pouch, and I thank you," she said and tied the pouch closed. She stood to her feet clasping Mashire at her belt—a sword grown to full size! Dana looked about for her waves. Instead she saw rising out of clover, four rays of light, four colors beaming.

"What were winds, then waves—behold them now, Queen Dana, your rays!" Ibbur pointed. "Wind to water to light!"

The rays spun together rising as a shaft of light. In their spinning Dana thought she heard sounds, a hum or buzzing whir. Or were there words? A song? Light glinted off her ring, four colors flashing on gold. Would the ring now sing out its charm? She waited. But no, the ring kept quiet. Dana was bewildered.

"Patience, my queen. Your ring holds great magic, but yields it slowly. Take heart, it will come."

The four spinning colors lighted Dana's eyes. She smiled softly, bowed her head, took a deep breath and looked farther about. A thicket of hawthorns ringed the glade like a wreath. All was hushed, deep in silence. Dana held her breath listening. . . . No rustle of leaf. No birds astir. No droning bees. She strained after something to hear until her breath burst her lips—

In a rush, voices broke from the trees. Cheers and hurrahs of delight. "Queen Dana, dear queen! And Ibbur!"

"The leaves—are they talking?!"

Ibbur spread his arms, spinning joyously on one heel. "As with blades of grass, so with leaves!" From behind each leaf there poked a face, tiny as Ibbur's and silver, or gold, blue or sheer as moonlight.

"Angels!" Dana gasped. Like windswept leaves they descended, gliding, flitting, drifting on air. They slid down shafts of light or fluttered on wings soft as spider's lace. Some were mere wisps, shining from within. Others seemed formed of rainbows, sprinkled with powdered jewels. The tiniest dashed to and fro in a twitter, pausing and peeking like dragonflies.

They alighted and assembled around Dana in two circles, one within the other; thousands of tiny faces, smiling, excited, singing:

> *Our queen is come,*
> *by holly,*
> *to right a woeful wrong,*
> *A star-crossed,*
> *doomful folly, to take a moon*
> *so young.*
>
> *To seize our moon,*
> *by yarrow,*
> *it grieves our heart*
> *full sore,*
> *Evil bent on sorrow,*
> *sown at Dana's door. . . .*

Tiny feet shuffled, slow-stepping sideways. And so the circles turned, moving around Dana as two wheels. Dana was the hub. From the center she watched. One wheel turned within the next, each in different directions, so that Dana was dizzy with delight.

From high in the trees came the trill of fiddles. Crisp, cutting chords. Drums thudded. Beats throbbed. The circles quickened their shuffling pace. Tiny arms swept the air, legs kicked. A dance unfurled. And a thousand slight lips, green, blue, clear, and golden, continued their song:

> *Torn away,*
> *by brookweed,*
> *borne away,*
> *by broom,*
> *Stashed away*
> *by wicked greed,*
> *when Var*
> *kidnapped our moon! . . .*

Tiny bodies bent in a sweeping bow. They straightened and some flew off, to where Dana couldn't see. But as they left, others came—or were they the same ones returning? Dana couldn't tell. There was a constant going and coming as the circles spun. Now the circles broke off one from another—two, then three, then four, until there were seven, then eight.

Odd and outlandish, but wondrous, Dana thought. Angels! Unlike I ever imagined . . . and yet, somehow I feel I once knew them, but when? Before my first steps, before my first tooth and words. Before . . .

> *Vile Var,*
> *by hazel,*
> *and Zar*
> *and Tar,*
> *his kin,*
> *Evil born of evil,*
> *switching face and skin.*
>
> *Shifting shape,*
> *by cherry,*
> *twisting, changing name,*
> *Shatter!*
> *Scatter!*
> *Bury!*
> *Dana's endless flame! . . .*

Heads bowed. The dance slowed and almost ground to a halt. The mood darkened and for a moment Dana felt her own heart sink. Then a crowd of fiddlers leapt from the trees. They were larger than the others, much larger even than Dana and awesome to behold. For their bodies shone like bronze and were ever changing: shining oxen, leopards, lions, and fish changing one to the next, on and on without pause, while their faces were like those of people.

Dana gawked as down they swept, each on four broad wings of light. Their fingers were flames dancing upon fiddle strings and their bows were bolts of lightning. The fiddlers formed a ninth circle around Dana, hunching over quavering strings, stirring the dancers to quicken their steps. . . .

We, the ones,
by woodbine,
past the earthen night,
Veiled by stars
and moon shine,
bearing Dana's light. . . .

Drum beats resounded in the trees. The fiddlers struck high, capering chords. The dancers broke step, jumping, twirling, spinning on toes, slapping feet, flapping wings, each in his own frolic, or in bucking pairs or skipping groups.

The air shimmered with joy, such spirited, sparkling joy, as Dana had never before seen or felt, or—but hadn't she? Her heart leapt in her chest. She knew she had! This very unbridled joy . . . before and before and before. At the Spring of Beginning . . . and when she'd stood in her towers, moons and suns at her fingertips. Joy unbounded! As around her the merriment grew.

From the trees came gusts of windblown tune. Pipes! High melody lifting hearts to rapture. Pipers descended, ten in all, sliding down Dana's rays to alight at her feet. Prancing, they formed a tight inner circle about her, heads reaching her knees, lips piping their tune. With them streamed the rays, four colors of light flashing, skimming the ground like flying hoops.

To this circle bounded Ibbur doing handsprings among the

pipers. Others too joined close about Dana as voices rose with new force:

> *Sworn to serve*
> *by balsam,*
> *to ever bear our star,*
> *Against the dark destruction*
> *of Var!*
> *and Zar!*
> *and Tar!*

Tiny feet trampled the three names, trounced them with dancing steps. The drums in the trees thudded deeper and louder. The circles quickened. The rays spun faster about Dana. Ibbur and the pipers and the others among them became a whirling blur.

Now the rays and two inner circles lifted and spun off from the glade. Dana felt herself rise above the trees in a gyroscope of color and piping sound. Dizzy joy and merriment! Not a worry or care. Dana's head spun with it all. Ibbur's smiling face swirled before her, spinning like a merry-go-round. Whirling . . . and gradually slowing . . . rising to an airy, floating room . . . as the whirling lessened, then stopped.

"To Dana, Queen of Angels!" The roomful of voices broke upon Dana's ears. She looked dizzily around. Curtains ringed the room in blue, purple, and scarlet; the finest twined linens, embroidered with silver. On deeply carved tables burned lamps of fragrant oils, incenses and spices, candles set in golden holders. Their many flames flickered casting glow and shadow, silhouettes of faces, bodies, wings.

Glasses clinked and were lifted, glistening all about. "From below and below and below she's come!" spoke a voice. "Here! Here!" others answered. "From after and after and after! To before and before and before!" Joyful laughter abounded.

Surrounding her, Dana saw a circle of shining faces. The pipers were there, and Ibbur, and others of varying sizes, colors, and shapes of body. Wings quivered above heads. Tiny wisps of light flitted like glowflies. The fiddlers, fiery and bronze, sat shimmering against a wall, fiddles resting on their knees. Above them all hovered Dana's rays.

"Queen Dana, we welcome you with outspread hearts!" The largest of those standing spoke with a voice like song. "In moonless night, our hearts never dimmed. As never we've doubted your return." The speaker's face, lion-like, shining amber light, turned to Ibbur. "And Ibbur, our angeline triumphant! Who would've guessed?" Short, stifled laughs erupted into cheers and the pounding of tables as Ibbur, blushing crimson-green, was hoisted upon shoulders.

Glasses were lifted. Several of the assembly—with faces of chubby children, Dana noticed—flew overhead refilling each glass with a golden, honey-like liquid poured from crystal jugs.

"To Ibbur of high and low places!"

Again titters fell to cheers, "To Ibbur!" as he was passed from shoulder to shoulder, and finally to Dana. Upon her shoulder he stood, as a brimming glass was passed forward and thrust into Dana's hand.

"Should I drink it?" Dana whispered to Ibbur. "What is it?"

"Liquid song, my queen. Perfectly safe." He laughed. "Don't you remember? You were weaned on it!"

Dana lifted the glass to her face. The room grew hushed. She sniffed at the rim. Familiar? Yes . . . something of the scent of that moon-pink fruit . . . but older still . . . a freshness of secrets once known. Dana breathed deeply and touched the glass to her lips. Sweet flow! The liquid streamed like light, filling her mouth as air through a straw. Each swallow was a breath and a memory, taking her back to beginnings. . . .

To when the princess stood in each of her towers, hand extended to each of the moons. Then, explosions of light, of water, of wind and of dust! There came a sharp-toothed mouth growing bigger, ever wider, crushing, slashing fangs. A mouth in a face that was hidden. Three times Dana felt herself falling. . . .

But before it all, there was a pinpoint of light. Nothing more. It shone as through the eye of a needle: a sharp, piercing beam. Dana traced it in her mind and seemed to find herself balanced upon it, a tightrope walker on a beam of light. With sure-footed step, she saw herself alight from the beam to Light Castle. There she stood, bathed in light, while at her fingertips spun a moon and sun—as one!—shedding brilliant light.

It all raced quickly through her mind, but to Dana it seemed she stood there forever . . . until the sharp-toothed mouth appeared, yawning, gaping in shadow. It opened and devoured, swallowing her down. Dana shuddered. She thought she heard a whisper, a breath at her ear, a voice, a song. Terror vanished. Birds, thought Dana sleepily, whistling and wings. Or humming . . . yes, hummingbirds! Or, no—

Dana felt as if she'd just opened her eyes, but her eyes were already open. The pipers were playing. Each tone sounded in her ears, so clear and precise it seemed she could see it. For each tone was another color of sound. Ten sounds in all.

Impossible! Dana thought—but yes! She'd heard, yes *seen* them before. Five of the tones reminded her of the five sounds played on the hand that had crumbled. Anavak's hand! Inviting, she'd thought, and oddly familiar. Of course! The tones were part of an old song, a song once as familiar as her own hands, all ten fingers. Five tones and five more, just as the ten pipers were playing. From before all befores! Now she could hear them, see them, remember them.

Upon Dana's finger her ring began to spin like a tiny hoop of light. As it whirled it whistled, first one piper's tone. . . . Then of its own it jumped to the next finger and began playing another piper's tone. Again it jumped and again, ten times for ten fingers and tones, each like a song in itself. Dana watched and listened. Each tone seemed to spin its own color. Not red. Not yellow. Not blue. No combination of these. Yet each color was familiar. She'd seen them before, each another color of joy.

Dana held out her hands to Ibbur. "Ten sounds, Ibbur, just as the pipers are playing! And I knew them long ago."

"Indeed, my queen. Ten joyful tones, and each a part of the Song of the Heart. Together they'll lead you through the Mountain of Light to the Spring of Beginning."

"And then?"

"And then, Queen Dana, you'll know what to do."

"As Anavak said."

"Indeed."

The pipers blew ten blasts. The largest of Dana's hosts spoke again with song-like words. "Six sparks our queen has regained." Wings fluttered excitedly amid hurrahs. "And not without peril, dangers faced and faced down."

"Queen Dana the Brave!" came a chorus of shouts.

"Are we not thankful, thankful beyond measure for the valor of our queen?" Murmurs and shouts of agreement stirred the hosts. "As we bask in her light and her deeds, are we idle?"

"Never!"

"Have we idly awaited her return with wings folded, sharing none of the work?"

"No! Impossible! Never!"

The amber-faced speaker turned to Dana with widespread wings. "You see, our queen, to herald your return, we've endeavored to act by your example. And so"—with a sweeping gesture of arms and wings—"we give you, Queen Dana, your seventh spark!" Two pudgy faces rose on fat stubby wings. Between their hands stretched a cape of spangled light. "Taken from the back of Var himself. May he freeze in his own darkness!" Sneers and scornful laughter overflowed as the spangled cape was draped across Dana's shoulders.

Dana touched the cape gingerly and felt a static charge beneath her fingertips. She was flustered, stammering her thanks, "I—I—"

"Some words from our queen!"

"Queen Dana!"

"Well, I—am thankful and amazed!" Wild cheers petered to an alert, listening silence. Dana could hear the slightest flitter of wings and flickering flame. She wrapped the cape tighter. "You're all so kind." Tears welled in her eyes. "Strange as it is, I—I feel I've known you—from—from before and before! Yes, I have known you—and the Song of the Heart from so long ago." Excited whispers rippled through the hosts. "And now—now I've come this far, as Anavak insisted. As everything, I think, insisted! With Ibbur's help and the sparks' charms, even when I didn't know how or exactly why, or what was before me—or behind me." The assembly looked on, eyes shining, glinting, gleaming like stars.

"Each spark I've found—or that found me!—is a gift, a charm working its magic. And I've never known what to expect." Dana lifted her arms, spreading her cape. "Yet each spark brought me what I needed. As it turned out, what I needed most at the time." Light sparkled across the cape, spreading wider with Dana's rising arms. "And so this spark—" She felt a peculiar sensation running down her arms from shoulders to fingertips. "This spark you've given me is a—gift t-two times"—her head began to bob—"whatever magic it—it—holds!!" Dana quickly tried to finish her words of thanks, for she'd begun rising through the room, as if weightless, her cape arching and flapping like wings.

"Hail Dana, Queen of Angels, Queen of Worlds!"

Dana hovered above their cries, astonished, her rays streaming about her. Ibbur strutted proudly across her back saying, "Your seventh spark, my queen—the power of flight. Now learn its uses—fly!"

Dana flapped and flew, forward and back, awkwardly at first, but gradually feeling her wings, gliding, spiraling, soaring above radiant heads. Her rays spun in hoops and through these Dana dove, barrel rolling, looping, flying lazy eights as Ibbur hung on. And her hosts, those with wings, sprang into flight, joining their queen.

The room filled with wings, fluttering, flapping, shining joy and delight. The pipers intoned their ten sounds. The fiddlers sprang from their haunches, leaping like lightning, striking flame upon strings. A dance of flight fell out. Airy abandon! Glasses clinked. Jugs poured. Dana's ring jumped upon her fingers, spinning light and tone. Harmony reigned. All joined in the Song of the Heart.

But as they rollicked and romped with Dana marveling at her newest spark, there came a sudden clanking off-key sound to break the revel. Music and merriment ceased. The curtains parted with a slicing whoosh as in rushed sharp shadows, dark forms, searing heat, screeches, curses, and foul stench. A hundred cruel eyes burning like coals. Bat-like reptiles filled the room as locusts breathing fire. The curtains scorched and burst into flame, leaping black, leaping red. Through this fire passed a gaping mouth filled with teeth, hollow and sharp, like a cave covered ceiling to floor with knives.

"Var!" cried Dana's hosts. "Evil and his hordes! Demons!"

Joy gave way to turmoil, flailing wings and thrashing claws.

"Come for my cape!" blasted the mouth. "But what do I find? Why, the Queen of Thieves! Thief of Sparks! At last to devour!"

The mouth opened wide as the room, raging fury, dripping fire. "Crush them, my legions! Tear wings! Break hearts! Scatter all defenders! But leave the queenly prize for me."

Demons dashed gnashing teeth, spitting poisons. Dana's hosts streaked like squadrons of light. Her rays formed into beaming shields, butting demons. The fiddlers formed a circle around Dana swiping broad stinging lightning bolt blows. The mouth was at bay, teeth fencing fiddle bows. Lightning crackled, teeth cracked. The room grew hotter with Var's rage.

"Queen Dana, you must make your escape!" shouted Ibbur, climbing over her shoulder.

"But Ibbur—my angels! They need me!"

"They need you alive, loyal queen! Flee now!"

"How, Ibbur, where?"

"Fly, dear queen. Straight up and out!" as he ducked down her collar.

Dana looked overhead. A canopy of stars filled her vision. Without hesitation she sprang upward into flight. And with two great flaps of her cape, Dana left the battle far below raging into silence.

Chapter Sixteen

GATES TO BEGINNING

Trailed by her rays, Dana soared like a comet streaking a four-colored tail. Her winged cape flapped with the grace of an eagle, but with strokes far more powerful. As a spark of moonlight she flew, beaming past shards of the Mountain of Light.

To one side burned black fire, hollow and hot, lapping like flaming seas. To the other side black fire burned too, but empty and cold, like oceans of icy night. Dana glanced neither way, but rushed headlong, eyes fixed on a distant point.

This way, of course! thoughts spoke in her head. The way of the white raven, when I saw it fly off from Anavak's cave. This way, I'm certain. Up ahead!

Dimly-lit stars spiraled into a funnel-like passage. Through this passage Dana flew, willful and determined, a queen on the wing, eyes fixed like the white raven's.

As she flew the spiral, shrieks filled her ears, and hammering cries of "Die, lost queen, lonely death!" Dana sped on, uncowed, unflinching, while the shrieks grew louder, raspier, and battering. "Blood, hated queen! A taste of your blood!!" Dark forms crossed her path—Var's demons and shades spraying venom and curses, clutching, slashing claws. Yet they could no more grasp Dana than they could her rushing rays, so fast did she fly.

Past Var's hordes Dana emerged into part-light, out an opening tight as a keyhole. Pale sky spread before her in a sea of haze. Down depths she flew, descending through clouds, slowing, gliding to land. On drifting sands she finally alighted, folding her wings in blue-purple desert. A great mound of sand loomed before her, higher than a tower.

"What place is this, Ibbur, do you know?"

Ibbur's head peeped from Dana's sleeve. He sprang to her shoulder and eyed the sandy hill. "A place to test your power of song, my queen; to test all that you've learned and remembered."

Dana scanned the mound thoughtfully, one hand upon Mashire at her belt. Her four rays had begun circling the high hill of sand. A soft breeze blew past her ear. A whisper. A sound. The first piper's tone, thought Dana, remembering. She twisted the ring on her finger. The ring spun with a whir, glistening, whistling color. The breeze blew stronger with the same sound. Dana's rays circled faster. Sand lifted on wind.

Grain by grain, the mound stirred and shifted. Wrinkles appeared. Ripples in sand. Sweeping. Whipping in wind. Granule by windful the sandy hill eroded, dwindled, and shrank. Dana shielded her face with her wing-like cape, squinting to see. The mound peeled like an onion, layer by layer. And before Dana's eyes, each layer revealed something more. . . .

Windswept sands at the top unveiled golden bricks, one then another, built one upon the other. Layers fell away to uncover a tower, half in ruin, rising from the mound. Dana looked on as whistling wind peeled away more: other towers, columns, and golden walls, half tumble-down pillars and turrets. All became unburied before her eyes. Desert ground kept shifting, lifting, dancing on wind to the piping of Dana's ring. Buildings seemed to grow from the ground. Mansions. Chambers. Wall after wall, unveiled. Everything golden, or so it seemed through the windblown sand. But as wind and sand dispersed, Dana saw more clearly. . . .

Where the mound had stood, there were now walls within walls—forming circles within circles. Each rose high above Dana's head and shone not of gold, but of hazy tarnished light. Far within the walls of light were mansions—half-shining in golden light, partly hidden, as though seen through a screen. The mansions too formed a circle. At its center shone a structure much larger and brighter, but also of hazy light, with ten towers rising from its corners. Light Castle! Dana knew without asking. She'd seen it all before, long before. She was thrilled to behold it again, and by her own magic! But to see it in ruin choked her joy. For the only things standing whole were the castle's outer walls. And these, Dana knew, kept her out.

"Ibbur, I must get in!"

"Of course!"

"But how?"

"There was a time, my queen, when you'd simply walk in, through walls and all."

As he spoke, Dana pictured herself doing the very thing Ibbur described. "Yes, Ibbur, I remember that. Like a dream, but real! Though somehow I know I can't do that now."

"Then you *do* remember! Memory re-grown! And wise you are not to attempt it. For to pass through walls of even dim light requires ten sparks. Not eight. Not nine, but ten. Without them, you'd be burned in a flash. Turned to vapor!"

Dana shivered and reached for her pouch, then stopped, a new idea bursting. "Ibbur, the cape! I'll fly over!"

Ibbur slowly shook his head. "Think again, Queen Dana. Magic too has limits. Remember?"

Dana wasn't sure that she did. Why not fly over? she thought. She imagined herself taking flight, rising above the first round wall. But as she came to the top and prepared to cross over, the wall grew taller, leaping with flames.

"You see," said Ibbur, "that way, too, you'd be burned."

Again Dana shivered and reached for her pouch. Which way in then? she thought, as if asking her sparks. And they seemed to light her thinking, for an answer came—ten gates!

"Correct, Queen Dana."

"Indeed!" Dana laughed. "Can you read my thoughts, Ibbur? Have you always?"

"Not each and every one"—Ibbur paused—"but the loud ones, yes." Dana's lips parted to speak. Before she could utter a word, Ibbur said, "Please, dear queen, that's all I'll say about it for now. We've gates to find. The first and nine more."

"That shouldn't take long, dear Ibbur," said Dana, spreading her cape. Again her seventh spark became wings, sparkling plumes on which she rose.

"Don't be foolish, Queen Dana!" cried Ibbur and he dashed down her sleeve.

Dana flew the bounds of the outer wall, her rays following at her heels. Shortly, from winged heights, she spied what she was after and glided gently down to the first gate.

Ibbur emerged, straightening his jelly-cap. "Clever queen, for a moment I thought—"

"You don't think I'm foolish, do you?"

Ibbur smiled sheepishly behind Dana's hair as she folded her wings and approached the gate.

Unlike the walls which were of dim light, the gate was wrought of wood. It stood broad and tall, hewn of thick cedar with hinges of gold. Massive posts, also of cedar, held it in place. On the posts Dana saw carved symbols—or were they letters?—overlaid with gold.

"What do they mean, Ibbur?"

"Hidden names, my queen."

Hidden names, Dana thought to herself, recalling . . . "Ibbur, the giant said something about them, when it found you up my sleeve. It knew who you were and threatened you with secrets and hidden names." Dana reached her hand up to a gatepost. "These?"

"Zar's threats can be believed, my queen."

"Whose names do they spell?"

"Ancient names, Queen Dana. Lost in time. Before all befores. The most ancient of names."

"And Zar knows them," said Dana, fingertips grazing a golden letter. "Then Var knows them too." She turned to Ibbur. "How can he use them to hurt you?"

"The names—as you once knew—contain the oldest magic. Those who know them tap the greatest power to do good or evil."

"Then, Ibbur, I've got to remember them!"

"Pass through these ten walls, Queen Dana, and you shall."

The gate. Easy to find, but to open? Dana stepped up to it and pushed . . . and pushed harder. Nothing. Next she pulled and yanked on its golden handle, but the gate remained rigid as a tree.

A spark, thought Dana, one of my charms. Which one? Her hand went to Mashire, knowing the sword could pierce anything. But cut the gate to pieces? Dana's heart told her no. Then as she listened to her heart, it told her other things too: the sound of a letter, the meaning of a symbol. The ones on the gateposts! Ancient, out of time. Before time. Letters and symbols into sounds, music and colors. A song. The second piper's tune! Dana listened from within and twisted the ring on her finger. Instantly it jumped to the next finger, spinning a new color, whistling a new tone of the Song of the Heart.

Gateposts sizzled and ignited. Letters and symbols began to burn with sound. The gate glowed and shook, and then, as if rammed by a great force, it sprang open.

The ring grew quiet, settling on Dana's finger. "Well done, knowing queen," said Ibbur. Dana smiled and stepped carefully past the first of ten gates beyond the outermost boundary of Light Castle.

Chapter Seventeen

WINGS OF STONE

The gate closed with a rushing force. Dana stood within the outermost wall of Light Castle, steeped in shadow. A strip of sand ran like a track between the outer wall and the next within. Opposite the first gate was a second, also hewn of cedar, with other symbols and letters carved into its posts.

Ibbur jumped to the ground where the four rays glowed in a huddle. Small rounded stones and shards of pottery lay partly covered in the sand.

Dana looked up and down the desert track, then knelt down picking up a shard, turning it over in her hand. She studied it, eyes staring deeply, drilling through it, past it, back in time . . . into herself. "A river ran here," she spoke slowly, sounding far away. She shook her head, as if shaking away sleep, and turned to Ibbur. "A river of light! Between these walls, Ibbur, rivers flowed, circling endlessly, until Var—until Var swallowed them down!"

"And they'll flow again, Queen Dana, if you succeed at your task." Ibbur balanced upon a rounded pebble, arms out at his sides like wings.

Without pause, Dana strode to the second gate and twisted the ring on her finger. Again it whirled and spun off to the next finger, whistling the third piper's tune. The gateposts glowed. Letters burst into flame. The gate began to tremble, golden hinges gleaming with the third color of sound. Song of the Heart! And with a blast, the second gate sprang open just as the first.

Ibbur scurried like a lizard, catching up to Dana and her rays, as the gate closed behind them with a crash.

Dana found herself in a second desert track, between the second and third walls of light. Before her loomed the third gate. In front of the gate was a figure, larger than Dana, hunched and perfectly still. It appeared as a statue in alabaster or white marble, mostly hidden by arched wings.

"An angel," Dana whispered, "an angel of stone."

"Of stone?" Ibbur was doubtful. "We shall see." He crept to the figure and slipped under its white shining wings.

Dana heard a muffled voice—Ibbur's. To whom was he speaking? The statue? Now another voice spoke in murmurs. Words passed, muted under wing. Gradually, they rose in pitch, one voice and the other, till a veiled quarrel reached Dana's ears. What is he up to? she thought. Arguing with a statue?

The other voice grew louder, irritated and angry. "It is deep, deep, who can find it? Deep I say, deep! Who can find it?!"

Ibbur made a reply that Dana couldn't make out.

"Deep I say! Who'll find it? I dig in the name of the queen!"

Ibbur responded in pleading tones.

"Forthright and true? Fah, fah!" replied the voice. "I can't believe it. Deep I say, deep. Go away!"

Ibbur emerged from beneath the wings, a frown on his tiny green face.

"What is it, Ibbur? Who?"

Sand began to fly furiously from under the wings. The figure appeared to be digging as it had said.

"She's the guardian of this gate and has been since before the destruction." Ibbur shook his head. "But she's gone mad. Frozen with grief and longing! A stiff-necked madness has overtaken her. All she knows is to dig. It's all she has left."

"But for what is she digging, poor thing?"

"Wisdom. She believes if she finds it, Queen Dana will return."

"Then tell her I'm here!"

"I did. She won't believe me. She's off her wing. Frozen in madness!"

Sand continued to fly wildly from beneath the stone-like wings. "Dig deep, down to depths!" wailed the voice. "Deep! For the queen! Distance! Direction! Correction!" Words flew with the sand and with the rhythm of the digging in a sing-song, gone-mad chant:

> *Oh queen!*
> *Oh wisdom!*
> *Take measure,*
> *measure of ten,*
> *without end!*
> *Deep to begin—deep at end!*
> *Depth of good—depth of evil!*
> *Measure above—or below!*
> *Down I go*
> *for Queen Dana!*
> *East—then West!*
> *North—or South!*
> *Down to the middle*
> *of nothing!*
> *To harmony,*
> *wisdom, dear queen!* . . .

"I'm here!" Dana ran to the figure, tears streaking her face. "Poor thing, dear thing, I'm here, right here!" But the guardian ignored Dana, or didn't hear, lost in her digging and frustrated chant.

"Unbalanced," said Ibbur, shaking his head.

Dana embraced the stone-stiff wings, pleading and imploring, "I've returned, understand? Please understand and stop digging! Queen Dana's returned!" Her tears fell hot upon the wings to form rivulets in folds of stony feather. And as the tears ran down, the feathers twitched. Wings stirred as flowers awakening in spring rains. Dana's tears ran to the wing tips; tiny waterfalls leaping to the ground, splashing at the figure's feet.

The digging suddenly stopped. Wings fluttered and lifted, stretching like a swan's. White-faced beauty peeked out. Hair seemed to pour like milk. Eyes shone as pearls regarding Dana. "Queen Dana? Could it be?" lips sparkled and spoke.

"Yes, please believe me!" Dana cried. "Here, see, here is my sword, Mashire! My sparks and Ibbur."

"I know nothing of a sword. And of sparks? They were taken! Yet your voice is a song and—Ibbur, you say?" The pearly eyes opened wide upon him. "As you insisted, faithful green! But I wouldn't listen. Oh little angeline! Of you I've heard tell, before and before. Gone to fetch the queen? From the depths? Is it so?"

"Yes, dear angel, it is!" Dana urged. "I've come back."

"Sweet song! Then it's so. Queen Dana has returned!" The guardian swept her wings to launch body and robes into flight. "Joy! Oh wondrous, wondrous joy!"

"Come down at once!" shouted Ibbur.

"Harmony and joy!" sang the guardian and her wings swept higher.

"Heed the walls!" warned Ibbur.

"Elation! Elaaaation . . . !" came the voice rising with delight, soaring higher.

"Come down!" called Dana.

"She's flighty, still mad," said Ibbur, "but now with joy, poor fool. Balance!" he yelled at the top of his voice.

"Jubilation, true queen!" The shining figure descended streaking white light.

"Look out for the walls!" cried Dana.

"Euphoria . . . !" The guardian shot down like a falling star, unmindful of danger, delirious with joy.

Dana's rays leapt upward rushing as lifesavers to a drowning swimmer. But as a frantic swimmer can hamper help, so the guardian entangled her would-be savers.

"Euphooriiiaaa!" she called, sailing over a wall.

"Stop!" screamed Dana.

All efforts were useless. The guardian topped the wall. Light exploded. Flames reached up in fiery waves, and farther with pure heat . . . till in clear flash, the guardian was engulfed, gone, vanished in an instant. A shooting star lost.

Ibbur hung his head. Dana stared, heartbroken, sorrow-sore.

"She couldn't be helped, Queen Dana," said Ibbur at last.

Dana remained silent, brooding.

"Some angels, dear queen—you should know—go even quicker than that. Each moment creates us by the thousands, simply to sing the Song of the Heart and in the same moment expire."

"But why, Ibbur, why?" Dana's voice broke.

"You know better than I, Queen Dana. To utter the Song of the Heart is no small thing. Some moments play forever, up and down through the worlds, holding everything together."

Dana gazed up at her rays untangling and circling where the guardian had vanished in flame. "She felt so deeply. Such sadness, such joy."

"Dear queen, even joy must know its bounds, lest we destroy ourselves. For an angel must balance between wings. One wing is fear—call it grief, despair, longing. The other wing is love—joy, kindness, compassion. So many names for love. Between love and fear we find our balance, tilting one way and the other, learning to fly straight. That's why the heart is in the middle. So is the mind. They must be balanced between wing tips, in harmony, in song! Otherwise, fear turns to stone. And love without bounds burns itself out."

Ibbur pointed to the hole where the guardian had been digging, already filling with shifting sands. "She wasn't the first to lose herself to fear and then to love."

Dana mulled it over quietly . . . then resolutely stepped past the hole to the third gate. "We're going through, Ibbur. Two more sparks to find—and worlds to repair."

"Queen Dana of Song!" hailed Ibbur and sprang for her pocket. As before, Dana twisted her ring. A new color of light spun with the fourth piper's tune. Again the posts glowed, the letters sizzled, symbols flared—and the third gate burst open as the others had done.

Chapter Eighteen

DEMON SANDS

Two steps past the third closing gate, Dana sank to her knees in sand. "Hunh!" Her voice hung in the air. She tried lifting her feet but couldn't. It was as if her sneakers were cased in stone. With each squirming movement, she sank deeper, sand burbling and sucking her down.

"Quicksand!"

"Steady, my queen," Ibbur called from her pocket. "Don't move!"

"Don't move?! But I'm sinking!" Boggy sand lapped at Dana's thighs.

"No quick motion. Be calm."

"Calm!" Dana struggled with her legs, sinking lower.

"Yes, calm! Balanced! The quicker you move, the quicker you'll sink—the quicker we'll sink!—and drown in your fear! This is Var's doing, to be sure. Don't lose heart! You must outthink him."

Outthink him, outthink him, yes, yes, think, Dana heard in her head. Her heart pounded in her ears. She could see her rays streaking frantically nearby over the surface of wet sand. She tried to spread her cape, her wings, but their tips were soaked in sand and wouldn't open. Next she looked down at Mashire, blade covered most to the hilt. Could you slice through this? she asked in thought.

"Mashire won't do, not here," said Ibbur. "Waste no motion!"

Fear crept at Dana's hips. Her vision began to blur. She reached for her pouch—comfort there, but no fitting charm. Sand sloshed at the bag's ties like greedy fingers, poking, prodding to get in. "Keep away!" Dana screamed in a frenzy, forgetting herself, pushing sand from her pouch. With each push she sank lower, sand gurgling up her waist. She imagined it filling her mouth. The taste of fear!

"Queen Dana, control yourself! Don't let fear overcome you! Var tests you now as he has all along. For he needs to know your limits to do battle! Move ever so slowly through this mire and think . . . what limits of mind, of heart, of body. Move slowly. Balance and think."

With nothing else to hold to, Dana held to her thoughts . . . all she'd come to know: her charms, hidden names, secrets in song. Anavak. Winds. Angels! . . . as she inched with the least amount of motion, the slowest possible swim through muddy sands. Limits. What limits? Balance and fly! Sand bubbled up her shirt seeping toward her pocket.

"Easy . . . easy . . . ," coached Ibbur climbing gingerly from Dana's pocket to her shoulder.

Dana paddled ploddingly like an ancient turtle, holding her mind fixed on slowness. Inch by creeping inch . . . slow flight through quicksand. Think, think and glide. . . . No limits. I can do this. Feel flight. . . . Heart soar! . . . Body move!

Little by little, Dana relaxed to her task. Calm enfolded her limbs and bore her through ooze. Fear fell away, even as sands slopped under her chin and Ibbur climbed to her head.

"Queen of Striving!" encouraged Ibbur as Dana neared the fourth gate in the fourth wall of light. Her rays circled above her head. Dana smiled despite the danger, sands trickling at the corners of her mouth.

"Your ring now, brave queen!"

With slowest motion, Dana raised her arm through the swallowing sands. Her hand reached the surface . . . then stuck there, fighting greedy guzzle. "Let go!" she cried. Like the mouth of a cruel calf, sand slurped at her fingers.

Dana could taste it: sand overflowing her lips. Yet it tasted more of curiosity than fear. Will I smother or drown? she wondered. Are they the same? The sand seemed to lull her, making her sleepy . . . closing her eyes . . .

"Awake, Queen Dana!" Ibbur called, clinging to gloppy

strands of Dana's sinking hair. "Var strikes you with slumber. You'll be sleep-drowned!"

Dana's eyes fluttered, straining to open. Sand splashed up her nose. She felt weighted, eyelids and all sinking down.

"Wide awake, my queen! Pull! Free your hand, your ring!"

My hand, Dana thought sleepily, is this how Anavak lost hers? Now mine too? Taken by Var? And the sparks . . . sucked down in quicksand?

From deep inside Dana, a voice spoke up, "No!" Old and withered, but knowing and strong. Anavak! "The sparks are yours, Queen of Beginning, as is your ring, as is your hand. Now and forever—or never!"

As if by command, Dana pulled with new force against the guzzling sands. Her lion's heart pumped in her chest. Her mind pulsed. With a gurgling slosh then, her hand pulled free, fingers splayed like a cat's claws, swiping, sparkling, nails flashing light. Where her hand had been, a gash opened in the quicksand oozing foul-smelling creatures, sandy blobs reeking muck, burbling curses, "Sunken queen! Swallow death!"

"Sand demons!" shouted Ibbur.

Sand-covered limbs sloshed like octopus arms, tentacles tugging, sucking Dana down. Her head went under. Sputtering, she came back up. Demon limbs wrapped around her neck. Again she went under. Sands closed over her head burbling, "Fie! Fie and die, Queen of Drowning!"

Moments passed with Dana submerged. Finally, a limb rose from the muck, then another . . . then a third one dripping sand. The three struggled, wrestling arms, until one tore free. On its hand spun a ring—Dana's! The ring flashed color, jumping fingers, piping sound. The fifth piper's tune! Letters sparked on the gateposts. Song of the Heart! Hidden names!

The fourth gate burst open like a ruptured dam. Quicksand surged past Var's demons and the fourth wall of light. Dana was carried through, arm upraised, ring piping, chin bobbing above the splashing sands. On her head rode Ibbur. "Conquering queen!" he proclaimed as behind flowed Dana's rays streaming like banners of victory.

Chapter Nineteen

SHIFTING GROUND

The sodden sands dried as a flood in retreat. Dana sprawled on the ground coughing and sputtering from her mouth and nose. Ibbur did the same, hacking like a fallen bird, "Cah! Cah! Demons!"

Slowly they revived. Dana took a fistful of dry sand, running it through her fingers, watching it trickle down. She stood up wobbling, then found her balance, stomping her feet for the feel of solid ground. Her nostrils flared drawing fresh breath.

Ibbur slapped sand from his clothes with his red jelly-cap. He cleared his nose and spat, then looked up at Dana. "Secrets in light!" he cried gaily. "Breathe your triumph, dear queen!" and he sprang to her shoulder.

Dana smiled fleetingly and eyed the fifth wall of light. It shone as the others with its cedar gate and carved posts. "Five gates and five more," Dana said and strode toward it. But as she came to the gate, the wall vanished—and reappeared in the distance.

"Ibbur, it moved!"

Ibbur squinted his tiny black eyes. "Var."

"Yes, Var." Dana shifted Mashire in her belt, and again began walking toward the fifth wall of light. At her side beamed her rays: four silent colors.

The drying sands became parched, hard and cracked, crunching beneath Dana's feet. At first the ground seemed barren, empty of anything save sand. But as Dana walked on, she saw what seemed to be shadows, small ones, flitting over the ground. Farther on, watching closely, she began to see more clearly: not shadows, but small creatures. Lizards scurried over the desert crust, stopping and going, zigzagging and slipping down holes.

With creeping flesh Dana hurried on. Panting, she reached the fifth wall for the second time. She raised her ringed hand at the gate. Instantly the wall vanished to again reappear in the distance. "Ibbur," said Dana in dismay, "what kind of evil game is this?"

"As I've said, Queen Dana, Var doesn't play games, evil or otherwise. He has taken your measure and finds your powers greater than he thought. For your powers grow while his remain unchanged. He must stall for time to gather his forces. He'll strike when he's ready."

Again Dana set out for the fifth gate. Lizards darted past, confusing her step. She had to set each foot down carefully, so carefully that soon her feet wearied and her mind became muddled by the squirming beneath her feet.

How will I ever reach the wall? she thought. As if in reply, her four rays beamed upright at her side twisting themselves into a long braid, straight as a pole, spinning four colors.

"Behold, Queen Dana, your walking stick of light!"

Teetering on the edge of falling, Dana took hold of the lighted stick. She leaned upon it as a third leg, righting herself, steadying her step to again reach the fifth wall.

Warily she approached the gate. Supported by her stick, Dana raised her hand, but the gate vanished for a third time and reappeared in the distance yet again. "No!" Dana shouted. Slowly she walked on. For the first time since drinking Anavak's tea, Dana tasted thirst. Her mouth dried. Her tongue stuck. Her lips cracked.

The desert ground rippled with movement. Lizards and their shadows, more than before and larger, slow-moving and fast, crowded Dana's path. She stepped over and around them: sand-lizards and skinks, stumps and girdle tails, fleeting throngs at her feet. Sweat drenched Dana's shirt. Her skin crawled. Don't trip, don't slip! she pleaded with herself and tried not to think of the outcome if she did . . . to fall among them, squirming. Please no!

"Steady, brave queen," urged Ibbur. "Balance. Think. . . . Must I remind you? Fly!"

"My cape!" Dana cried. "Why didn't I think of it before?"

"Fear dims thought, my queen. It deadens the mind, sinks the heart, cripples the hand, and clips the wings! It is Var's greatest power."

"But didn't you say that even the lion knows fear?"

"And what did I say he does with it?"

"He—he acts to possess it!"

"Yes, and I also said that in the end you'll find there's no cause for fear. Only wonder. Only awe. For you are no mere beast, but Queen Dana of Beginning, before all befores. Before even fear! Know this: A lion does not fly. A lion does not understand with mind and with heart. A lion is but one spark. He does not restore worlds. He does not gain wisdom. Queen Dana does!"

"I do!" said Dana. "And I will!"

"Will indeed! Before all befores you'll come to will."

Dana had spread her cape and taken flight. Radiant joy and sparkling wings propelled her. In her hand was her stick of light; on her shoulder, Ibbur. Balance and harmony filled her so, there was no room to ponder what Ibbur had meant by the last thing he'd said.

On swift wings Dana once again reached the fifth wall of light. She stood before the gate, arm upraised, when the ground beneath her began to rumble and pitch. An earthquake, she thought, but too soon; for though the ground shook, the cause was more dreadful than an earthquake.

The ground seemed to come alive, rolling and tossing. Dana was thrown face-down. Land exploded about her. As mountains break violently from flatlands, the ground swelled and burst with bulging forms. Creatures emerged. Bodies and heads, scaly skins, gaping mouths, spitting tongues—snakes! A sea of serpents, wriggling, twisting, shedding earth.

"To flight, Queen Dana!" called Ibbur as Dana struggled to her feet already spreading her cape, flapping her wings. But she didn't rise, she couldn't. She was bound and anchored. Snakes had twisted around her ankles, holding and squeezing. The ground slithered in a tangle of vipers and adders, pythons and mambas spitting, spraying venom, flashing fangs. Boas encircled Dana's legs with crushing coils, climbing higher.

"Don't let them reach your waist, brave queen!"

From the midst of the tangle there sprang four cobras, bigger than the rest, rising straight upward. They towered above Dana, like shadows swaying, spreading their necks into wide, hooded flaps. Their fangs dripped poison. Their eyes squinted hate. Behind them rose a squirming mound. Snakes heaved and surged as a huge spiny head broke through. It reared on a body bigger than a dozen of the others, with a cobra's hooded flaps, a python's skin, and a rattlesnake's tail. "Var!" shouted Dana. But how? she thought . . . Var wears no masks!

"Correct, clever Queen," Ibbur said hurriedly, reading her thoughts. "It's not Var himself, but his weapon—a spark, to be sure!"

Var's weapon stretched to full length then descended like an avalanche.

Balance, Dana thought. Unflinching, she drew Mashire and held the sword before her. The serpent's head swooped down to within inches of the blade—then stopped, hissing hate with Var's voice. "Dare to strike me foul queen and my hordes will strangle your breath! What will become of your worlds then, Queen of Ending?" The beast spread its jaws. Knife-like fangs glistened with venom, widening their bite. Burning eyes met Dana's. The serpent's tongue darted with menace, flicking at Dana's face, licking at her skin. At the same time, Dana could feel the boas winding round her hips.

If they reach my waist, I'll be crushed, she thought . . . so I must slash them off—but if I move to strike them, Var's weapon is open to strike me. What then? If I strike his weapon first, those four cobras will pounce and the rest will follow. Dana considered her choices as the boas crept higher . . . and reached her decision, impossible as it seemed, thinking to herself, I have no choice! . . .

Down came Mashire—

Instantly, Dana's four rays unraveled: The walking stick divided into parts, four colors, each one expanding, reshaping, forming anew, growing heads, scaly skin, fangs. Rays into snakes! One blue, one red, one yellow, one green.

"You've lost—!" sputtered Var's voice, head flying from the serpent's neck, severed by Mashire. The head fell hissing into the squirming mass of snakes. Turmoil! Dana sliced the boas from her legs as the cobras dove to attack.

They neared Dana, hoods flapping slaughter. In their paths were four lighted mouths, jaws leaping like fire. Dana's rays! Snake met snake. Light consumed dark. Down red, down yellow, down blue and green, the cobras were swallowed. Each lighted snake then swallowed more of Var's hordes. Down lighted gullets they went hissing their last.

From all sides snakes darted flaring fangs. Dana struck down head after head, slicing bodies and bellies with flurries of cuts. Mashire streaked like lightning in her hand. Both the blade and her skill were sharper and surer.

Heads flew off Dana's sword. Necks, bodies, and tails writhed and spurted cold blood. Dana trod their twitching backs wielding Mashire. All that neared her tasted her blade. Now the battle began to slow; fewer snakes on the strike. The four lighted snakes devoured anything that still slithered. Split heads and jaws lay at Dana's feet. Headless serpents jerked in spasms. Dana stepped through the gore occasionally slashing a snake on the rise. She panted for breath, heart thudding in her chest.

Ibbur thrust his head above Dana's collar, surveying the slaughter. "Conquering queen!" he hailed. Dana wobbled on her feet, Mashire grown heavy in her hand. She leaned on the blade to keep from collapsing. "Blood—and more blood," her voice cracked.

"Var's demons' blood, Queen Dana, and his weapon's."

"Yes, I know." Dana cleared her throat and shook her head. "Var the Destroyer of Worlds! I know him. I knew him! And I know I must defeat him or be defeated. But it's sorrow I feel, not joy."

"Queen of Heart! Queen of Feeling! You are as you must be. But do not neglect the glow of triumph. Feel as you must, but gather your spark."

As he spoke, Dana eyed her lighted snakes changing back

into rays above the headless form of Var's weapon. She wiped her brow and stepped closer. The grotesque snake head lay nearby, staring, mouth open, tongue stilled. Dana walked the length of its python body, treading its back, wider than a tree. The skin appeared as shadow till she neared the end where it tapered to a tail. There rested its huge rattle, silent and shining. Without hesitation, Dana severed the rattle with one cut and took it in her hands, hoisting its weight. She at once felt renewed, enlivened, empowered. Her eyes dazzled with reflected light.

"Var's rattle, Queen Dana. Your eighth spark, to be sure!"

"To be sure." Dana shook the heavy rattle. It seemed to sparkle with the softest, most liquid of sounds. Secrets, she thought . . . secrets here too. But what do they say? "What secrets, Ibbur?" she spoke aloud.

"Please, my queen, first learn the spark's charm. Secrets will follow."

Dana brought Var's rattle to the lip of her pouch and big though it was, it slipped easily inside, compressing as it went. Once more she stepped to the fifth gate raising her arm, half-expecting the wall to move. It didn't.

"Lift both arms," advised Ibbur.

The ring jumped from the last finger of Dana's hand to alight on the first finger of the next. A sixth spinning color—the sixth piper's tune!—and the names on the gateposts sparked into flame.

"Through gates to beginning!" piped Ibbur as the fifth gate sprang open. And Dana passed through, wholehearted and poised for whatever lay ahead.

Chapter Twenty

LAMP OF DARKNESS

Wide open wasteland spread before them, deserted and looming, without definition. Far as Dana could see, there was no sixth wall of light. Nothing but black sands stretched out into endless distance.

This time she didn't forget her wings. Dana began spreading her cape, but before her wings could open, the ground started flowing like water beneath her feet.

It reminded Dana of standing in surf at the seashore, spent waves rushing back to sea past her legs. Though not quite, for at the seashore it always felt as if she were rushing backward away from the sea. Now the feeling was different. Dana felt herself rushing forward—and it wasn't just a feeling, but a fact. The ground came rushing to meet her, hurtling at her feet with the speed of a rotating globe. Dana sped onward, gliding, surfing through sands.

"The worlds have waited long enough!" Ibbur called, head jutting from her collar. "Var's hold upon them is slipping!" He held a tiny green hand over his jelly-cap, keeping it safe from gusts.

Wind whipped Dana as she sped on and on skating over wild space. Skies went from pale to gray to black and back again, over and over, quickly and more quickly, changing with each instant, till it seemed to Dana that time too was rushing underfoot. Amazement and joy filled her. She could see her rays keeping pace at her side, and she laughed, thinking, I'm traveling at the speed of light!

"And why not?" asked Ibbur.

"Why not indeed, Ibbur, Reader of Minds!"

Ibbur blushed purple, laughed and opened his mouth in song:

Seventh spark's charm on sandy sea,
Flying cape in harmony,
Sark I-iddle-du, lily Lu-lee,
Wings to balance regally!

Eighth spark's charm on rushing sea,
Rattle's . . .

Ibbur's song came too swiftly through the rush for Dana to understand it; high-pitched words packed too closely together. "Sssweeee . . ." was all she could make out, whistling off Ibbur's rounded mouth, as day cycled to night and day again, then stopped—abruptly at night.

Sand ground to a halt. Dana was lifted off her feet soaring through darkness, whizzing headlong through thick blinding night. Black wind pressed at her face. The dark flight seemed unending, until she felt herself plunging, then crashing to the ground. Now she was skidding through sand, careening head over heel. Finally she tumbled to a stop and slowly, dizzily sat up.

Ruffled, but unhurt, Dana spat sand from her mouth. Inside she could feel her belly lurch and she thought she'd vomit, but she couldn't, she was empty. A gnawing hunger filled her. With it came a sudden foreboding. She called out in alarm, "Ibbur! Ibbur, are you okay?" No reply. Dana's hand went to her sleeves, searching one then the other—empty, then her collar and pocket—all empty! "Ibbur, where are you?! Ibbur!" Her voice rang thinly in the vastness of night, as if darkness itself swallowed each word. "Ibbur! Hear me!" Dana searched frantically through the sand, not daring to walk about lest she step upon Ibbur in the dark. "Ibbur, please! Answer me!"

Dana thought she heard laughter, shrill and harsh. It sniggered in the dark and faded to a hollow faraway patter, then was gone. Dana's skin tingled. An empty hole seemed to open in her chest; a feeling so lonely and real, she thought her heart might slip out. Her hands reached up as if to hold things in place, and she felt her heart beating rapidly, worriedly inside. "Oh, Ibbur," she whimpered and knew he was gone.

What will I do? she thought. Find him! But where? And what if he's hurt? Dana stared blankly into the black stillness, sinking in self-pity. Fear started up her spine. She began to shudder, then stopped—thinking . . . Var's greatest power— fear! But before all befores I knew no fear. Now even in darkness I must face him. But how? Dana's head bowed. A faint light caught her eye—the pouch! Her hand moved to her belt and there found Mashire shining dimly. And in the sand a short ways off, a pale stirring—four rays! Shaded by darkness, yet still they shone, and Dana knew: how else to face Var, but with light!

She emptied her pouch onto the sand, gathering her sparks. Together they glowed as an opening in the night. Like a tiny clouded moon, the sparks glimmered dimly.

Again there came laughter from behind the darkness. Snide sniggers sounded off in the distance, but instead of fading as before, they grew louder . . . closer. Soon Dana could see eyes surrounding and encircling. Blood red orbs glared out of blackness. Laughter teased and broke into shrieks and rasping howls. Amid the din Dana heard words. "Cursed Queen! Thief of Sparks! Death is yours!" The din swelled to a thunderous roar rushing at her with the force of storm winds. "Strayed queen!" they teased and taunted:

Into Var's lost Lamp of Darkness,
Stray you as insect to web!
Back to the center of nothing,
Where Var will Dana behead!

Four shells surround to confound you,
Stoked with black fire and dread!
Back to the center of breaking,
Dana the No One is dead!

Burning like coals of hunger and hate, the eyes circled in.
Were they demons or creatures or beasts of the night? Dana
couldn't tell. Var's Lamp of Darkness, she thought to herself . . .
the opposite of light! Dana's hair bristled, her heart pounded as
she tried to keep her thinking sharp, unclouded by fear. She
reached for her sparks, a tiny shining moon, and prepared to
take up Mashire for battle. But as her hand tried to grasp the tiny
moon, a voice spoke suddenly from within its glow. . . . "Queen
of Beginning, seize Var by the tail!"

Dana was certain she'd heard it, yet at the same time she was
sure she'd heard nothing but the yowling curses closing around
her. The voice seemed to speak out of silence. . . . "Reach in,
princess who has grown to be queen!"

Dana was spellbound, thinking . . . not Anavak, not Ibbur.
Then who?

The beastly cries rumbled closer. "Lost Queen!"

Quickly, Dana thrust her hand to the center of the sparks'
glow. "As a snake sheds skin, so a queen sheds doubt," spoke
the silent voice.

"The rattle!" Dana cried out as she withdrew her hand. And
as fruit is picked from a tree, Dana plucked the rattle from the
tiny moon of sparks.

The surrounding eyes flashed like points of lightning. There
was a frenzy of bloodthirsty shrieks. The circle tightened. Dana
could feel the heat of hot stares, the breath of hidden mouths.
With one hand on Mashire, the other holding Var's rattle, Dana
was trembling. Was it in fear or defiance? She didn't know
which, nor did it matter, for the trembling spilled over into
action. The rattle began to shake in her hand. It shook rapidly,
then violently, twisting in her grip, giving off a spray of
clattering cinders. Like tongues of black fire, cinders darted
from the rattle sputtering sounds of the night, rasping songs of
the Lamp of Darkness.

As if in response, the howling shrieks stopped. Blood-red
eyes halted all around. The night became silent and still.
Then in a whisper, heard and unheard, the voice spoke
again from the glowing, moon-like sparks. . . . "Well done,
Queen Dana. Var's beasts yield to the sound of your

mastery. Now gather your sparks and find the angel Var has taken."

"Then Ibbur is alive—taken by Var!"

"Be on your way, Queen Dana of Worlds. Five more gates to the Spring of Beginning and time is running down."

Dana gathered the sparks and shrinking rattle to the opening of her pouch. "Where will I find Ibbur—and Var?"

"Find them where you will . . ." and the sparks spilled from Dana's hands into the pouch in a murmur of words and rattling sound fading to silence.

The circle of blood-red eyes blinked and stared; cowered and obedient beasts, tamed by the rattle. Dana tied her pouch. She spread her cape, intending to fly, though uncertain how she'd find her way. "Away and aloft!" she called into the night.

Dana's feet never left ground. Instead the ground stirred as before, rolling forward to meet her. A space opened in the circle of blinking eyes and Dana sped through it, skating again across dark open wasteland, trailed by her rays dimly shining.

Chapter Twenty-One

BLOWER OF LIGHT

Night cycled to twilight, just before daybreak, as Dana and her rays reached the sixth wall of light. The ground slowed and gently came to a halt beneath her feet. Before the sixth gate she stood—but she wasn't alone.

In the predawn mist Dana saw the outline of a figure sitting before the gate. "Another angel," she whispered under her breath, half-expecting Ibbur to confirm or deny. Her heart sank when he didn't. Cautiously, she approached. She was surprised to see that as she neared, the figure remained only an outline, contained by a transparent border of something like skin that gave it shape, but not color.

In its clear lips, Dana saw a pipe or flute of some sort, held there by delicate see-through hands. The pipe was silent, the hands unmoving, the figure perfectly still. Even as Dana came closer, she could not detect the slightest rise and fall of breath. Another statue? she thought, but of air, not stone? But no, the other wasn't a statue after all. And this one? If Ibbur were here, he'd know. I'll just have to ask, Dana decided and blurted out, "Who are you?" Her words seemed to fall away unheard. She leaned in closer and repeated, "Who are you?"

The eyes blinked open, clear and seeing. The lips parted from the pipe. "Queen Dana! Queen of Worlds, is it really you? Tell me you're not some illusion of Var's."

"I am—I mean, I'm not—I mean, it's me!"

"As I breathe and blow!" The pipe bobbed on smiling lips. "And where is Ibbur? He was bound for the Mountain of Dust to fetch you, dear queen."

"He did! But now he's gone, taken by Var in the Lamp of Darkness."

"Gone, you say?" The figure shook its head. "Taken by Var, perhaps, but gone? Never! Ever watchful is Ibbur."

"But you see he's not here," Dana tried to explain. "I need to find him!"

"Forgive me, Queen Dana." The figure stretched out an arm and fingered Dana's sleeve. "He rode in here did he not?"

"Y-yes," Dana stammered.

"Therefore I see what I see!" The figure walked around Dana fluttering transparent robes. "Perhaps you've forgotten."

"There's so much to remember!"

"Worlds to remember, dear queen! I've kept my place and I know. Ibbur I've known too, down through the worlds. So remember this: Ibbur clings like skin, deeper than skin, deeper than heart or mind. It is not in his nature to be gone from you. He's attached too deeply!"

"But he's not here!"

"Yet he's present, Queen Dana. Many talents has Ibbur and tricks numerous as Tar's. So that even when taken from you, a part of Ibbur unseen still clings within."

Now Dana recalled what Ibbur had told her in the belly of the sea beast, his words echoing in her head. . . . "No one is alone, ever. Not the slightest blade of grass . . . and certainly not a queen!" So clearly did she hear his voice that Dana was sure Ibbur was present. But when she looked, he wasn't there. A sudden fear seized her. "Ibbur's in danger!"

"Grave danger, dear queen! For if Ibbur is kept apart—in parts!—too long, his power weakens. And you'll weaken too as Ibbur weakens in you."

"Then how shall I find him?" Dana was anxious to get where she was going.

"Arm yourself."

"I have eight sparks already, plus all that I've learned and remembered."

"What do you remember?"

"It's too much to tell!"

"Then I'll ask," said the figure. "Who are you?"

Dana was annoyed. "Queen Dana!" she said hurriedly.

"From where did you come?"

"From before all befores."

"Good, good! Now, why are you here?"

"To find the lost sparks and restore the worlds."

"Exactly! And to where are you going?"

"To the Spring of Beginning!"

"Precisely!" The figure clapped once and kept its hands clasped. "You do remember, dear queen. Now one thing more. Ibbur must have shown you which comes first—action or thought?"

Again Dana recalled what Ibbur had said in the belly of the sea beast, his words resounding in her head. . . . "Action occurs first in thought, then in the hand. Mind first, my queen. How did you exit the locked closet? . . . With thought!"

"Thought comes first," said Dana. "Action occurs first in the mind."

"Exactly!" The figure unclasped and reclasped its hands. "Think it, then do it! Yes? Though when a queen possesses her thoughts, she may think it and instantly it's done. Is this so?"

"Yes it is," said Dana, "but I'm still learning how."

"How? Practice. Remember to think. But there is something else too. Something I must show you. So if you would, Queen Dana, one more question: Before thought, what is there?"

"Before thought?"

"Yes, my queen. What comes before thought?"

"I—I have no idea!" said Dana growing frustrated.

"Precisely, almost."

"Precisely almost what?"

"You said it—idea. That's almost right. Idea is the smallest thought, but it's still thought. Something else comes first. And that something is called will, the spark to action."

"Will!" cried Dana with sudden remembrance. "The voice that spoke from the silent glow told me I'd find Ibbur where I will! And Ibbur too, he used the word, will. Before all befores he said I'd come to will."

"Before all befores, precisely! But first you must master the power of your own will—and I'll show you how."

The figure sat still as it had been when Dana first saw it, transparent in its robes. See-through hands brought the pipe to the outline of its lips. "The Blower of Light am I, wise queen, and light—you'll now see!—begins with will."

Transparent lips closed slowly around the pipe's stem. Wondrously, the figure kept speaking with lips unmoving. . . . "Will, Queen Dana. What is it exactly? Deeper than thought. Deepest! Higher than mind. Highest! Now watch."

Above the figure's head air began to stir. It was difficult to see, though Dana did see it. For her eyes saw more keenly now than before. She saw the air form into a tiny tornado spiraling above the see-through head.

"What you see, Queen Dana, here above me," said the Blower of Light, "is the stirring of my desire, the spinning of my decision, the movement of my will."

"I see it," said Dana with eyes fixed.

"Now, what do I desire, what do I decide, what do I will?"

Dana looked on, not knowing what to say. Though she thought deeply, no answer came to her. It was only when she stopped thinking and looked long into the twisting air that an answer came to her like a flash—"Light!" she said. "You want to make light!"

"Precisely, Queen of Knowing! As I'm the Blower of Light, my will is to make light. Light is my desire! My decision is to send forth light. Now you'll see how it's done. . . ."

As Dana watched, the twisting air spun down into the figure's head. Dana saw it enter the see-through skull. "See, Queen Dana. I bring my will down into my body, first into my brain. Here is my mind, the seat of my thoughts. Now my every thought is to send out light. I think to myself, how will I do it? And I realize, my thought is not yet complete. I must bring my will down lower. . . ."

The Blower of Light sat calmly in thought. Dana saw the twisting air spin down through the see-through face and lower still to the Blower's throat. Then it spun down the throat to the chest where Dana saw it enter the Blower's heart. There the twisting air began to glow like a flame unfurling on a candle.

"See, dear queen," said the Blower of Light, "how I've

brought my will down into thought and even deeper into my heart. Here my will glows with warmth and feeling. Here my thoughts shine. For now I'm thinking not only with my brain, but also with my heart. With the wisdom of my brain and the understanding of my heart my will finds balance. Now I am prepared to bring the spark of my will into action. . . ."

Dana watched as the twisting flame spun down from the heart and divided to enter the Blower's lungs. She saw the lungs expand with the glow and suddenly collapse. Then, like a glowing wind, the flame rose upward from the lungs back through chest and throat to the Blower's mouth.

"Now my will is my very breath and I've merely to blow," said the Blower of Light. Dana thought she felt a breath on her neck as the twisting flame left the clear lips and entered the pipe. "See, dear queen: my will presses through the pipe, gathering force and potential. . . ." Dana saw the flame speed to the end of the pipe. "To exit and expand, dear queen, in all directions. . . ." A bubble of light began forming on the end, taking shape, growing like a balloon.

"And so the breath of my will comes to rest," said the Blower, "in a vessel of light." The bubble of light dangled at the end of the pipe growing larger and larger till suddenly it popped in a shower of tiny disappearing sparks. Dana tried grabbing for them, but they vanished in her fists.

"They're gone!" she cried.

"Precisely, Queen Dana! And precisely because I tried too hard. One must take care not to push or hurry one's will. All thoughts must be relaxed. All concentration must be relaxed and effortless. Will it and it's done."

"Then if my will is to find Ibbur," said Dana, "I must will it completely, but I mustn't insist."

"Precisely, Queen of Balance. Instead, calmly watch your will find its course. See it out of the corner of your eye: a fleeting bird. You've only to reach out and grasp it. Even as you begin to grasp it, your will is already done. Calm self-mastery. But there is one more thing: One may only will for the good. Only good thoughts and actions carry the power of will."

"It is for the good," said Dana, "for the good of worlds that I find Ibbur and the last spark in the Mountain of Light. How else to stop Var's Lamp of Darkness from swallowing all light, all water, all wind, and all dust?"

"Queen Dana of Purpose and Cause. Assert your will now and overcome darkness!"

Dana closed her eyes and looked into the darkness beneath her eyelids. At first fear crept under each lid: worry over Ibbur, separation and loneliness, doubt. Her thoughts became confused. Var's face, Zar's and Tar's loomed before her . . . teeth sharp as knives, sea beasts, demons, ants, pumpkin-men, snakes, and two-faced giants, all spitting blood. "Powerless queen!" Their shrieks filled Dana's ears.

Dana struggled with her thoughts, trying to see and listen past fear. Lion's heart! Cunning queen! She fixed her mind and heart on balance, on memory, on . . . will. In her vision now there appeared the glow she'd seen in the Lamp of Darkness, the one that had spoken in silence. In this light, the faces and masks of evil vanished, their curses fading beneath the silent voice. . . . "Queen Dana, reach boldly for your will. Shed fear. Before darkness and fear there is only awe, only wonder. Before all befores. Spark of sparks. Cause of causes. Dana in her towers once knew. You'll find action at the depth of beginning."

Dana saw her thoughts untwisting, floating into the glow. Thinking passed from her, then ceased. Dana's mind became blank. She looked out into whitest light, for though her eyes were closed, light filled her vision.

Out of the corner of her eye then, she saw a rush of wing and feather. A swallow? Dana reached for it, but too late. Fleeting will! Off it sped, quicker than light. She saw no trace until it returned in a flash, wings shimmering rainbows of color. At the edge of her vision Dana saw it and darted her hand into its path as if to catch a ball. She felt the bird's breath across her palm. Swiftly but gently, Dana closed her hand in time to seize the bird by its tail.

Through whitest light, she found herself flying. By the barest, hindmost barb of the swallow's tail, Dana held shakily to her will. Will to see Ibbur! Will to save worlds! Dana's will came twisting toward her as wind off the bird's back. Twice her grip slipped and twice she grappled higher up the bird's tail. Finally with her grasp more secure, balanced upon the tail, Dana began drawing her will to herself as the Blower had done.

Holding fast, yet relaxed, she let wind wash over her. Gusts came spinning, blowing through her mind, and deeper through her heart, opening passages down through Dana, way down into breath. And when her will had filled her lungs full as two balloons, with no place else to go, it turned and rose out the way it had come. Dana's will rose to her mouth as the Blower's had done. As it reached her lips, she blew. . . . Will to see Ibbur! Her breath echoed like a piping tune over water. And the swallow shot forward as a spear slicing through light and space on a path to nowhere.

"Farewell, brave queen!" came the Blower's call. "And remember: Hold fast, but not too tightly! Effortless and relaxed is a queen's hold upon her will. . . ." The Blower's call faded, blending with the piping of Dana's breath, into the distance behind her.

Holding by instinct, mind blank and open, Dana trailed her will blindly, her four rays beaming at her heels. Sheer light opened out in all directions. Endless light. Yet from its midst, a still brighter light shone. Dana flew headlong toward this brightness. As she neared, the ring upon her hand jumped fingers. Looming before her was a barrier. The sixth wall of light! Dana was certain. Her ring sounded the seventh piper's tune. Will to save worlds! Light flashed with explosions of color. The sixth gate opened to permit her passage, then closed behind her. The piper's tune ceased.

Past the sixth gate, darkness reigned. Dana entered a space filled with howling curses and foul-smelling stench. Willfully she sped on, clinging to her will amidst cries of "Lost forever queen!" Demons wove webs in her path, laughing gaily, wagging tongues like two-pronged forks. Tiny imps, the smallest and meanest of Var's hordes, spat mini-globs of poison. Fear shouted in the dark, "Ibbur is gone! Dana is done!" Dana's grip faltered then corrected itself, but not as firmly as before.

Under this barrage of evil, Dana's will was shaken and began to come undone. Her hold upon the tail kept slipping. Balance

fell away. Gradually Dana's mind drifted back into thought. . . .
Don't push, don't hurry, she reminded herself, recalling the
Blower of Light's words. . . . "Effortless and relaxed is a queen's
hold upon her will." Yet this was more difficult than Dana had
imagined. In the face of darkness, evil abided, mocking her will,
upsetting her calm. Dana's hand slid down to the tip of the
swallow's tail. Desperately she gripped tighter, but the more
tightly she gripped the less relaxed she became. The more force
she used, the more slippery became her will.

Thoughts came flooding Dana's mind: Where am I? Who
am I? Awake, asleep, or dreaming? She began sinking under
questions, smothering in confusion and disbelief. Shadows of
self-doubt crowded her will and choked her breathing. Var's
imps swarmed her. "Lost and forgotten queen!" they shrieked.
"Before thought, what is there? Nothing, fool queen. Nothing!"
Dana cried out, "Ibbur!" and the darkness replied with
sniggering scorn.

Dana tottered in flight, balance lost. Will, she thought. . . .
Will to see Ibbur! But her thoughts hung in her head, no longer
reaching to her heart and breath. Her grip came loose. The tail
of her will sped off and away. She was falling. Down through
dark space her thoughts reeled with the Blower of Light's
words. . . . "If Ibbur is kept apart—in parts!—too long, his power
weakens. And you'll weaken too as Ibbur weakens in you."

"No!" Dana shouted into space. "I still have my sparks!"

She tried flapping her wings, but they felt awkward and weak,
flagging uselessly at her sides. Dana's rays too had weakened
and slowed, trailing far behind dimly in the distance.

"Fading light! Fallen queen!" came the taunts of Var's hordes.

"Oh, Ibbur," Dana moaned, falling helplessly down dark
space. "Ibbur, I need you . . . !"

Chapter Twenty-Two

QUEEN OF WILL

How long and far she fell, Dana couldn't guess. All during her descent, she tried to regain strength and balance, to re-grasp and hold to her will. Yet she couldn't. As the Blower of Light had warned, Dana weakened as Ibbur weakened within her when kept apart too long.

The farther Dana fell, the more crowded became her thoughts and the greater her doubts. Perhaps this is only a dream after all, she considered . . . all of it, Ibbur included. I've awakened from other dreams of falling, like I was catching myself, waking up in my own bed! Dana closed her eyes and imagined her bedroom at home: her windows and curtains, dresser, posters on the wall. Her body jerked. Now I've fallen into bed where I've been all along! Dana was certain. But when she opened her eyes, she was still falling through space.

If only I had held on to my will! Dana grieved. But I tried too hard. I felt it slipping and I held too tight! Without effort, said the Blower of Light. Yet even he couldn't do it. His bubble of light burst into pieces! So how was I supposed to hold on to something so delicate? You are Queen of Worlds, Ibbur would say. But Ibbur is weakening in me. I can feel it. I'm falling and it's not a dream. And now what? Where will I land? In Var's lap? Between his jaws? Or will I simply be crushed by the fall?

Enough thinking, enough! Dana told herself. To find my will I must go before thought. As the Blower said, will is deeper than thought, higher than mind. My will stirred to see Ibbur, but I pushed my will and desire too hard. Why? Because of fear. Because of love. Like the guardian of the third gate, I lost my balance. Too much longing! Too much fear! Love and fear must be balanced between wing tips, just as Ibbur said.

In these last moments—so close to bottom!—Dana's thoughts took a turn. . . . Then I'll will something else! Not Ibbur, not yet. First I must regain my wings. My will stirs to fly!

A tiny wind began swirling above Dana's head. She could feel it tickling her scalp. Stirring of desire. Spinning of decision. Movement of will. She knew what it was. For in the swirling wind, a swallow soared. Lightness on wing! Without thought, Dana reached for its tail. Instantly, the tiny wind blew down through her head. She could feel it enter her skull as she had seen the Blower's will enter his. With relaxed purpose she brought her will down into thought, to her mind and farther to her heart. Here Dana's will found balance. Thought began to leave her. Effortlessly she waited as her will entered her lungs to burn as the breath of fire. Every spark of her desire was flight and all she had to do was blow.

Simply blow. But how hard? For if the breath is too soft, the bubble of will won't form. And if the breath is too hard, the bubble bursts. Just calm, steady breath, Dana told herself, for my will to expand like a bubble of light.

She blew . . . and her breath seemed to fill her wings with light. Dana's wings grew and lightened like balloons, spreading at her sides, buoying her up. Will to fly! In her mind's eye, Dana saw herself clinging to the tail feather of a lighted bird. Falling became floating, and finally flying on revived wings. Softly Dana descended through dark space, calmly grasping and holding her will.

"Tighter, crippled queen! Hold tighter and think, think!" Again the voices of Var's demons shrieked. "Who are you, what are you, where are you? Nobody! Nothing! Lost!"

Though Dana heard their words, she had no attention for them. The taunts were as winds rushing past her ears, or as waves pounding a faraway shore. For Dana was completely fixed on her will—flight, only flight. No thought could enter from within or without.

Downward she flew, four rays closing from behind, brightening, reviving with Dana's will. The darkness below brightened to silver. Gray dawn opened like a well. Down this well Dana descended into dappled light, until at last she touched down.

Folding her wings, she felt the familiar crunch of crusty sand beneath her feet. Gently she released her will. It seemed to fly off to hover nearby, flitting like a hummingbird. Dana sensed she had merely to reach out and grasp it when needed. Will, desire, and decision would again be hers.

Will it and it's done, the Blower of Light had instructed. Dana learned and remembered, transforming will into action. Will to fly became flight. Before all befores, Princess Dana in her towers had been a master of will, spinning moons and suns and stars at will. Now Dana was regaining her mastery in spite of her separation from Ibbur. There was more to her power than she understood; more than even the Blower of Light knew to tell. For even as she weakened, Dana regained and transformed her will. She had to. To find Ibbur and free him required her to— and more.

Dana had descended to find herself once again within the walls of light surrounding Light Castle. Before her stood yet another gate, but which one? The seventh, Dana thought. . . . I passed through five with Ibbur and then one more as I grasped my will for the first time, before I fell. "This must be the seventh," she said to herself.

"To be sure!" came a voice from atop the wall.

Dana looked to see—"Ibbur!" Her flesh tingled. "How—what are you doing up there?! You'll be burned!"

"Nonsense, caring queen. Not I."

"But you said so yourself! You saw what happened to the guardian of the gate! Ibbur, come down!"

"The guardian was unbalanced. She didn't know how, but I do. So do you!" He laughed and sprang along the top of the wall, walking on his hands, kicking his heels, while singing:

> *Why doubt what you see, Queen of Balance?*
> *With ease you may leap to my side,*
> *As you will it, it's done by your talents,*
> *So leap with your will as your guide.*

Should I try it? Dana considered. Ibbur hasn't been wrong yet, though at first he warned me gravely about the walls. But that was before I learned balance, before I learned to grasp my will and to make it real.

> *Lose thought and fear, Queen of Knowing,*
> *Spring to the height of your charm,*
> *Skip along walls bright with glowing,*
> *Your will shall protect you from harm.*

As Dana watched, he did handsprings on the lighted wall without a care as to being burned. He seemed perfectly safe. I've only to will it, thought Dana . . . as I willed to fly, and I did. As I willed to see Ibbur, and he's here!

So with calm decision, Dana emptied herself of all thought and again brought her will into balance . . . then into breath and she blew. . . . Yet she remained upon the ground. Again she blew, with no effect.

"Ibbur, I can't. It's not working!"

"Try harder, brave queen!"

Harder? thought Dana . . . harder doesn't help. Holding harder to my will only makes things worse. That's how I lost hold of my will and began falling. With ease, without effort, said the Blower of Light—and with ease I regained my wings!

"Hold tighter to your will, my queen!" came the tiny voice atop the wall. "Will to fly over walls! Will to join me here!"

"Tighter?!" shouted Dana. "Tighter doesn't work! Harder doesn't work! Ibbur, don't you know?"

"Of course I know!" he replied, standing on his head. "I'm upon this wall of light, am I not? I'm not burning, am I?"

"No, you're not." With thoughts confused, Dana decided to give her will another try. Again she relaxed and shed all thought, reached for her will, brought it into balance, into breath and calmly blew. . . . Again nothing happened. A thought then entered her head. Dana remembered what the Blower of Light had said about will working only for the good. Suddenly she knew what she was facing—and it wasn't for the good. A cold chill seized her.

"Ibbur, how did I exit the locked closet?"

"How, Queen Dana?"

"Yes, how. Tell me quickly!"

"How? What does it matter?"

"Answer me!" she demanded.

"Very well . . . with a magic key!"

"Var!"

"Var? Where?"

"You!" Dana pointed.

"Me? Var? No, I swear it! I'm Ibbur, see?" He spun on his toes and bowed. "Come along, my queen. We have worlds to save!"

"No, on second thought you couldn't be Var."

"See?"

"Var is all evil and wears no masks. So who are you?"

"I've told you. Ibbur, who else?"

Dana squinted. "You're a demon!"

Instantly, the little green man changed. The tiny body lengthened like an uncoiling serpent. Arms and legs grew, hands and feet sprouting leopard-like claws. The face stretched into a snout, lips curled back to expose monstrous fangs. Eyes expanded to the size of saucers, bloodshot and bulging. A hoarse voice screeched from widening jaws, "Right you are, clever queen. Dead right!"

Var's demon sprang from the wall, leaping down upon Dana. At once Dana drew Mashire.

"Cruel queen!" The demon fell upon Dana's sword squealing, claws flailing as Mashire pierced its belly through to the back. Black blood spewed from the demon's mouth burbling with curses. "Meet your end between walls!" The demon gasped its last and lay still.

Sickened, Dana withdrew her bloodied sword. She thrust it deep into the sand over and again to cleanse the blade of the demon's stain. As she did so, she felt a peculiar sensation at her back. Dana turned, Mashire at the ready, and came face to face with the sixth wall of light advancing from behind. Her breath caught in her throat. The wall was almost upon her, inching closer like a lengthening shadow. Dana spun to face the seventh wall and saw that it too was inching toward her from the front.

Without pausing for thought, Dana raised her ring before the seventh gate. The ring jumped fingers spinning with a new color of light sounding the eighth piper's tune. Still the walls advanced from fore and back narrowing the space where Dana stood.

Open! Dana thought to herself . . . please! The walls pressed forward. "Please! Why don't you open?"

Even as she said it, Dana knew: Var was nearby. The power of his darkness was stronger, holding the gate shut.

But I have my charms, Dana thought . . . the Song of the Heart in my ring and the power of my will before thought. If only I can grasp it!

With walls creeping toward her, Dana banished all thought and reached out for her will. Calmly then, and seemingly heedless of the crushing danger, she grasped it by the tail, brought her will into balance, into breath and blew. . . . Will to open! Dana's ring spun faster, brighter, louder with the eighth piper's tune. Song of the Heart! The gateposts glowed and ignited. Carved symbols sizzled, letters sparkled. Still the two walls pressed with Dana sandwiched between. . . .

Relaxed in her desire, unruffled in stillness, alert in her calm, Dana held gently to her will. Out of the corner of her eye she could see it, a fleeting bird in halted motion, waiting, expectant of outcome. . . . Thwack-boom! The seventh gate burst open with a peal of thunder. Queen of Will! Dana bolted through, flanked by her rays, as the walls came crushing behind her.

Caught in the crush was Var's demon, a limp, hideous form squashed between walls, mashed to a stinking black ooze. While to the sound of colliding light, Dana entered the seventh desert track, not knowing what she'd find.

Chapter Twenty-Three

RING TOSS

The seventh gate slammed behind Dana with a booming blast to her ears. Steps away was the eighth wall of light shining golden and inviting. With hands upon her ears muting the blast, Dana lifted a foot forward. Before her foot came down, a gash opened in the air. As if from nowhere, demons and tiny winged imps charged from the gash, folding out of air to attack like maddened wasps.

Dana spread her cape. She beat her wings, but found them heavy, as if her feathers had become weighted. They had. "Var!" she screamed, feeling the weight of his evil upon her.

Dana's rays quickly joined in pairs at the underside of each of her wings. Green and blue, yellow and red mixed and shone like sunlit air to light her feathers, to lighten Var's evil. Slowly Dana rose, wings beating faster as scaly hands clutched at her feet and tore at her sneakers.

The demons rose too on leathery bat-like wings, surrounding Dana, clinging to her. Above the tugging of their claws, Dana raised her ringed hand. Var's imps scaled her arm in a swarm rushing one over another.

Will to open! Dana tried to focus her attention on the gate, reaching out before thought to catch a bird on the wing. Desire and decision! Queen of Will! Dana's ring jumped fingers spinning color and sound. The ninth piper's tune! Word and symbol ignited. Flames danced upon the posts. The eighth gate crashed open and Dana flew past, hounded by demons, covered with imps.

The very air seemed to explode as the gate banged shut.

Before the ninth lighted wall Dana hovered on wing, swathed by imps pinching and clawing up her arm. With her rays to boost her, Dana held to her will. Imps clung to her hand, clambered up her fingers, clutched at her ring. Yet her heart and mind remained balanced, in restful resolve to open.

Dana's ring jumped from her finger spinning into the air. Color and sound! The imps leapt with it and so too the demons charging the ring like hungry bats, grasping with the fingers of evil. Dana swiped some away, but there were too many to hold off. One then another seized the ring, another and another, struggling, tugging this way and that, until one demon gained possession and flew off.

"No!" Dana shouted going after the ring, her will shaken. She drew her sword, facing the demon. "It's mine!"

"You want it?" The demon spat fire.

"Give it!" Dana demanded.

"Here then!" And the ring was tossed to another.

Dana pursued her ring, brandishing Mashire as demons and imps formed a circle around her. Each time she strove against one, the ring was tossed to another. "It's mine! No, it's mine!" raspy voices taunted while the ring was passed about. Dana lashed out with her sword, striking demons swiftly in succession, but the ring was tossed from hand to evil hand.

Frustration and anger welled within her as Dana charged the circle cutting down her foes, one by one. Yet their number seemed to increase. When exhaustion finally overcame her, Dana paused at the center of the circle, catching her breath, ignoring the demons' taunts. She closed her eyes, and drew a long, deep breath.

"Nap time, princess?" a demon called out. The others joined in laughter. Dana, however, heard nothing. Inside she'd again become silent. In silence she began drawing her will into balance. Calm attention. Purpose. The ring!

The taunts grew louder. "Dream on, ringless queen! May your dreams be nightmares of Var!"

Dana stirred not an eyelash. Demons and imps snickered about her. All but one. This one, more clever than the rest, was unsettled by Dana's silence. He suspected her of tricks. "Awake,

Queen of Deceit!" he shrieked. Still Dana heard nothing. "Awaken her!" he rasped to the others. "For while she sleeps she plots treachery! In Var's name, stop her!"

As a hangman pulls tight his noose, the circle closed to squeeze Dana in a stranglehold of evil. Crushing bodies, smothering wings, choking limbs rushed in. . . .

In the thick of their rush, Dana brought her will into balance. With calm breath she blew . . . ring of song! On wings of light her will flew out amid the rushing horde. In the same moment her will returned, Dana's ring speared upon its beak. Calmly, she returned the ring to her finger. Up it jumped now, spinning color, piping sound—the tenth piper's tune! The names on the gateposts began to glow. With an explosion of will, letters burst into flame and the ninth gate swung open. . . .

While at the center of their fast-closing circle, demons and imps met with a crunch, head against head. Dana heard their hateful squeals ringing past the gate as she passed through, having left them behind at the moment they'd come together.

Into the ninth desert track Dana now flew, ring upon her finger, rays tucked beneath her wings. Blistering wind struck her as the ninth gate closed. To Dana it seemed that she passed through a wall of fire or the doors of a furnace. Heat scorched her clothes and seared her eyebrows, nearly igniting her wings. If not for her rays, enwrapping her like towels of light to dampen the fire, she'd have perished in flame. Instead she flew protected, shielded by light, into a barrage of wicked cries. "Burn! Melt! Blaze! Queen of Witches!"

Through shimmering air, thick and waving with heat, Dana saw flames streaming over ground, leaping like a river of fire. Her eyes opened wide and hot. For above the flames, tied and bound, a figure dangled, surrounded by demons poking and prodding with sticks.

"Ibbur!"

The hanging figure made no reply, but jerked helplessly at the end of its rope.

Chapter Twenty-Four

BATTLE OF WILLS

With her rays as a shield against the heat, Dana swooped on lighted wings to the near bank of the flaming river. There she hesitated, uncertain whether the dangling figure was truly Ibbur or a decoy fashioned by demons.

The demonic hordes hissed, "Taste torture, fool queen! First Ibbur, then you!" And they laughed, poking their victim.

Decisively, Dana brandished Mashire and called out, "Let him go or you'll taste my blade!"

"Go back, brave queen, it's a trap!"

"Ibbur!"

"Back away, Queen Dana! Do not test the River of Fire without your ninth spark!"

"But I have the power of my will!" Dana shouted above the vaulting flames. "The Blower of Light showed me!"

"Past the ninth gate, you're in Var's domain! Here his will holds sway and yours is powerless—so long as Var holds the ninth spark—!"

"Stifle him!" shrieked the demons and pounded the tiny figure, gagging his mouth.

Fury rushed through Dana. She nearly sprang from her spot, but held herself back, heeding Ibbur's words—if Ibbur's they were. For she couldn't be certain—or could she? I might try my will and see, she thought to herself. If I will Ibbur to be free and he appears at my side, I'll know. If he isn't freed I'll also know.

So Dana brought her will into balance. She grasped her will by the tail and held it. Calm breath filled her lungs and she blew. . . . Will to free Ibbur. . . .

When she opened her eyes, Dana remained as she'd been, alone on the bank of the River of Fire. A feeling almost forgotten then seized in her chest—fear!—as Dana suddenly understood she was without her power of will.

Gray skies darkened. A parched wind blew. Flames jumped like whips of fire lashing in the wind. The bank where Dana stood swayed underfoot, and began softening, melting, oozing red and black, molten as lava. Dana took flight above burning ground, shielded by her rays, not knowing which way to fly.

Thunder crashed with a force to peel back the sky. From behind torn layers of cloud came a spreading black mass . . . opening, unfolding as a wing cracking an eggshell. It emerged and divided becoming two dark leathery wings blotting all light from the sky. Only the flickering shine of burning ground remained by which to see. And by this light, reflecting orange against the winged sky, Dana saw a single giant eye in a head of black fire: Var.

Her throat tightened. Instinctively Dana's hand reached for her pouch. Sparks! But which would serve? All. They must! Without her power of will they'd have to.

She gripped her pouch and felt the throbbing of her sparks within. Each still held its charm, beating like a heart, pulsating beneath Dana's fingers with the force of its own magic. "You are mine, and no longer Var's," she spoke softly, and each spark seemed to reply, silently, with a tingling in Dana's fingertips. She felt the tinglings run up her arms and spread through her, coming to rest in her head, her heart and belly with a jolt. And Dana remembered: Before all befores she'd known no fear. In the place that was no place before beginning, there had been no evil, masked or unmasked. There had been no Var.

Dana took courage in memory. To the darkened sky she called, "Release him, Var!"

The sky crackled with lightning and laughter. A hole opened like a maw dripping red in the head of black fire. "Gladly, Queen of Empty Demands! After you've returned my sparks!" Flames leapt from Var's jaws wagging tongues of fire.

Dana didn't reply. She felt a stirring inside, a whisper like the rustling of leaves, and she knew it was her second spark, cleverness asking, why should Var be making deals? Why doesn't he just take what he wants? Why? Dana asked herself . . . because he's afraid he'll lose! He's been testing my powers all along, as Ibbur said. Now even with the ninth spark and his power of will, Var is doubtful.

Dana felt her confidence soar. She rose higher on wing and whispered to her rays, who seemed to whisper back, still enfolding her as a shield.

"Keeping secrets from Var, selfish queen?" Var rumbled and spat out a thunderous laugh. "I think not!" The great wings flapped and descended like a falling sky. The eye in the head of fire loomed closer, staring, burning like a star.

Dana remained cloaked by her rays, her back to Var. In hushed huddle she conferred as if speaking with herself or to a voice within.

"Queen of Tricks! There is no hiding in my domain!"

Dana was silent. Her rays concealed her in stillness as clouds veil a moon. Finally one ray, the red, flew off. It broke from the others, streaming for the horizon to vanish on the edge of darkness.

Now Dana spoke out. "I said release him, Var!"

"I'll release him, foolish queen, I will, and serve him up to you as a puny steak charred on a grill!"

Dana pointed vengefully with Mashire. "Then I'll destroy you Var. I swear I will!"

"Lost queen!" shrieked Var. "You have no will!" And he laughed explosions of hate. Then to his demons, Var rasped, "Cook him!"

The demons tittered gleefully, lowering Ibbur's rope.

"No!" shouted Dana. "Wait!"

"Hold him!" Var dove to within striking distance of Dana. There he hovered, one gigantic eye staring hate from his face of fire. Between them shone Dana's three remaining rays, an armored suit of light, shielding, protecting.

"Have we had a sudden change of heart, fickle queen? Dear, tender-hearted Dana, who would sacrifice her sparks for the sake of one pathetic angel? Give them here then!"

A second ray, the blue, now broke away from the others and beamed to soar like an eagle above the River of Fire.

"Desertion in the ranks, abandoned queen?" Var opened wide his fiery mouth in a shout of cruel pleasure. His single eye glowed brighter, staring, dilating with hate. "See here, forgotten princess," he hissed. "My eye sees through you as you weaken beneath my gaze. And what do I see? Fear! Loneliness and loss! Longing for a home you'll nevermore see. Boohoo, forsaken queen. Or should I say princess? Or is it Dana, just sweet little Dana wishing to be home in bed? Wake up, Dana. You're dreaming! Worlds to save? Ha-haw! You've been had, little girl, by illusion and fancy. Ibbur the angelic twerp? Anavak, the one-handed enchantress? Wisps of dreams. You knew them when? Such lively imagination. You've known them never! Awake and watch them vanish!"

As he spoke, Dana locked on to Var's gaze. So long as she held his baleful stare, she seemed to sense or know, his words wouldn't penetrate. Var denied Anavak, but it was Anavak who'd warned Dana to hold every stare, as she'd done with the two-faced giant and now again with Var. When the time comes, do not falter, Anavak had said, or all would be lost. So Dana held her attention hard on Var's eye and found she could see through his lies.

"If none of this is real," Dana replied, not shifting her gaze, "then neither are you, Var, nor your threats. I'm home in bed as you say and you're nothing but a nightmare!"

"True, true, clever girl! So you've nothing to lose by handing over the sparks."

"Never, Var—not even in a dream!"

"Fool! Give them here, homesick girl, if you're ever to see home again! Or shall I offer up your angel as toast? My legions are impatient for a little fun!"

Dana's rays, green and yellow, parted ever so slightly before her. "The ninth spark, Var. I'll have it now," said Dana.

Var flourished his great wings and spat fire. "Guffaw! Insolent queen! To think I'd hand over my most precious of sparks! My waiting is over!" Var called to his hordes, "Sink the midget!"

With screeches of delight, the demons let go the rope from

which Ibbur dangled. At the same time, Var darted a leathery wing tip between Dana's rays. Then snapping back his wing, Var yanked the pouch from Dana's belt.

Demonic cheers rose in gloating chorus. Var's hordes fanned out in all directions. As bats scattering from a cave, they overspilled the sky with dark wing and shadow. Dana and her two shielding rays were quickly surrounded. Demons swarmed in bunches scratching and clawing, overwhelming the rays, penetrating Dana's shield. Still, Dana held Mashire, swiping her blade at head and wing, severing anything that neared. By now, her swordsmanship had grown beyond all bounds. Mashire revolved in her hand with a spellbinding force, spinning and cutting like a deadly baton. But for every demon that fell away, ten more came on the attack.

Ibbur plunged helplessly above the River of Fire to the splashing flames below. Tied and gagged he dropped through crowds of demons jeering, "Poof! To angel dust!" Absorbed in their taunts, however, the demons didn't see, nor did they hear the whiz of color and whirring sound passing among them. "Splash and burn!" they squawked as the highest spray of flames spattered Ibbur. His binds and his clothes caught fire. Deeper into flame he tumbled soon to be consumed, when of a sudden, a blue streak crossed the path of his fall—Dana's ray! And plucked from fire, Ibbur was carried off. Cool blue light draped him and doused his burning ropes and clothes.

Demons converged instantly on the streaking ray. From all quarters of sky they thronged. Yet none left off attacking Dana. In two squadrons they flew in a blitz of demonic might.

Above the field of battle hovered Var crowing triumphantly, pressing Dana's pouch in the pit of a wing. "Destroy them, my legions, and take the sparks that remain—the sword, the ring and winged cape! Hear me! And take her hands with them!"

The demons were without number. Like devouring locusts they flew in clouds, selfless, with a single mind to do Var's will. Dana sliced them away until her arm wearied, then without pause passed Mashire to her other hand and continued her fight. But her strength was not without limit. Ten times she passed her sword between hands and her muscles grew hot, straining, aching, and spent. Still there was no slowing of demons. They pursued Ibbur and the blue ray tirelessly. The most swift and agile caught hold and climbed aboard, treading the ray, grappling to take hold of Ibbur. It seemed only a matter of time before demons overwhelmed Dana and Ibbur both.

Then on the horizon where darkness met shadow, a streak of red began to glow, separating the two. Like a rising sun, the glow radiated, expanding out. As the red light grew, it also neared. Head-on it came like a crimson comet—Dana's ray!—and not alone. On its tail rode an army, warriors of light; figures in gold and silver, alabaster and bronze. More flew behind, shimmering on rainbow-colored wings.

With a sound of great rushing, they approached the field of battle. At their lead flew a figure in sparkling robes, golden, with eyes of jewels. A horn of bone was held to its lips. The trumpeter. At its sides flew winged beasts with great, smiling, bull-like heads and copper hooves that swiped the air striking fire. They entered the fray, horn blaring ten sounds to rattle air and wing. The song reached Dana in mid-swipe of her sword and the tones charged her swing with new force. Pipers' tones. Angels! Song of the Heart! Dana, emboldened, swiped harder and faster.

Into black sky thick with demons, the lighted forms streaked with a clash of wing and claw. Amber faces met swarthy snouts. Demon mouths bared fangs across swan-like backs. Razor-edged shadows slashed. Fur flew and feather. "Wipe them out!" shrieked Var above the warring broil. "For evil's sake, finish them and inherit their worlds!"

Treading the blue ray, Var's demons wrestled silver-winged figures. Jagged claws pierced sparkling plumes. Barbed arms and legs sliced brutally. Demons and lighted figures fell, but others quickly took their place. To one end of the ray the demons pushed, nearing Ibbur. "Crush him!" called one. "Weaken his witch!" Ibbur, his bounds burned free, painfully dragged himself away. The demonic crowd followed and pounced. But now diamond-edged swords in sparkling hands came down with the sharpness of flame. Demons fell in heaps. Yet the hordes were undaunted. In greater number they alighted upon the ray and increased their attack.

Around Dana there had formed a ring of lighted figures. Each swiped a fiery sword and held a glowing shield. Guardians. Their swords spun like wands of light. Their shields shone like moons and suns. Demons amassed in swarms to penetrate the protective circle. Defiantly they flew against the guardians, but no longer could they reach Dana.

To the blaring of the trumpeter's ten harmonious sounds the battle raged. The weakest of combatants perished by sword, by claw, by flame or fang, plunging down into fire to be consumed. Finally only the strongest engaged the strongest, claw to hand, wing to wing, shadow to light. Wound opened upon wound, yet neither attacker nor defender fell.

Above this deadlocked battle, Var peered down and at long last saw his chance. With one great flap of wing he flew over Dana's guardians of light and swooped low to face her within the lighted circle. Dana's rays shone between them, yellow, green, and red returned, shielding their queen.

"Surrender, Queen of Angels Fallen and Falling!" Var rasped and laughed a spray of scorn. "Yield your ring, your sword and cape and save what's left of your wretched hosts!"

"It is you, Var, who'll yield!" shouted Dana. "Surrender the ninth spark or your head to my sword. The choice is yours!"

"Brazen mite! Dare you defy my power and dominion?!" Var opened his red blazing mouth. "With one fiery breath you'll blister and burn!"

Through the shielding light of her rays, Dana could see into Var's burning maw. Flames danced like a thousand hungry knives. Will his fire burn through my rays? Dana wondered . . . and presently, she found out. . . .

Var's heated breath left his mouth. As a blanket of fire it flashed against Dana's rays and seemed to set them ablaze. "Now burn beneath your shield, stubborn girl. I'll collect the rest of my sparks when you're an ember!"

Without pausing for thought, Dana thrust Mashire through her burning shield. Flame parted as a curtain for Dana to pass through. And as a stone flies from a sling, so Dana now flew unswerving at her target, Var.

Mashire struck hard into one of Var's great wings, opening a gash of black fire. Var only laughed. Dana reeled back and again flew forward, this time striking Var's other wing. Again Var laughed, black flame pouring from his wounds. "Do you think you'll harm me with pinpricks, princess? Endless fire pours through my veins! With burning blood I'll consume you!"

Dana ignored Var's words and struck again. Mashire's blade came down squarely on Var's head. Dana watched, expecting to see the head cleave in two, but it didn't. Black fire gushed from the wound and sprayed her. Yet Var remained whole and unharmed.

"Defeat is yours, young witch! What powers have you in my domain? None! Your sparks fail and abandon you!"

Dana struck again, a fourth time. Her blade swept across Var's flaming mouth slicing red fire from black. Var's fiery lips curled viciously, spewing curses. And again he laughed to show his contempt. "Give up, losing queen. Your task is hopeless! Can't you see you're no match for Var?"

Dana struck once more, harder than before. She lunged with Mashire, piercing Var's skull of fire. Her jagged blade drilled a hole that poured forth flame as torn flesh yields blood. Still Var remained uninjured, his fire endless and undiminished.

"Five swipes, reckless queen. Need you more proof of your powerlessness?" Var jeered.

Dana had backed off. She hovered on wing opposite Var turning Mashire in her hand. Her eyes were closed. A small smile crept across her face.

Var's mouth twisted in flames of rage. His horrible eye bulged hot. "Why do you not fear me?!" he shrieked.

Dana's eyes opened slowly. "For the same reason, Var, that you do fear me." Her words were calm and assured.

"Fear you?! Queen of Nothing, Queen of Dreams!" thundered Var. "I fear you not, nor your angels, nor your sorceress, nor—" Var halted his words.

"Nor what?" demanded Dana. "Why don't you finish?"

"Nor nothing!" insisted Var.

"Nothing is right!" countered Dana. "Before all befores there is nothing to fear! Nothing! No thing. No place. Nothing to see, or hear. That is the nothing you fear. And so you know why I no longer fear you! Because I know who I am and from where I come. Because I know why I'm here and to where I'm going! Queen Dana of Worlds! Princess of Light! You do remember me, Var. From before all beginnings I have come. From before will itself! And to that place which is no place I am returning."

"To ashes you'll return, Queen of Scorched Fleas!"

Var erupted in a hail of black fire. Raging flame bombarded already burning skies as a hurricane batters an ocean. And at the center of the fire-storm, at its heated core, Var's eye swelled like an expanding star. Hot gases, blue and white, hotter than fire, radiated out. The very air quivered with heat.

Dana found herself choking for breath, her throat scorched, lungs seared. Her head lolled, growing faint for lack of air. Mashire bobbed in her hand. Consciousness wavered. Vision fluttered.

"Conquered queen!" exulted Var. "Artless princess! To think you'd restore the worlds I've taken! What have you learned since I destroyed your towers of light? You've learned only to forget—and you too are forgotten. Now perish in the fires you once held in balance. Queen Dana of Beginning? Ha! Begin your sleep of death!"

But now on the edge of mind, Dana saw or thought she saw . . . tattered robes, green-black with age . . . a bent back—and listen . . . the faint sound of a voice riding on wind, a creaking call . . . "Queen Dana, don't falter! Attack Var at his source and there find your spark!"

Dana's head whirled with dizzy heat; a blur of seeing, hearing, understanding.

"Able queen!" came the voice, nearer. "Remember! Act! How does a queen hold a stare? Steadfast! Without blinking, or all is lost!"

Dana's head jerked back in wakeful knowing. Anavak! Here? Yes, in mind and heart . . . sensing, feeling. . . . "To action, Queen Dana!"

Stirred from defeat, Dana came to herself. "Var!" she cried. "Your evil is done!" On a path of fire she sped forward, Mashire pointing the way. Through flame Dana flew as a diver swims watery depths unscathed.

"Meet your end, Queen of Moths!" roared Var. "Blind flight to devouring flame!" Fireballs of spittle shot from his mouth.

Dana sped on, heedless of warning, two hands upon Mashire in single purpose—Var's source. Depth of evil. Correction! The guardian of the gate's mad chant! Balance . . . thought Dana, pointing Mashire's diamond tip. I've merely to think it and it's done. Even without my power of will, I still have thought . . . a queen's thought to action . . . and—Dana struck!

"Wicked queen!"

Fire convulsed and burst forth in waves as Mashire pierced a heated membrane. "Destruction!" Ruptured light gushed black. "Queen of Hate!" cried Var. "Precious eye!" Like an exploding star, Var's eye blew apart in a rampage of light. "Legions! Shades!" On rising flames Var's wails sounded with the uproar of ten thousand thunders. Blind rage spewed. "Blacken her light, devour her flesh! Smite her hosts! The blinding witch shall not retake what is mine!"

Through whirlwinds of flame flew Var's demons, slashing, tearing, stabbing with teeth and barbed limbs sharp as swords. Dana's hosts returned blow for blow, cut for cut. Upon the blue ray they rode with Ibbur, fending off the hordes with flashing blades of light.

Var swept the sky blindly feeling about for Dana with wings of black fire. "Taker of sight!" he bellowed. "Would you hide in my darkness? Still I'll find you!" In one burning wing tip Var held out Dana's pouch. "Your sparks, thieving queen! Retrieve them if you can. Closer, here!"

At the center of her circle of guardians, Dana heard Var, but only as a faraway whisper. Her attention was elsewhere. For as she'd withdrawn Mashire from Var's eye, skewered to her blade was a radiant stone. It shone translucent and hot, brilliant and pearly-blue. She knew what it was—moonstone!

Sliding the stone from the blade, Dana gazed at it and through it into skies and oceans, seeing past breathless heights and down endless depths. In that limitless blue there appeared to Dana words and symbols, letters like those on the gateposts, now etched in blue space. Secrets . . . she thought. . . . Hidden names! Dana spoke them in her head as she would her own name or her own secret thoughts. Quickly as she spoke them, however, the words left her, receding like an echo. So too did her thoughts fleet away, fading into blue . . . until thought fell completely away and all that was left in the vastness of space was the moonstone itself. Dana grasped it like a floating feather and knew at once that what she'd grasped was will.

"Here!" cried Var as Dana reeled back through space, back through depths to the center of the circle of guardians. "Your sparks for the taking. Come closer, Queen Dana."

Dana clasped the moonstone in her hand. Her arm shook as though she held a great weight, yet the stone felt weightless. "Precious will," she whispered and as the words passed her lips it came to her fully . . . Var's most precious of sparks. Dana unclasped her hand and regarded the shimmering stone, her throat grown tight, her eyes damp. The ninth spark to be sure! Without doubt she knew its charm—will!—for she could feel its power surging through her. Will to restore worlds!

"Your pouch, little girl," called Var through his darkness, "and the sparks herein. Come, come. Any or all I offer in trade for the eye you've taken, most precious eye! Or better still. Join with me in darkness and we'll share the sparks and worlds together. Rule with me, Queen Dana, as Queen of Darkness! Such power as you've never known!"

Moments passed. Dana made no reply. "In silence you spurn me!" shouted Var. "Very well. The sparks then. How many do you want?"

Dana remained silent, gathering her will to herself even as Var felt the loss of his own. For without the ninth spark, Var's power and force drained from him as water down an unplugged pipe. "Two for one. Three for one. Four!" cried Var, his voice cracking, emptying of will. Frantically he fumbled with the pouch. "How many are here?"

"None."

"Queen of Lies!" Flaming wing tips tore at the pouch and plunged in. "Impossible!" cried Var as his wings came up empty. "None!" A piercing wail erupted from Var's throat of fire. It sounded and convulsed with the agony of ages. So deep and pitiful a wail that Dana herself felt moved to compassion.

"Cruel, false-hearted queen!" shrieked Var, his fires shrinking. "My destruction shall be yours!" Laughter poured hysterically from his burning maw. "Nine is not ten, do you hear? In the end your gain shall be nothing! My faces will devour you and your worlds. Wait and see!" And he flung Dana's pouch to the fiery waters below.

Dana watched Var's flames wither, contracting like spent blooms. Mouth and eye socket shriveled, caving in upon themselves. Black wings shrank, curling in from the ends like drying leaves.

When his flames had withdrawn to a single ball of spinning fire, again Dana heard Var's crazed laugh. It began as a cackle, grew to a shriek, and rose in pitch to a squall, then over the edge of laughter it slid into howling sobs.

Again Dana was filled with pity at Var's twisted throes, but it was a pity short-lived. For no sooner had her sympathy been aroused than Var's ball of flame exploded from its center. Evil came asunder. Whirl-blasts of fire filled Dana's vision in a hailstorm of burning debris. Each nugget of flame sounded with a laugh or a wail falling around Dana's head, filling her ears. Words fell too, each as a tiny broken wing of fire. "Shades!" "Demons!" "Destroy her!"

In the chaos of raining fire, Var's demons flew helter-skelter seemingly lost or drunken. They lashed claws and razor-edged wings flailing this way and that, striking Dana's hosts and invisible foes or each other. Demon pounded and slashed demon wildly and mercilessly until all had either fallen or blindly fled.

The remains of Var's black fire fell noisily, flame by flame, curse by curse down to join in the rush of the River of Fire below. Gradually then, drip by blazing drip, the sky opened from behind its cover of fiery dark.

Dana hovered on wing among her guardians, bathed in silvery light. From above there now fell, not flame, but a fine, milky-white rain. Dana held her face to the sky and opening her mouth joyfully received the sweet shower upon her tongue.

Nearby flew her rays, red, yellow and green, fires quenched, fluttering as pennants. Her hosts soared in brightening sky, warriors of light shining as moonflowers in a field of grass. In twos and threes they flew, busily gathering up their wounded, the afflicted leaning upon the swift. While in the hollows of their wings and upon their shields, guardians caught the milky rainfall and fed it to the broken and torn. By these rains, Dana and her hosts were revived and healed of the wounds of battle.

When she'd had her fill, Dana lowered her face, dripping wet and flushed with joy. Before her flew the blue ray tracing lazy eights and spirals. Upon its spine sat Ibbur, restored to himself, singing cheerily, enjoying the ride:

> *Ninth spark's charm on flaming sea,*
> *Moonstone gained, will to free,*
> *Park I-iddle-du, lily Lu-lee,*
> *Var's eye taken, preciously!*

"Ibbur!" cried Dana and with a rush of wing joined him upon the ray.

Ibbur bowed deeply with a sweep of his cap. "Queen of Worlds! How far you've come to beginning!"

The blue ray carried them down to where the ground below no longer boiled and burned, but formed a firm lighted bank bordering the River of Fire.

"We have a river to cross, brave queen," said Ibbur, adjusting his jelly-cap, "and one more gate to the Spring of Beginning!"

Chapter Twenty-Five

FOUNTAIN OF LIGHT

Dana's four rays beamed about her as she stood with Ibbur and a throng of hosts on the riverbank. Before them surged the River of Fire, full to overflowing, sloshing flame above its bank.

"Ibbur, can it be crossed?" Dana turned the ring on her last finger. She held up her hand. The ring was silent and still. "I've already used the ten tones in the ring. And what about the last wall of light? It's not possible to fly safely over without all ten sparks—you said so yourself."

"Where are the sparks, Queen Dana?" asked Ibbur. "Where is your pouch?"

"Here, here!" cried a guardian, gold-tipped wings fluttering excitedly over the heads of the throng. With fingers of light she passed the pouch to Dana. "I saw it falling and thought it a wounded bird or an angeline."

Dana turned the pouch over in her hands, lightly touching each charred weave of grass as one would a wound to the flesh.

"Are the sparks contained within?" Ibbur inquired anxiously.

Dana opened the pouch, shaking it over the ground.

"Empty!" Ibbur was aghast.

A slight smile crept over Dana's face.

"Sly queen!" Ibbur jumped to her shoulder. "You knew it was empty! Now where are the sparks?"

Dana unfolded her wings. "One," she said. She thrust Mashire into the ground and announced, "Two." Next she gave a wave of her ringed hand. "Three," she said, enjoying the suspense.

"And the rest?" demanded Ibbur. "Where are they?!"

Dana lowered her eyes to her flannel shirt.

"Your sleeve!" Ibbur leapt down Dana's sleeve, vanishing from sight. Shortly he emerged laughing delightedly, juggling nuggets of light in his hands. "Count them!" he called tossing one after another into Dana's pouch. "Six is all, plus three is nine!" Ibbur jumped back to Dana's shoulder as she tied the pouch to her belt. "When did you hide them?"

"Before my last battle with Var. I thought it best for him to think he had the sparks," explained Dana, "and my rays agreed, didn't you?" She glanced at her four colors of light, each ray flushing brighter at her words and look.

"Well done, clever queen. And did Var know before his end that he'd been fooled?"

"Yes," said Dana recalling with some discomfort the pity she'd felt for the evil that had tried to destroy her.

"Then this explains Var's raving madness, his utter loss of face. To think he had the sparks only to find he'd been tricked by one he thought less powerful. You dashed his pride and conquered his will."

"That's it!" Dana hastily opened her pouch removing the last spark, the shining moonstone. "I have the power of will now for certain! Therefore I may will our way across the river and it's done!"

Ibbur frowned and shook his head. "Know this, Queen Dana: Will too has its limits. Though it's true that a queen's will is action itself, it is but the first step in making things happen. Will is like the arm that draws the bow or the hand that releases the spear; it gets things started in the right direction. But much can happen after the spear leaves the hand. A thousand tiny actions of motion, space, and wind, the forces of the worlds—the cooperation of a thousand angels!—are required to guide a spear to its target."

Dana pointed to the hosts all around her. Those on the ground sat quietly preening. Others hovered overhead spinning spirals or soaring in squadrons watching the play of light on their wings. "I have a thousand angels, Ibbur. Far more than a thousand!"

"Were the will of Queen Dana and the efforts of her angels enough, you could will the tenth spark and regain it now. But there is much you don't yet know or don't yet remember. To cross Var's River of Fire requires a force of will much greater than your own. The power of that will is contained in the ring, in the Song of the Heart, and in the hidden names. Together these brought you through the nine gates. But the ring for now has spent its charm. So your will must reach higher than before. Therefore I ask: Before will, what is there?"

"Before will?" Dana tried to think the question through, but she quickly became confused in her thoughts. Past thought, she reminded herself, and before thought to will . . . a bird on the wing. Grasp it! Once more Dana grasped her will. Again she heard the voice that had spoken to her from the silent glow. . . . "Before all befores you have come to will."

"The voice that spoke out of silence!" blurted Dana to Ibbur.

"Before the voice and before silence. Before will itself!" insisted Ibbur.

Dana's heart raced. Once again she saw herself in her mind's eye, stepping and sliding down a beam of light to alight upon a tower of Light Castle. Her heart leapt to tell Ibbur. "I recall a single beam of light!"

"To be sure! And from where does the light stream forth?"

"I—I don't remember!"

"Don't you?"

"From before all befores!" Dana was flustered, almost feverish. "From nothing—" she stammered. "Everything—Beginning!"

"From before beginning, it streams, Queen Dana. The beam of light came from the Fountain of Light beyond all beginnings. From beyond even the Spring of Beginning! There is the source of all will—the higher will!—hidden from all eyes, cloaked in its own mystery. It was the higher will that set everything in motion and maintains it. Behind worlds it remains hidden: the cause that willed you to be, the one that made you queen."

Dana's forehead furrowed. "I don't understand. If that cause has a will greater than my own, then why doesn't it use that will to regain the sparks and restore the worlds itself?"

"Because you're the hammer."

"The what?"

"The hammer the builder uses to drive nails. The house

doesn't get built without you. Only you, Queen Dana, could ever regain the sparks of worlds lost to Var. Such is the way things were formed at the beginning. For you, dear Dana, are the daughter of the king."

Dana opened her mouth to speak—no words came. Slowly her lips closed, thoughtfully, wistfully. When finally she spoke, her voice was thick with tears. "I don't remember him."

"When the time comes, Queen of Feeling, you will."

Dana grew silent again, pondering. . . .

Ibbur continued softly, "The Blower of Light showed you how to reach for your will and grasp it. But for will to work requires a balance of need and desire, power and skill, and finally, persistence. Without the determination you've already shown—the persistence of a queen!—you'd never have come this far. By the power of your will you must reach farther to grasp the higher will at its source."

Ibbur paused looking into the rushing flame. "We must cross this River of Fire." He turned back to Dana, his tiny mustard seed eyes searching hers. "How do you suggest we do it, Queen Dana?"

Dana still didn't know. "You say my will must reach farther than it already has. I wonder . . ." Her words trailed off sinking deeper into thought. How high can that be? I've learned to grasp my will as a bird in flight. Now the bird must fly higher. Higher I think than even angels fly. Yet how would a bird reach such breathless heights? Not on its own. No, it must have help. Angels? Angels alone aren't enough. The ring, then. But the ring is spent! Then the hidden names. What are they? I saw them on the gateposts. They raced through my head as I withdrew the ninth spark from Var's eye. Now they're gone! And what's left?

Dana felt a rush of blood to her head. Song of the Heart! It brought me through the nine gates. Each opened to another piper's tune. By the Song of the Heart my bird will soar! On wings of song my will shall fly higher!

"Song of the Heart!" cried Dana, her eyes shining. "The trumpeter! It was he who blew the blasts of the Song of the Heart that brought our battle to victory. By the power of secrets hidden in sound and by the force of will, the River of Fire can be crossed!"

"Queen of Knowing!" hailed Ibbur, leaping to the ground. Then, "Trumpeter!"

From the crowd of shimmering wings and heads, the trumpeter flew forward bearing his horn of bone. At river's edge he stood, fiery current licking at his feet of pure gold. Dana's hosts grew hushed. All that could be heard was the ripple of wind over wing and the streaming rush of flame. "Song of the Heart," Dana spoke in a whisper as she brought her will into balance . . . will to cross the River of Fire.

Between platinum lips, blue-white and aglow, the trumpeter held his horn. He blew. . . . Tones poured forth in a cascade of sounds tumbling one over another like a liquid rainbow—a bridge of pouring light. To her joy and wonder Dana not only heard, but saw each tone as another color of sound.

With great care she took her ninth spark, the moonstone, and gently opening her hand, swept her arm toward the trumpeter's bridge. As a swallow springing from its perch, the spark took wing. Reaching after it, Dana felt herself pulled into flight, holding once again to her will. Together they flew to the highest bend of light in the trumpeter's bridge. There her will flew off and Dana herself seemed to vanish into light.

So completely did she vanish that not only could she not be seen, but Dana vanished also to herself. Thought and sensation dropped away. She was lighter than a speck . . . weightless . . . thinking nothing . . . feeling nothing . . . nothing! . . . as if she had never been.

She was light itself, nothing else. From behind the light then a voice called, "Queen Dana of Worlds!" Dana heard nothing. She rode—no, she had become!—a beam of light and as light she beamed past the voice, past the light as past a barrier, and into a void of spaceless space. Then out of the void, above the noiseless, endless expanse, there appeared the tiniest pinpoint of light. From this point, light trickled forth as water from a fountain.

Slowly Dana came to herself as a sleeper awakening from a dream of endless floating. In stages she awakened, before thought, before mind, heart, and breath. Toward the far-distant tiny point, Dana sped as light returning to its source.

As she neared, the pinpoint of light seemed to widen like the pupil of an eye. Through this eye Dana entered as if diving into an ocean of light. Light washed over her in boundless, rhythmic waves. Each wave carried a sound that broke into a thousand sounds and a thousand colors. Delighted, Dana swam through the spray marveling at each color and sound. She rode the waves and laughed into the spray of jeweled light.

All at once, the ocean of light began retreating as waves from a shore. Light withdrew from its center outward leaving in its wake a vacuum, a circle dark and empty, outlined by a single ring of light. As Dana watched from the dark center, a beam of light streaked inward from the lighted ring. The beam was simple and fixed, pure radiance, pure energy in motion. As it went, it traced nine more circles bounded by rings of light—circle within circle. And in the space between each circle was darkness, empty and void.

Watching the beam streak to the center, Dana knew without question that she'd seen it before, and the pinpoint of light and the infinite ocean as well. In memory she saw herself walking the beam, then leaping to a tower of Light Castle. It was the same memory she'd had among the hosts who'd offered her the honey-sweet liquid. She'd recalled it again on the bank of the River of Fire.

This beam comes from before beginning, Dana spoke inside her head. From behind the Fountain of Light, from before all befores it comes! With calm assurance Dana knew she was looking deep into the fountain from which all beginnings flow. And somewhere behind the fountain, cloaked in light as with a robe, was the higher will, the source of all beginning. There behind the Fountain of Light was the no place from which Queen Dana had come. She knew it, though she couldn't remember it.

There came a slight touch upon Dana's hand, stirring her from reverie. Out of the corner of her eye she saw it—a fleeting flash. In the same moment she reached and her fingers closed over a warm beating body. Feathery down pulsed in her hand. Will of wills! Dana brought her hand to her face. A soft glow shone through her fingers. She leaned closer and inhaled deeply, breathing in the light as air through her nose. Through mind it flowed and down through windpipe to heart and lower to Dana's lungs. Her lungs filled with light, pure and balanced. Dana blew. . . . Radiant breath rose through her to shine from her lips. . . . Will to cross Var's river to the Spring of Beginning!

Instantly, Dana found herself carried down, not falling, but riding on pouring light. In her hands she cradled higher will, a golden shining eaglet. Liquid light swaddled and caressed her down the path she'd come. . . . Past ten circles of light and the infinite ocean of light. Through the pinpoint of light Dana exited, marveling at the vastness of beginning behind the tiny glowing point.

Down through the spaceless void she was carried, past the barrier of light, past the voice that called, "Queen Dana of Worlds!" Out of silence it sounded. Again Dana lost all sensation. Again she was light itself, streaming back down. Back to the hearing of sounds. Back to her hosts. Back to Ibbur.

Sensation returned. "Queen of Light!" hailed her hosts as Dana rejoined Ibbur beside the River of Fire. Before them, the trumpeter's song still arched and spanned the river as a bridge of light streaming color and sound. Dana held quietly to the higher will she'd brought down and with a gesture outward from her chest she released it. Along the trumpeter's rainbow it flew to cross the river with desire, purpose, and higher will.

"To the tenth gate!" shouted Ibbur. "To Light Castle make haste! Worlds await us, brave Angels of Light!"

Ibbur sprang for Dana's shoulder as Dana spread her winged cape and took flight over the River of Fire across the trumpeter's bridge. At her side flew the trumpeter himself, his armored breastplate reflecting the flaming river. Behind them trailed Dana's hosts, guardians and warriors of light flying in dignified splendor.

So long was her train that Dana reached the tenth wall of light before the last of her company had started across the arched bridge. Those at the back heard the trumpeter's blasts sound again. In the far distance, they saw the gates of the tenth wall of light spring open and Dana pass through.

Chapter Twenty-Six

LIGHT CASTLE

A great courtyard of meadows, rolling hills and gardens opened to Dana's full sight past the tenth wall. Among the hills were mansions arrayed one after another fanning out in a wide circle. At the center of this circle, rising high above the mansions, Light Castle stood gleaming dimly. Dana could see its ten towers rearing in decay skyward. From the base of each tower a pathway ran out to one of the mansions, each a brick-work of sapphire radiating outward as the spokes of a wheel.

At the highest tower of Light Castle, Dana spied the shining eaglet, the higher will she'd brought down. For a moment it hovered, then sped off in a flash, shedding part of its light as a layer of skin. This remaining light swirled into flight and returned to Dana as her own will on wing. It alighted in her hand as her ninth spark, the moonstone.

Breathing deeply, Dana returned the spark to her pouch. She looked about with eyes wide at the faded grandeur before her. Each of the structures, once steadfast and iridescent, was presently in ruin, roofs caved in, chambers collapsed, light dulled and clouded. Towers slouched and bent even as they strained upward. Fields and plantations were charred, trees broken and leaning, grasses dried to straw.

Without blinking her eyes or shifting her gaze, Dana spoke in troubled tones to Ibbur. "When I first glimpsed these ruins from outside the ten walls, I was determined to regain the last sparks and restore things to the way they'd once been. Now I have nine sparks and Var is defeated, Tar and Zar too, and yet nothing seems changed."

"Not so, Queen Dana," responded Ibbur. "Changes have been occurring since first we flew from your window on the back of the white raven. For each spark regained and each memory recovered there have been shifts in the worlds far below and far above the surface of things, at the lowest depths and at the highest realms. You yourself have changed—returned to majesty!—and for each small change within the Queen of Worlds there is a matching change in the worlds through which she moves, above and below."

"I'd like to see them," said Dana still staring fixedly ahead.

"You will."

"When?"

"After you've entered Light Castle and done there what needs to be done."

The last of Dana's hosts were filing through the tenth gate. Throughout the courtyard, guardians and warriors of light frolicked merrily on wing or gamboled on foot in dancing circles round the mansions and Light Castle. The tiniest caught rides on others' wings high-stepping recklessly across star-bright backs from wing tip to wing tip. Dana herself was swept into a romping dance around Light Castle. Her rays followed overhead, twisting colors of motion. Dancers spun and dipped stepping buck-and-wing, then sprang into air and floated back down. Upon every tongue was the Song of the Heart rising airily, filling the courtyard with sound and light.

Ibbur too was caught up in the rollick, doing a Castle walk across Dana's shoulders, when suddenly he stopped. His eye had been drawn to a gap in the boundary of Light Castle. Quietly he left the dance. On closer look he saw that the gap opened where a great doorway had been removed. "This way!" he cried. His tiny voice was overwhelmed by the rollicking hosts, but one, then another did hear and joined in his call, "Angels of Light! This way!"

Dana's hosts crowded the opening. Above their heads flew Dana with a guardian at each arm. Nobly and gallantly, they set her down before her hosts. Brilliantly they shone, attentive and silent. Ibbur spoke. "Here the threshold of Light Castle once stood!"

"Huzzah! And again it shall!" shouted a guardian from the back of the crowd. "Huzzah!!" cheered the hosts.

"I'd thought that if ever we returned," continued Ibbur, "the threshold door would be difficult to find, hidden from us by Var. But it seems Var left in haste and planned to return before we did."

"At the bottom of evil there's a fool!" came the guardian's voice from the back. Laughter coursed through the hosts.

"Indeed!" agreed Ibbur, jumping to Dana's shoulder. Her four rays shone at her side, quivering light and anticipation. Ibbur whispered into Dana's ear and Dana stepped to the threshold. "Hold your positions," he told the hosts as Ibbur, Dana and her rays entered Light Castle.

The boundary of Light Castle enclosed an inner courtyard of once stately, formal gardens. These were now overgrown, wild and weed-choked. Trees lay toppled across pathways. Others lay fallen over fountains and statues crushed by the trees' great weight. Jungles of vines clung to half-lighted stones and twisted up the Castle towers gripping with tendrils strong as anchors. Dana shuddered recalling the pumpkin-man's smothering reach.

"Don't trouble yourself, Queen Dana, over the evil that has been," comforted Ibbur. "You'll only cloud your will. Instead, set your will to repair and rekindle the light that was."

"You do read my thoughts, Ibbur. And still I wonder how."

"Not thought, my queen, but higher than thought. For I began and begin to know you before thought."

"By my will, then? Is that how you know what I'm thinking? By knowing my will?"

"Not by your will alone, Queen Dana. I know you and am attached to you by the higher will." Ibbur smiled. "You're my blade of grass."

A small laugh escaped Dana. "So you're the angel who tells me to grow."

"Exactly."

"And have I?"

"Grown? Why, yes! By leaps, by worlds! Do you remember?"

Dana's eyes scanned the gardens gone to seed. "I do, Ibbur.

More than I ever dreamed, but there's much I don't remember too. I recall stepping from a beam of light"—Dana pointed—"to that tower right there. I know it was that one. Once it was the brightest. But before that, way before, I recall the point behind which the beam had its beginning."

"The Fountain of Light."

"Yes. And these gardens. I walked here. But where was Anavak then? And you? And the king? I don't recall his face at all."

"Those things and others too you shall remember at the appointed time." Ibbur looked around the inner courtyard drawing a deep breath, heavy with relief. "This is the first time we've entered these gardens since Var destroyed our worlds." He shifted his gaze to a great round hedge at the middle of the courtyard. "My queen, do you remember the hedgerow circles?"

Dana looked intently at the ring of overgrown shrubs. At first they looked like any bushy overgrowth, but as Dana kept looking she found her vision penetrating the thick mass of branches and leaves. She saw through the circular hedge, deeper to another hedge, and deeper to a system of paths through the hedgerows. "Ibbur, it's a puzzle, a maze!"

"A labyrinth, to be sure!"

"What purpose does it serve?"

"That which does not belong, can't find its way through."

"Through to what, Ibbur?"

"Tell me what you see, Queen Dana."

Again Dana peered through the tangle. As her eyes reached farther, leaves seemed to sway. Branches parted from her line of sight. Dana's skin paled then flushed with excitement. She seemed overcome. "Spring of Beginning!" she cried.

"Seeing queen! Do you know the way through?"

"But why not fly over?"

"Because the space above the maze is deathly space. Nothing passes over, neither angel nor demon, but its existence ends as if it never had been. The same for Var. The same for you."

"Did Var ever find his way through?"

"Many fools, evil and wise, have tried."

"But did he?"

"It's been said that none but Queen Dana could ever."

Dana stared ahead as if spellbound. "We're going through, Ibbur. The daughter of the king has returned!"

"Hail, Queen of Worlds!" cried Ibbur, waving his red jelly-cap.

In that instant it seemed to Dana that she too could read minds—Ibbur's. So before he spoke again, she spoke for him, calling, "Here's off!"

Ibbur dove for Dana's sleeve. "Here's after!"

"I'm off!" cried Dana.

"I'm after!"

Leaves rushed. Branches parted. Along pathways Dana darted through the hedgerows followed by her rays. As she went it seemed she remembered every curve and cornered turn. Each leaf and twig was as familiar as if she'd known it by name. Where pathways had become overgrown, shrubs swayed at her approach. Whispers of delight passed from stalk to branch. Those she passed swooned in ecstasy at her closeness and those she neared waited with bated breath.

Memory grew around every curve. There was Anavak on silver-toned wings leading a procession of hosts through the Lamp of Darkness. There was Ibbur—also on wing! There was the ocean of light, and far above it, wheels of light; wheels within wheels humming as they turned, spinning in balance as gyroscopes in space. At the wheels' center was a massive chair, a throne of sapphire, and a form sitting behind a curtain of fire. Dana squinted to see its face, but the form vanished. Again she saw the hedges whizzing by and in the far distance, a spray of light.

She noticed bent forms crumpled into corners of hedge. What are they? she wondered. Frightened, Dana lapsed into thought. . . . Like bodies dead and still. Suddenly she knew. Demons and angels! Foolishly they'd entered and became trapped in the maze.

Dana had passed through nine circles of hedge and was counting the tenth when the hedges suddenly gave out. She emerged into a clearing at the center of the maze landing on her belly. Her first thought was of worry for Ibbur riding in her sleeve. She righted herself and peeked inside. . . . "Ibbur?"

"Forever watchful, my queen." Ibbur smiled and jumped to the ground, jauntily cocking his jelly-cap.

"Ibbur, if you don't mind, whatever happened to your wings?"

"My wings, Queen Dana?" Ibbur flushed crimson-green.

"Yes, coming through the maze I remembered you too once had wings."

"But you don't recall what became of them?"

"No."

"Then, no matter."

"But Ibbur, I don't mean to pry. It's just that—well, when I first met the angels and drank their golden liquid, they hinted at things that made you blush."

"Never mind, tender queen. It's of no concern now." Ibbur turned away as if he'd spoken enough, then hesitated, and added, "Never risk your balance, Queen Dana. Devotion too has its bounds. That's all."

Dana asked nothing more. An uncanny silence washed over her. All questions dropped from her mind. Ibbur too became hushed. Stillness seemed to surround them, drawing in from the innermost hedge to the center of the clearing. There Dana saw what only moments before she hadn't noticed, as if a veil had been lifted from her eyes. . . .

At the center of the clearing grew a tree, different than any other. It had a trunk that met the ground, but its roots grew above, reaching up in reverse like branches. They extended far into gray sky then vanished into clouds. No limbs could be seen. Dana and Ibbur moved closer, coming to rest at the foot of the tree.

Wondrous as the tree was to Dana, adding to her wonder was a shining object that she now saw encircling the tree at its base. Where trunk met ground, a golden crown ringed the tree as a bracelet upon a wrist. Dana saw that the crown had ten points and that each point had a hollow at its end like the setting for mounting a jewel. She'd seen it before, she was certain, but where? Dana flashed on memory to a sandy shore, drilling for fresh water with Mashire . . . before the giant emerged from the sea. She'd seen down the wellspring to her own shining face, and her head had worn a crown studded with sparks. But the sparks had spun free and vanished! Now Dana knew: the crown had been hers! And here it was again, ringing the tree.

A lightheadedness seized her. Dana's throat felt tight, her breathing labored and short. Her heart raced. She was shaking, words stammering from her lips. "This crown, Ibbur, I—I wore it long ago . . . long before the worlds were destroyed—when I stood in the brightest tower of Light Castle. There I held the moon and sun in balance! Ten sparks filled my crown then—before—before Var's evil took hold!"

"Princess of Light! The crown was yours. And each of its sparks was a seed that birthed worlds! Most precious and pure, most lasting of sparks. These were the ones that remained when the worlds were destroyed. These are the sparks you have gathered, less one. Sparks to restore worlds!"

"Truly! So I know what I must do! As Anavak said, when I've reached the Spring of Beginning I'll know what comes next."

"By Anavak's word, it's so!"

"Yes. But where is the Spring? I glimpsed it through the hedgerows—a spray of light that filled this space." Dana was breathless. "Now where is it?" Feverishly, she began examining the crown, its points and design, searching. Below each point she found symbols, letters etched into gold, much like those she'd seen on the gateposts. Dana touched them, rapt by a sensation of static jumping beneath her fingertips.

Next her hands explored the ground where the crown encircled the tree. Fumbling, she found four tiny holes arrayed as the points of a compass. Her rays, hovering nearby, took keen interest in these holes too. Like fingers themselves they poked and prodded, each lingering at the rim of a different hole as a cat at the door of its home.

Peering down the holes, Dana found her mouth growing parched. Her tongue felt thirsty and thick, her gums dry and droughted. Queenly thirst gnawed through her, reaching down her throat and belly until she was hollow and drained. When her thirstiness reached bottom with no place left to go, Dana dizzily stood up, wild-eyed, facing Ibbur. "It's here, Ibbur. Here! These holes together are the Spring, but they'll not flow until I act. Action at the depth of beginning! That's what the silent voice told me when I first grasped my will."

"Queen of Memory and Light! As once you knew and have come again to know: there's no way to convert darkness into light except through action."

Dana was kneeling over the crown hurriedly untying her pouch. Gingerly she emptied its contents to the ground. Six nuggets of light spilled out, lighting Ibbur in their glow. In trembling hands Dana raised a spark. "Var's rattle," she said, feeling of its weight in her hand. She brought the spark to a point of the crown—then stopped to consider. "Does it go into any point, Ibbur, or a particular one?"

"My queen, I'm sure I don't know." Ibbur peeked over the top of the crown. "They all appear the same. Yet everything in all worlds has its exact place; above all, the sparks of beginning." He looked encouragingly at Dana. "You must trust that you know."

Dana's hand was poised above a point. She held her breath. Shakily she let the spark slide to the tips of her fingers . . . then she let go. The spark remained in her hand as if stuck there.

"That mustn't be its place," said Ibbur.

"No . . ." Again Dana held her breath. She brought the spark to another point and let go. The spark floated from her fingers and slid readily into the point. Dana released her breath. "That's one, Ibbur." She took up another, feeling of its nature and charm. "This one is cleverness—my second spark, but let's see. . . ." She lifted the spark to an empty point of the crown, let it go, and watched it float readily into its setting.

"Clever queen!"

A short giggle of delight slipped from Dana's lips. She reached for another spark, gently rolling it in her fingertips. "Moonstone, Ibbur—my will. Dare I let it go?"

"Will was already yours, Queen Dana, before you regained the moonstone."

Dana chose a point, and closing her eyes . . . she released the spark. With a flash of light it flew from her hand to ease snugly into the crown.

Three times more, Dana lifted a spark from her pouch, named its charm and returned it correctly to its place in the crown. She re-tied the empty pouch to her belt, then reached for the ring on her finger. "Song of the Heart," she whispered, holding the ring on a fingertip, lowering it to the point she'd chosen. As it neared the point, the ring seemed to shrink into itself, and as a nugget of light, it floated securely to its setting.

Next Dana reached back over her shoulders to remove her winged cape. It shimmered in her hands as a blanket of stars. Gently she lowered it to the crown as one lifts an infant child to its crib. The cape billowed and twisted upon itself. It wound into a rope and began to shorten, retracting like a turtle's head into its shell. It collapsed into a nugget, floated down, and as a single spark of light it came to rest.

"Well done, artful queen. And the ninth?"

Dana's hand had already closed round Mashire's golden hilt. Now she hesitated, her will hanging in doubt.

"You're reluctant to part with Mashire, I know," said Ibbur. "As Anavak would say, how could it be otherwise?"

Dana ran her hand along the flat of the blade, studying its zigzagging shape, committing every inch of Mashire to memory. The sword shone golden bright, grown in battle to full length and power by way of Dana's skill.

"Of all the sparks, Mashire's the one that has helped me feel most protected and strong, most like a queen! It seems that forever we've been joined at the waist. Paired to battle evil."

"Like moon and sun paired at the beginning, Queen Dana— one shone within the other and the other within one."

"But evil divided them!"

"Correct. Yet it isn't evil now that divides you from Mashire, but higher will, higher good. In fact, there's no separation at all. For the charms bestowed by the sparks may not be taken from you. They've worked their changes from without and within. They've become companions of your will. Please, Queen Dana, don't mourn a loss that isn't."

"But I could never do what I've done—slaughtering demons and beasts!—without such a weapon as this!" Dana held Mashire before her as if to cleave the air.

"Queen Dana, hear me! The Thunderbolt is yours! Mashire isn't a mere something to hold in your hand. The Thunderbolt is held in your belly, in your heart, mind and breath. Deep at the center of your will! It isn't physical force that gives power to Mashire's blows. What is indestructible in Mashire is also indestructible in you. It's the energy that pours from the Fountain of Light to fill the Spring of Beginning. That force existed before Var, before evil, before Zar and Tar and the masks of evil. Before worlds! Before the separation of things into opposites: moon and sun, night and day, good and evil."

Ibbur pointed to the roots of the tree reaching skyward. "All things are rooted in the same place—no place. There they spring from the same source, the same beginning."

"Even Var? Do you mean to say that Var too, in all his evil, comes from the same source as—as angels?"

"Without doubt, Var was part of the whole. He's root and branch of the same tree. And so are his offshoots: Zar and Tar and their many masks. Checkerboards of evil and good. Patchworks of evil masking as good, good masking as evil. You'll find, Queen Dana, that even with careful pruning, evil may grow back."

"But, Ibbur, I've destroyed them all!"

"Queen Dana, you're forgetting the Mountain of Dust and the many twisted faces of evil that thrive there."

"Then I'll destroy them too!"

"You shall! But if you don't completely know your enemy and the source of his power, you may likely destroy your own self in the process! Then all would be lost."

Dana fell silent in confusion. With all she'd remembered and learned, somehow she felt she knew nothing. She and Mashire were one, sprung from the same source: this is what Ibbur insisted. So there was no giving up Mashire, only realizing that the Thunderbolt and her charms were held within. But didn't Ibbur also suggest that Dana and Var were one? For Var too had sprung from the same source. Before all befores, hadn't they been one?

Dana didn't have a chance to voice her puzzlement. Ibbur heard her thoughts and readily replied, "It's true, my queen, you and Var are one. That's why you felt such pity for him, he who clamored to destroy you! And he may yet do just that, if you refuse the whole truth. For your greatest weapon lies hidden. In deepest memory it slumbers. Many more edges and sharper ones has it than Mashire. To claim it and hold it, however, you must be willing to let Mashire go."

Dana found the meaning of Ibbur's words as fleeting as her will before she'd learned to grasp it. It wasn't that she didn't understand what he said. Rather, it was difficult to hold on to that understanding. She turned Mashire in her hand. The sword wasn't difficult to understand. She knew from experience what Mashire could do. The Thunderbolt could cleave mountains and drill pathways between worlds! But what could the weapon that was hidden within do?

"You'll never know, Queen Dana, if you're not willing to find out."

Chapter Twenty-Seven

MOON AND SUN

Dana gazed ashen-faced into the light glinting off her sword. Her chest heaved as slowly she raised Mashire by the handle, blade pointing down. Reluctantly, in numb hands, she lifted the blade until it was poised above the crown.

"For all that you've done," Dana said through quivering lips, "I'm grateful." She kissed the widest flat of the blade and closed her eyes. Dana took a breath and quickly, decisively thrust Mashire down through the ninth point of the crown. As the diamond tip touched its setting, Mashire shrank, collapsing in length. The blade, which had grown so gradually in stages, shrank speedily to the length of a dagger. It became as Dana had found it, a jeweled pin, before shrinking further to a nugget of spark.

Dana let go her breath. As she did, the symbols below the points began to glow. Each symbol flashed fire, seemingly lighted from behind as keyholes to lighted chambers. There followed a loud cracking sound. Dana saw a split open in the tree, jagged and dazzling as a bolt of lightning. She looked on astounded as a great bird, glistening white as day, exited the split. With a single flap of its huge wings, the bird alighted to a root of the inverted tree. It blinked once and fixed its fiery eyes on Dana. "White raven," Dana whispered and met its stare with dropped jaw.

"Catching flies, Queen of Worlds? I wouldn't think you'd have the time," came a voice from behind Dana. "Ah, but Queen Dana is not bound by time. Isn't that so, Ibbur?"

"Anavak!" Dana cried out turning on her heel. "You're here!"

"And where else? I wouldn't miss this moment for—for worlds!"

"But how?"

"By way of light and wing—never you mind. Only feast your senses and more on mending. For the changes you've wrought sprout before you!"

From the sky fell droplets of rain, some like the milk-white rain that had fallen at Var's defeat, but also pearly drops of rainbow-colored rain. Each droplet flickered as it fell and upon reaching the ground transformed. Where each droplet splashed down, a shining figure took shape in swirling patterns of light.

"Angels of Light!"

The figures formed into circles ringing the inner courtyard with the tree at their center. Within the circles, seedlings sprang from the ground, grew and flowered. Young shoots burst forth and matured quickly through the stages of growth to become saplings, then trees. The hedgerow circles grew luxuriant, manicured and shining with the deepest holly green. Barren ground sprouted stalk and stem, tuft and greensward. Long-forsaken flower beds bloomed with periwinkle and foxglove, baby's breath and featherfew. And from behind each bloom, each petal, leaf and blade there peeked a tiny, shining face.

The lighted figures circled one way and another as Dana's hosts had done when she'd first entered the Mountain of Light. Among them, Dana recognized faces and forms she'd seen or known before: golden, smiling faces with armored bodies of chrome; wispy, web-like figures woven of filaments of light; towering, star-bright forms with bodies like candlesticks, wicks for necks, and heads of flame.

With dance-like steps they shuffled as the others had done in the glade. Music played off their lips and sounded from their wings—ten tones rising and falling in an order forever new and varied. Upon their tongues was song:

> *Promenade to admire and adore,*
> *As above, so below and before,*
> *By light of our queen,*
> *Reclaim and redeem,*

> *Remember what was and what for,*
> *Four worlds for Dana,*
> *For sure! . . .*

The song was sung in a round. Each circling ring of hosts began and ended and began anew, overlapping words and tones. Above their heads, from shining hand to shining hand, they passed Ibbur. On the words, "For sure!" voices rose and Ibbur was tossed from one circle to the next amid throaty cheers of victory. . . .

> *Escapade to inspire and restore,*
> *Queen Dana returned to her door,*
> *Beginning as one,*
> *First moon and first sun,*
> *Replace, revive and restore,*
> *Four worlds for Dana,*
> *For sure! . . .*

Among the circling hosts danced Dana's four rays, weaving patterns of light. One then another flew off into newly leafed trees and returned carrying riders. The riders, ten in all, reached into folds of light at their hips and withdrew long, narrow tubes. These they brought to their lips and blew . . . ten tones upon pipes! Pipers of song! Dancers leapt upon air. Circles rose and spun gaily to the Song of the Heart.

With each rotation the circles spun higher. The ten pipers now led ten rings of hosts, circle within circle, in airy carousel-like sprees. Among them skipped Ibbur, while Dana and Anavak watched from below.

"Ibbur of many talents!" called Anavak into the sky. She turned to Dana. "Why don't you join him?"

"Join him? How? I've returned my wings to the crown."

"Ibbur must have told you, did he not? The charms cling within you, close as heart or belly."

Dana reached over her shoulders, feeling for her wings. "But Anavak, you see they're not here."

Anavak laughed her shrill, cackling laugh. "I do? Ho-hum!"

The slightest breeze stirred her green-black satin robes. "I see so much else!" And with these words, Anavak lifted from the ground as a crow into flight. "Feathers are for pigeons, my queen."

"Anavak, show me!"

"Ah, but Queen Dana, you're the one who showed me!"

From the back of Dana's mind, memory suddenly spilled forward. . . . Anavak and Dana in a tower of Light Castle; something tiny falling through the air. Ibbur! Dana sprang from the tower quick as light to catch him in her hand. She hung in air, wingless, calm and balanced. Then it was Anavak, young and resplendent with the scent of honeyed milk, asking, "How, Princess? How did you do it?"

"How did you, Queen Dana?" called Anavak, hovering above Dana's head.

"On wings of will!" cried Dana, eyes alive with remembrance and knowing. Dana looked back over a shoulder and where before no wings had been, there now shone wings of purest light. With a flap of glitter and sparkle, Dana joined Anavak. Together they ascended the heights until they reached the circling hosts. Coming upon the outermost circle, Dana was reminded of the ten circles of light she'd seen in the vast ocean behind the pinpoint of light. In memory she once again saw the beam that had traced those circles. Now Dana knew what to do. . . .

Leaving Anavak behind, she streaked toward the center of her dancing hosts. In her wake was left a trail of colorless light, pure and fixed as the beam in her vision.

Past the tenth circle of dancers, Dana came to rest, stepping from her beam as in memory to a tower of light. From this tower, Dana looked out upon a kingdom of light. There were seven palaces and gardens, marble halls and chambers filled to overflowing with lighted hosts.

In lavish brightness Dana closed her eyes. When again she opened them to squint out, she found herself standing before a gate to the first palace. Towering above her was the keeper of the gate rising as a lofty peak. His eyes shone as torches with lashes of lightning, while his skin burned as fire without being consumed. In each hand he held the reins of a dragon-horse, straining at the bit, nostrils flaring and ablaze. Across his great forehead flamed the name, Birur. Dana stepped toward the gate.

"Back away, Queen Dana!" The gatekeeper's voice broke like thunder. "Now isn't the time!"

"But isn't the king at home?"

"The king is no place!"

"How then may I see him and when?"

"After and after and after!" With each "after," spit-balls of fire flew from the gatekeeper's lips. "Don't dawdle, Queen Dana." He turned his mountainous back, dragging his beasts toward the palace. Before he vanished into light, the gatekeeper turned to face her. "Dust awaits, Queen Dana. Rectify!" And he vanished through the palace walls.

Dana tried lifting a foot to follow, but found it rooted to the ground, immovable. She closed her eyes and summoned her will, brought it into balance and blew . . . will to enter! Her feet never budged. Instead, she felt overcome with queasiness, a sudden nausea that filled her belly. Her head was dizzy with light, palaces and gardens spinning about her. Then light dispersed and Dana found herself in dark, empty space.

Only her queasiness remained, and now worsened. Dana's head pounded, her stomach cramped. A fever raged through her, bringing spastic shakes. She willed it to end, but it didn't. Her muscles tightened and throbbed. Dana was convulsing from belly to throat. Waves of upheaval coursed up, violent throes that reached her mouth and in a final heave broke out. Belching from Dana's lips came a sphere, a globe of light flashing as a star. Like a balloon it expanded, bloating before Dana's eyes. And as her sweat-soaked skin cooled, Dana saw the dark, empty space swell with light . . . to fullness.

"First moon!" a voice spoke in her head. "First sun!"

Anavak! Dana was flushed with joy and sudden craving. A longing seized her to join the light of the first moon and sun, to draw toward it, to enter and vanish. She spread her lighted wings.

"Queen Dana, no!"

Dana faltered briefly, then redoubled the beating of her wings.

"Return, Queen of Worlds! Return to your hosts and complete your task!"

"But here, now! Moon and sun!" Dana spoke blindly into light. "Just one embrace! How can I not?"

"By cause of worlds you mustn't! For with one embrace you'll be no more!"

There came a tugging at Dana's belt. She felt pulled back. Behind her head—the faint strain of pipes . . . muffled stomps and cheers. "Queen Dana, your hosts!"

Dana hung in doubt, her will divided. She felt drawn to this moon-sun as one is drawn home. Yet she also felt drawn away from the light, back to her hosts. The sounds of celebration grew louder. Dana could hear the song of the dancers:

> *Serenade to excite and allure,*
> *Back to dust or to light long before,*
> *Which way to complete?*
> *Above or beneath?*
> *Retreat or retrieve one spark more,*
> *Four worlds for Dana,*
> *For sure!*

Dana heard and decided. From light she had come and to light she'd return, but not yet. For there was still more to do to complete her task. One spark more remained in the Mountain of Dust. Who would retrieve it, if not she? No one else could. The gatekeeper had said it plainly: "Dust awaits, Queen Dana. Rectify!"

So with heart and mind in balance once again, Dana blew . . . will to rejoin my hosts! Instantly, the moon-sun receded in Dana's vision to a pinpoint of light. Dana found herself retracing the beam back through the ten circles of dancing hosts. She rejoined Anavak, Ibbur, her rays and hosts. And with ten dancing circles spiraling down, they began their descent back to Light Castle and the Spring of Beginning.

Chapter Twenty-Eight

SPRING OF BEGINNING

Merrymaking flowed down through the descending spiral. Dana's hosts flung themselves with abandon into their spree of dance and song, led by Ibbur:

> *Eighth spark's charm on rushing sea,*
> *Rattle's tameability,*
> *Tark I-iddle-du, lily Lu-lee,*
> *Beasts retreat so handily!*

> *Ninth spark's charm on flaming sea,*
> *Moonstone gained, will to free,*
> *Park I-iddle-du, lily Lu-lee,*
> *Var's eye taken, preciously!*

As she descended, Dana could make out changes in the sky. While before it had been gray and clouded, now the sky shimmered sapphire-blue beneath a beaded canopy of stars. At the highest heights shone the moon-sun from which Dana had reluctantly parted.

"Is it night or day?" Dana asked Anavak.

"Neither night nor day, seeing queen. For you've renewed moon and sun as one! In the Mountain of Light, night and day are also one, whole and joined as the source of their light. So it was at the start and yet again!"

As she basked in the blue of her descent, Dana noticed circle within circle of light shining from far below. At their center was a golden brilliance. Like a ring at the bottom of a pool, it flickered up through depths. Light Castle, marveled Dana, and rivers of light streaming between the walls!

From the center of that brilliance, Dana saw a rising spray of dazzling light. "Spring of Beginning," she spoke aloud as together with her hosts, Anavak, Ibbur and the four rays, Dana spiraled down to the shining ring through the spray of dazzling light to the foot of the tree.

"Behold, Queen Dana," proclaimed Anavak, "Light Castle restored to its glory!"

The Castle, which before had been in part-ruin, now rose complete with bricks of golden light. Higher still rose the ten towers of light reaching up into vast blue sky. Dana smiled broadly, her face and eyes aglow with reflected brilliance.

Her rays scurried about the four holes at the foot of the tree. It was from these holes that light sprayed, spouting like water jets, enwrapping Light Castle and all within its walls in a tent of multicolored light. Dana's hosts stood with open mouths, catching droplets of spray upon their tongues. Dana did the same, and to her delight found that each drop possessed its own taste and fragrance. The first tasted of cherry, the next of hazelnut, then came persimmon, radish and red pepper. Dana feasted upon a banquet of light. Her nose tickled with fragrances. She rolled the tastes together on her tongue and found that their mix was familiar . . . remindful of the moon-pink fruit and also of the honey-like liquid.

Anavak and Ibbur too drank down the tastes and inhaled the scents, gorging themselves with light. Long as they drank, no belly was filled. For the tastes were weightless and formless as light. Only when tongues and jaws tired did the company of celebrants cease feasting. Still many of the hosts drank on, for their nature was never to tire, and they'd been starved for light for so long.

While colors danced in the spray, sounds seemed to fly from the falling droplets of light. They rang out first as heartbeats, then as the whisper of leaves, next as bells and then wind. Finally they sounded out of silence, heard and unheard by Dana as the beating of her own heart.

Anavak withdrew to the tree, sitting back snugly against its trunk. The rays, which had entwined the Spring of Beginning, nosed up to her, nestling like kittens in Anavak's lap. Dana took a last swallow of light and contentedly sat down beside the old woman. Together in silence they watched the play of light and hosts, and savored sweet sounds and smells.

Finally, Anavak spoke. "You've done well, Queen Dana." With her one hand, Anavak stroked the four rays. "Your way was never to disappoint. Ah! Always striving!"

The rays shifted, stretching lazily across Anavak's lap and Dana's both. Dana stroked them, suddenly self-conscious of her two hands, eyeing Anavak's one. "Your hand—" Dana began and broke off.

"Queen Dana, please don't demure. We've known each other for quite some time." Anavak cackled. "I should say, in and out of time!" She waved her one hand in dismissal. "It's not for you to be timid," while with her stumpy wrist, Anavak continued stroking the rays.

"I found it in the belly of the sea beast!" Dana spoke in a hurry.

"Certainly, my queen. That's where I left it."

"Left it?!"

"Of course. After Zar ripped it from me."

"He did! But from that hand, Anavak—from the skeleton that remained of it!—I retrieved the ring of sound!"

"As destiny required! For it was your destiny to regain the ring, not mine."

Dana asked uneasily, "Then why did you try?"

"To inspire hope! Instead, I overreached my grasp, my purpose and portion. But enough of that."

"Anavak, I wish I'd come sooner."

"No matter." Anavak swept her handless arm in an arc. "Nine sparks, brave queen, see what you've done! Nine seeds regained to restore worlds!"

Dana's gaze followed the spray of light and her rollicking hosts. There was Ibbur leaping from light-drop to light-drop. For a long while Dana said nothing, then . . . "What about the worlds below this one?" she asked.

"Ah! As above, so below, Queen Dana. By your actions, the

worlds below this one have also been restored. In the Mountain of Water, sun and moon flow again, separate and divided as before. Days give way to nights in a world of watery substance.

"So too in the Mountain of Wind, where the third moon and sun shine again as wind! Sun blows the winds of daylight and moon breathes the winds of night—"

"And the Mountain of Dust?" Dana broke in anxiously.

"There too! Moon again reigns over dusty night and sun over day."

"I wish I could see them!" Dana started to her feet.

"By your will you shall." Anavak laughed taking Dana's hand, gently nudging her to sit. "As you already know, in the Mountain of Dust a single spark remains. Your task, you see, is not yet complete."

"But, Anavak! Moons and suns are restored in each of the worlds, you've said so yourself."

"Restored in part—in parts, my queen. For in the lower worlds, moon and sun are still divided. And as long as the last spark remains captive, Var still has hold in the Mountain of Dust. There opposites rule! Evil veils good and good masks evil. Only here in the Mountain of Light are moon and sun united as one. Yet even here their union is only makeshift, between-time. A temporary fix. Without the tenth spark restored to the crown, Var may still trespass. With all his masks and names—Zvar, Vzar, Tzvar!—evil may still over-spread itself."

With her single hand, Anavak gripped a hand of Dana's and brought it to the stump of her wrist. "You must be fully aware of the dangers before you. In the Mountain of Dust, more than any-where else, things are not as they seem. The worlds have been repaired—but not refined. Restored but not rectified at the root."

"Rectify!" shouted Dana with heart beating high. "That's what the keeper of the gate said."

"Which gatekeeper?"

"A giant with a name of fire burning on his forehead."

"Birur," said Anavak, "at the gate to the first palace. He sent you away did he not?"

"Now wasn't the time, he said. And afterwards you too, your voice held me back from joining the first moon and sun."

"Had you joined them then as you longed to, for your own sake alone, you'd have abandoned your worlds. Instead you've returned for completion. Unselfish queen!"

From out of the spray came Ibbur, dancing along droplets of light. He leapt to Dana's lap, then climbed on the back of the green ray, catching his breath.

"Dear Ibbur," cooed Anavak, "so happy in the presence of our queen."

Ibbur grinned and closed his eyes.

"Now I'll tell you, Queen Dana," said Anavak, "what you must know before you go on. Birur has already told you, but his words are few and hot-headed. Rectify, he said, and now you'll know what it means."

On the back of the green ray, Ibbur softly dozed. Dana stroked his head through his red jelly-cap.

"To regain the nine sparks, you've had to do battle," continued Anavak. "Each charm has served you, empowered you and brought you closer to the next. By wit, by wisdom and might you've subdued evil and conquered its forms in three worlds. And bravely! But in the Mountain of Dust it won't be enough to destroy evil. You may not simply sever its head or remove its evil eye. Var and his lower masks must be rectified. Evil must be converted to good. Wrong must be made right. Only then can moon and sun rejoin throughout the worlds. Only then can the four worlds make their return to one."

"I'm afraid it's easier to sever heads," said Dana. "Var didn't seem likely to change."

Anavak pointed into the heights of the tree where the branching roots disappeared into sky. "Past the highest reaches, all things have one root. In the Fountain of Light they join. This is what Birur meant by 'rectify.' In the end you must return evil to its source. If you aim only to destroy it, you'll fail."

Anavak stopped speaking to clear her throat. She caught the lighted spray upon her tongue and swallowed deeply. "Ahhh . . ."

Ibbur's eyes flickered, moving rapidly beneath their lids as in dreaming. His lips moved slightly and he spoke out of sleep. . . . "Weapon," he said softly.

"Ibbur, forever watchful," whispered Anavak.

Dana stroked Ibbur's tiny head. "When he insisted I return Mashire to the crown, he told me I'd find my greatest weapon within. I hope I didn't lose it when I vomited that moon-sun!"

"Nonsense! Your weapon lies well-hidden where the purest beam ends at the center of your visions. At that dark center, and within the silent glow contained in the Lamp of Darkness, there you'll complete your task—turning darkness to light."

"But Ibbur said the weapon was deep at the center of my will. In belly and breath. The places you mention are places I've been to, places I've seen."

"Places you've seen from within, my queen. Places deeper than dreams."

Ibbur stirred beneath Dana's stroking hand. "I've wondered," Dana said, "if all of this—you and Ibbur and everything else—is only a dream."

"Only? Who's to say that waking isn't a dream itself or that dreams aren't doors to things more real than dust or wind, than water or even light? Dreams are paths to hidden depths and heights! The purest of dreams, Queen Dana, are carried by angels. And visions? They're sixty times stronger than dreams. Visions are inspired by the king!"

"Then why can't I see him?"

"Is hearing not enough?"

Dana's ears began to tingle and of a sudden she knew what before she'd only suspected. . . . "It was the king who spoke from the silent glow. It was his voice that told me to find Ibbur where I will!"

"Of course! How could it be otherwise? Sound dwells closer to the king than sight. And sound out of silence is the closest. Why, time itself comes out of sound. The voices of song are the source of time. These things you once knew and shall know again."

As Anavak spoke, Dana watched the lighted spray of the Spring of Beginning descend in droplets of color and sound, tone and tone. She caught one on her tongue and savored its taste.

"A queen may taste what she hears and hear what she

sees," said Anavak. "Each sound, color, and taste adds to your knowledge and wakes the slumbering powers within. For asleep at the core of queenhood—past all the forms of all the worlds; past Var and the masks of opposites—is the secret of secrets, weapon of weapons—"

"Riddle of riddles," murmured Ibbur, eyes still closed and dreaming.

"Oh, yes!" agreed Anavak. "On the Mountain of Dust it's thought that the greatest of riddles is the passage of time. But time we know is the flow of song from the Spring of Beginning. No mystery there! Yet of the color of silence or the fragrance of sound, no one asks. For only Queen Dana may even ask the correct questions. Only Queen Dana may lift the veils and strip away the husks that hide and confuse. Only you, my queen, may penetrate evil to retrieve the last spark Var swallowed. But only when you've awakened the weapon of weapons within yourself may the spark be unbound and set free.

"And what is that weapon?" Dana blurted.

"Ah! Past all your senses you shall see, and touch and smell, taste, hear, and finally in the end, you shall feel and know. But not before you've returned to the Mountain of Dust, there to complete your task." With the smallest of motions, Anavak lifted her chin toward the roots of the tree. Before her motion was through, the white raven alighted to the ground. In the same moment Ibbur awoke. . . .

"Here's off!" he cried.

"Here—" Dana couldn't finish for the emotion choking in her throat.

"Not so fast, Ibbur." Anavak fixed deep, warm eyes on Dana and held them there, looking, penetrating.

Through eyes welling with tears, Dana returned Anavak's gaze. Her tears seemed to magnify Anavak's eyes of green jade and to wash between them with the ebb and flow of a tide. Waters welled and went and combined as one ocean, an ocean of silent, glowing light. Dana felt herself afloat at the ocean's center, drifting in timeless sea. Thought dropped away and will, and so too all definition.

Now upon the sea came floating four ships, each aflame in

black fire. On their sails were emblazoned letters and symbols—those that had appeared on the gateposts! Sea winds whistled in the sails with the sound of speech. Words? No, names. Hidden names! Dana heard each one as she had when she'd retrieved the moonstone from Var's eye. Now as then, she spoke them to herself, and as before they were gone in an instant—all but one. This one name Dana grasped and held firmly as if it were her own will, or her own heart beating in her breast. Her eyes flashed and widened with knowing, as before her Anavak blinked.

"Steadfast queen!" clucked Anavak. "So much regained to hold a stare. Back to time out of time when I'd blink first, and now again! Past any misgiving, you are prepared for your return."

Dana felt a rush of wind in her wide-open eyes. The white raven shifted restlessly, beating its wings. Dana blinked, and with a look spoke silently to Anavak. . . .

"Yes, I know, my queen," replied Anavak. "Hold fast to the name you've remembered, for no longer is it hidden from your knowing. Bind it to your will, to the muscle of your arm, and to your heart and mind. Like your charms, it will work for you. That name is the first and holds the greatest magic. Use it sparingly and only in direst need. Allow none but angels to hear you utter it. For it will speed your will to action, faster than before." With a flourish then of her mildewed robes, Anavak swung her arms high. The four rays stirred and gathered across the old woman's shoulders as a spangle-colored shawl. Anavak smiled slightly and nodded to Ibbur.

Ibbur sprang for Dana's shoulder, tipped his red jelly-cap and asked, "Are you ready, Queen Dana?"

"Then you *are* coming!" Relief settled in Dana like balm on a wound, slackening the pangs of loss she'd begun to feel. She turned to Anavak. "But you're not and neither are the rays?"

Anavak gave a wave of her hand. The rays bounded from her shoulders to alight as a blanket in Dana's arms. With caresses and whispers Dana held them tightly, then relaxed her hold and with a gesture outward sent them back to Anavak as a bride tosses a bouquet.

"Tender queen," said Anavak. "You feel as you must and

deeply, according to your nature. That can't be taken from you or changed. But know this: There is cleaving even in separation. Sometimes that which seems far-off and near-forgotten is most at hand. You've only to know how to grasp it, past worlds."

"Then I *will* see you again!"

"As a queen wills it, it's done!" Anavak clapped hand to stump. Instantly, Dana found herself upon the back of the great raven. "Above all," counseled Anavak, "maintain your balance between wing tips."

Dana glanced over her shoulder expecting to see the lighted wings that had carried her to heights among her dancing hosts. "But Anavak, they're gone!"

"From without, Queen Dana, but not from within. Do not forget that your wings and all your charms are held inside, deep at the center of will. Their source, and yours too, flows without end from the Fountain of Light. As above, so below!"

With those words, the raven sprang into flight. Dana and Ibbur rose above the company of hosts, looking down upon the flashing display of Light Castle, upon its rivers of light and surrounding walls and the rising spray of the Spring of Beginning. Sure and relaxed was Dana's grip on the raven's scruff.

Ten passes made the raven, circling Light Castle while Dana grasped her will. In the same moment, she grasped higher will too: a fleet lighted bird paired with her own. Together they converged at a point, where Dana blew . . . will to go home! And her breath was the sound of a name. . . .

"To the Mountain of Dust!" cried Ibbur.

"Queen of Worlds," came Anavak's voice fading to a thought in Dana's head . . . "Remember who you are and why you're there. For in the Mountain of Dust, the easiest thing is forgetting!"

Dana flew with the force of enchanted storm winds, faster than light or thought, faster even than will. In her ears was the Song of the Heart carried by the voices of hosts escorting her down through worlds. Down the Pillar of Light she wended, through the Mountain of Water; down the Pillar of Ice, through the Mountain of Wind; down the Pillar of Stars to the Mountain of Dust—all in less than an instant. For propelling her was the sound of a name, newly remembered, guiding her return.

Chapter Twenty-Nine

RETURN TO DUST

Next thing she knew, Dana was home in her room, her bed pitching furiously beneath her. She was gripping the mattress, sheets clenched in her hands, room lurching, head pounding, dizzy as before. "Will to stop this b—!" she shouted and before the last word was out, the bed stopped, becalmed and still.

Dana's dizziness was gone. She cast her eyes about the room . . . nothing seemed changed. Her nightgown still lay strewn over the back of her chair where she'd tossed it when dressing in a hurry. Her window remained open as she'd left it when she and Ibbur had bounded off into moonless night on the back of the white raven. But now—! Dana threw off her bed covers and rushed to the sill. Outside the sun shone in clear daylight skies. And out past rooftops, hanging once more as a pearl in the sky, was the daytime moon. Dana's hand shot to her sleeve— empty . . . and the other—empty . . . then to her collar and pocket—all empty!

"Ibbur!"

No reply came. "Ibbur!!" she shouted and hurried frantically about the room searching behind books, under clothes, in drawers. Her heart tripped in her chest—"Closet!" Dana yanked open the door. "Ibbur are you here?!" She was met with only stale silence. Dana swayed on her feet, dizziness returned, and sat down on the bed to keep from falling. She buried her face in her hands, saying softly to herself, "It was only a dream."

A knock at her door—"Dana?"—and her mother entered, flush from a dash upstairs. "Are you all right?" she asked, smoothing Dana's brow, feeling her forehead. "Your fever is down. What was that shouting?"

"A dream—I guess."

"And you've dressed. Please dear, don't work yourself up. Back in bed now and rest," she said, rubbing Dana's shoulders. Dana leaned back to lie down. As she did, her mother's glance fell to her belt. "Where'd you get the cute bag?"

"Bag?" Dana sat bolt upright grabbing the grass-woven pouch at her belt. "My pouch!" She flushed with staggering joy.

"A pouch then, I stand corrected." Dana's mother gave a short laugh. "It looks a little scuffed. Never mind about where you got it. You get under the covers right now and rest. That fever's made you excited. Understand?"

"Yes!" Dana threw herself under the covers, beaming delight.

Again Dana's mother laughed and shook her head. "I'm boiling that chicken. I'll be back shortly," and she left.

Dana hastily untied the pouch from her belt, turning it in trembling hands, reaching in to find bits of leaf and bark caught in the weave. "Witch hazel!" she cried out, giddy with joy. "Then it wasn't a dream—it all happened!" Again she searched her sleeves, her fingers fishing deeply into folds. From the seam of a shirt cuff, she loosened a tiny pile of lint or fluff. She pinched it tightly and withdrawing her hand saw pressed in her fingers . . . a tiny mass, red as fire—"Ibbur's cap!"

Dana smoothed it with care and grinning with high spirit set Ibbur's red jelly-cap upon a fingertip. With another finger she nudged the cap, cocking it just so, as Ibbur wore it. In memory she saw it soaring through the ant queen's chamber changing heaps of crumbs to sparkling jewels . . . and in her head she heard the Blower of Light's words. . . . "Ibbur clings like skin, deeper than skin, deeper than heart, or mind, or will." Behind the Blower's words came sifting others, faint but sure. . . . "No one is alone, ever . . . I know you and am attached to you by the highest will. You're my blade of grass."

"Ibbur," whispered Dana and carefully placed the jelly-cap in her pouch and secured it to her belt. Then she bounded from her bed to the window and peered up and down the street. All seemed the same—houses, gardens, trees and lawns—until, looking more deeply and intently, Dana saw what she was looking for: There! In a neighbor's tree, circling a bird's nest was a small group of lighted figures. And there! . . . busy among the leaves, tiny red-capped, bud-faced forms. And on her own lawn, dashing between grass blades, dancing on dandelions were countless shining faces. "Angels," uttered Dana as the door handle turned. . . .

"Back into bed, princess." Dana's mother entered with a tray of soup, toast, and water. "Your royal banquet is served." Reluctantly, Dana left the window and slipped slowly into bed. "Have some soup, you'll feel better. It's fresh."

"Soup?!" Dana's voice leapt with a start.

"Yes, soup. You *are* jumpy aren't you?"

"I guess, I mean . . . well, it's just that I'm not very hungry—not for soup!"

"Okay Dana, maybe later." She set down the tray. "Water then, and a nibble of toast. And rest!" Dana's mother smiled, shook her head and left.

Dana eyed the toast, feeling suddenly hungry. She took a quick bite and started to chew, savoring the buttery grain. But as she ground the bread between her teeth, Dana found its taste much more than toast. She rolled it on her tongue, tastes shifting and changing—sweet, then fruity, peppery, then rich—flavor flowing after flavor gushing in her mouth. Behind each taste, there's another, thought Dana . . . much more to a bite of toast than I ever imagined! To be sure! As there are worlds before worlds and veils behind veils! She jerked her head around— "Ibbur!"—thinking she'd heard him, and she had, but from inside her own head.

Dana scrambled out of bed, toast in hand, hurrying back to the window. She leaned out her head, certain somehow that Ibbur was nearby, perhaps rollicking in the trees with the others, or kick-stepping on a beam of sunlight. A hundred red jelly-caps flitted in the leaves. She squinted, searching among them for a capless golden-brown head. "Ibbur!" she called to trees and shrubs, but there was no reply save the whistling of wind past branches and stems.

Still Dana noticed there was something to the wind,

something about its movement and murmur that was different than before. Her ears pricked and she listened. . . . There came soft strains of melody, snatches of song blowing on pipes, whispered phrases of a song she knew well. Song of the Heart! As the wind played its sounds, it stirred leaf and blade in waves and patterns. Dana saw tangles twisting and raveling through the grass. Blades bent and flattened in the wind in curved and long shapes slinking up, down, and sideways. Like tracks, Dana thought . . . or tiny trails in the grass.

She followed the tracks with her eyes and saw that they flowed like the writing of a pen—a fluid, handwritten script. Blade by bent blade, motion by motion the writing came clearer to her, chasing away doubt. Dana watched and knew now with assurance that she wouldn't forget as Anavak had warned. For she knew who she was—Queen Dana, to be sure!—and from where she had come. Her task was certain: find the last spark and rectify worlds. No one could do it but her.

And as the last grass blade bent to complete the scripted message, Dana knew beyond question that she wasn't alone, ever. Not the slightest blade of grass was alone . . . and certainly not a queen! For etched in the grass was proof—words carved by the wind in flowing lines of script. . . .

Grow, Queen of Worlds!
Forever watchful,
Ibbur